MW00721531

# SIREN OF CHINA

西 施 传 奇

# OF
# CHINA

MICHAEL C. TANG

Better Link Press

This book is edited and designed by the Editorial Committee of *Cultural China* series.

Managing Directors: Wang Youbu, Xu Naiqing
Editorial Director: Wu Ying

Address any comments about *Siren of China* to:

Better Link Press
99 Park Avenue
New York, New York 10016, U.S.A.
*or*
Shanghai Press and Publishing Development Company
F 7 Donghu Road
Shanghai, CHINA 200031
Email: comments_betterlinkpress@hotmail.com

Interior and Cover Design: Yuan Yinchang
Computer typeset by Yuan Yinchang Design Studio, Shanghai
Printed in China by Shanghai Donnelley Printing Co. Ltd.

ISBN: 978-1-60220-204-7

First edition

*To my mother*
*Eileen Ge*
*and*
*my father*
*Qingan Tang*

# CONTENTS

# CONTENTS

# CHARACTERS

## STATE OF WU

Ho Lu - King of Wu
**Fu Chai** - King of Wu, Ho Lu's son
**Wu Yuan** - chief general, lord
**Bo Pi** - prime minister, lord
Prince Yiou - Crown Prince, Fu Chai's son
Wangsun Shong - army general
Wangsun Luo - army general
Mi Yong (pronounced *Mee Yong*) - army general
Gongsun Sheng - astrologer

## STATE OF YUE

**Gou Jian** - King of Yue
Lady Gou Jian
**Fan Li** - chief general, lord
**Wen Zhong** - prime minister, lord
**Hsi Shih** (pronounced *Shee She*, the first *shee* being slightly longer) - Yue girl
**Zheng Dan** - Yue girl
Yi Yong (pronounced *Yee Yong*) - senior minister, lord
Ling Gufu - army general
Zhu Jicheng - army general
Ding Hong - maid
Gao Lan - maid

# PROLOGUE

NO WOMAN IS more famous than Hsi Shih in Chinese history, and no woman is more beautiful than her.

Her life was caught up in the war between Wu and Yue, two antagonizing states in the fifth century B.C. in eastern China. The war brought forth a galaxy of extraordinary men—men of great ambition and great talent; it also immortalized Hsi Shih, the beauty of all beauties.

At the sight of Hsi Shih, a Chinese poet wrote, even the moon had to hide, even the flowers had to fold their petals in shame. The merry fish in the rivers and brooks were so astounded by her beauty that they sank to the bottom and the wild geese in the sky fell to the ground.

Surrounded by some of the most intriguing personalities of her time, Hsi Shih left such a vivid memory of herself that she became the most celebrated woman in popular legend. Her epic story was told a thousand and one times through the centuries and her name is synonymous with "beauty" in the Chinese language.

The story of Hsi Shih began in her birthplace, the State of Yue.

# CHAPTER ONE

## Death Row Convicts

THE NIGHT WAS deep and the oil lamp was burning low in the tent of King Gou Jian of Yue where the king and his chief general Fan Li were mapping out plans for defense.

In the year 496 B.C., King Ho Lu of Wu waged an undeclared war on Yue. Gou Jian knew this was in retaliation for what his father, the former king of Yue, had done a few years ago. When Ho Lu was away on an expedition in Chu, his brother, in collaboration with the former king of Yue, attempted to stage a coup d'etat in Wu. The attempt failed, and Ho Lu's brother fled. Since then Ho Lu had been keen on having his revenge on Yue.

But Gou Jian had not expected Ho Lu would come so soon. Barely a month had passed after his father passed away and he had just ascended the throne at the age of twenty-eight. The whole nation of Yue was in mourning when word came that Wu's troops, twenty thousand strong, had crossed the northern border. Gou Jian hastily gathered an army of seven thousand and rushed to Zuili*, a small town near the border, in an attempt to thwart the advance of the invaders.

"It's monstrous," hissed the king through his clenched teeth, his aquiline face clouded with concern. "That bastard of a Ho Lu has no sense of honor. He knows full well that we are unprepared."

"Ho Lu is shameless indeed," said Fan Li. "We must not allow him to succeed."

"But the odds are heavily against us, my general. Ho Lu's troops are well-trained and well-equipped, and they outnumber ours by far. To tell the truth, I'm rather worried."

"Sire, Ho Lu is not without a vulnerable point. For one thing, he doesn't have a good counsellor at the moment. His chief general Wu Yuan is staying at home. The man he took with him, his prime minister Bo Pi, is not half as well-versed in the art of war."

The king nodded. "Thank heaven, Marshal Sun Tzu has quit office." He was referring to none other than the author of the famous book *The Art of War* who had, until a year ago, served as Ho Lu's commander-in-chief.

"If we are clever, Sire, I do think we stand a fair chance of winning."

"You've got some plan up your sleeve, I suppose?"

Fan Li smiled.

"What is it?"

"We're going to win the battle through the effort of the sixty death row convicts that you've brought along."

---

* Present-day Jiaxing in Zhejiang Province.

"Pray how? They are no fighters, just tough guys to do odd jobs in the army."

"Neither did I expect they could be of such great value. But a unique idea has just crossed my mind. The fact is: the convicts understand that their execution is only a matter of time, that they are doomed to die in any event—and to die without leaving a coin to their folks. Now Sire, if you promise to reward their families with gold and silver on condition that they die to save the country, I believe the convicts will gladly accept the terms, and their death will be the prelude to our victory."

"I promise. Please explain."

"The strength of a disciplined army lies in its organization and leadership. If we form the sixty convicts into a dare-to-die team to disrupt the enemy's command center, their troops will collapse quickly."

As Fan Li elaborated on his idea, a smile began to light up Gou Jian's face.

Fan Li understood that the outcome of the impending battle would determine the survival or ruin of Yue and make or break the career of both the king and himself. A year ago, he was just a junior officer. But Prime Minister Wen Zhong spotted him, recognized his potential and recommended him to Gou Jian's father. During the interview, the old king was so impressed by his knowledge and intellect that he appointed him a senior officer. Shortly after the death of the old king, Yue's old commander-in-chief also died. The young king Gou Jian promoted Fan Li to be his successor.

Fan Li had good reason to be pleased with himself. He lost both of his parents very early. Brought up by his impoverished grandparents, he had tasted the hardships of life and was determined to achieve success for himself. Bright and ambitious, he had worked hard and studied diligently. Not only was he well-versed in classics but also in politics and the art of war. His mentor, Master Ghost Valley, was a renowned military strategist, and Fan Li was one of his best students.

The forthcoming battle would give him an opportunity to prove himself for the first time since his meteoric rise to the rank of chief general. He had worked out a meticulous battle plan and rehearsed it many times in his head until he was sure of its outcome. The king endorsed the plan forthwith.

Both men were dressed in white, white being the sign of bereavement. The king wore a white gown on top of a suit of sharkskin armor and Fan Li a white gown over a suit of armor made of rhinoceros skin. Gazing at his general, Gou Jian felt a slight prick of jealousy, for Fan Li was as handsome as he was smart, with his athletic form, well-chiselled features and large, intense eyes.

By contrast, Gou Jian had the looks of a human freak. Tall, thin and straight, he resembled a wooden post. Yet his movements were brisk and well-controlled. His beard was sparse, and his hair thin, but his brows were bushy—so bushy that they nearly covered his small, shrewd eyes. His sharp nose and protruding ears made his dark brown face appear thinner than it actually was, but his small head and long neck blended well with his lean figure. On the whole, he looked old for his age.

* * *

All was quiet in the twilight of the dawn. The deep silence was broken only by the footsteps of sixty half-naked men. Faces tattooed and stripped to the waist, they were marching from Yue's camp toward Wu's, each with a broad sword in hand, each wearing only maroon pants fastened by a straw rope.

The sun had risen when they came in view of Wu's camp. Thereupon they formed themselves into three rows—twenty to each row, with a distance of about thirty feet between the rows—and began to walk slowly on their knees, each raising the glittering sword and holding it horizontally above his head.

The strange sight caught the eye of a sentinel of the Wu army.

"Come on, men!" he shouted to his fellow soldiers. "Come and look!"

Many scrambled over to watch.

"Who are these people? What's the matter with them?" The viewers were bewildered.

More and more came to swell the curious crowd. Even King Ho Lu was aroused to join them, bringing with him his prime minister, Bo Pi, and his army general, Wangsun Shong.

"Could this be a trick played on us by Gou Jian?" Wangsun Shong turned to Bo Pi.

"Yes," said Bo Pi thoughtfully. "But what are they trying to do?"

Now the three rows stopped moving and calmly remained on their knees. The headman of the first row alone rose to his feet and took a few steps forward.

"Your Majesty! Illustrious King of Wu!" he said in a stentorian voice. "We who are about to die salute you! Our master, King Gou Jian of Yue, has provoked your wrathful indignation. Gou Jian pleads guilty. We, as his slaves, feel ashamed. We do not value our worthless lives. To expiate our master's shame, we are prepared to take our own lives—in your presence."

Thus saying, he swung his sword in a whirling arc and slashed his own throat. Instantly blood spurted and his body collapsed onto the ground. The remaining nineteen men of the same row immediately did the same, and their bodies all slumped and twitched in the throes of death while blood gushed out in streams.

The soldiers in Wu's camp had never before witnessed such a horrendous scene. They gawked, then yelled and shrieked. The noises they made drew more to the scene of horror.

*Brave men! They killed themselves to expiate the guilt of their master.* Ho Lu marvelled how Gou Jian could have slaves so loyal as to die for him in such a manner.

"Hail! Illustrious King of Wu! We salute you!" A loud chorus came from the second row of twenty men who also cut their heads and fell down in the same manner.

"What?" Ho Lu dropped his mouth. What was the idea of all this? A sense of hideous suspicion crept in upon his mind. He knew something was wrong. Definitely. But before he could put his finger on it, there was another volley of salutations—from the third row. "Hail! Illustrious King of Wu! We salute you!" Another twenty decapitated themselves and fell with an expression of excruciating pain on their faces.

The soldiers of the Wu army were petrified. They felt sick and their heads reeled.

*There is definitely something sinister about all this!* The king thought. It was at this very moment that Gou Jian's troops charged into Wu's camp with the speed of lightning.

The moment the sixty convicts left their quarters, King Gou Jian, following Fan Li's stratagem, set out with his troops, took a detour, rounded the foot of a hill, and came out behind Wu's camp. Fan Li had timed it so precisely that while the last batch of convicts were taking their own lives, Gou Jian's troops would charge into the unguarded rear of Wu's camp and win the battle. Instantly, the sky reverberated with drums and bugles and battle cries. Smoke shot up: Wu's camp was set on fire.

Ho Lu realized it was too late to put up an organized fight: his soldiers had not yet recovered from the shock of the mass suicide. Total chaos prevailed. In the midst of the confusion, Ho Lu found himself hemmed in by hundreds of Yue soldiers. A fighter of great stature and ability and a masterly swordsman, Ho Lu was past his prime; he was in his fifty-sixth year, and age had impaired his speed and stamina. He turned left and right in the company of his prime minister Bo Pi and scores of his guards, but was unable to break free. Yue's General Ling Gufu, brandishing a sword, was closing in on him. At this critical moment, General Wangsun Shong arrived with a band of horsemen. After a bloody melee, they tore into the enemy line and rescued the king and the prime minister. The sword of Ling Gufu, however, had already inflicted a mortal wound in Ho Lu's left foot: it was a poison-tipped sword.

In his flight, Ho Lu, his strength ebbing, grieved over the loss of half of his men in this engagement which historians called the "Battle of Zuili." He regretted for not listening to his chief general Lord Wu Yuan who had counselled him not to court opprobrium by breaking the traditional inter-state honor-code which forbade one state to attack another while the latter was in mourning.

King Ho Lu died on the third day after returning to his capital, Gusu*. Before he breathed his last, he murmured to his twenty-nine-year-old son, Fu Chai, who was kneeling tearfully by his bed, "My son, you must never forget my enemy and you must follow Wu Yuan's wise counsels."

"I will, Father!" Fu Chai pledged solemnly.

---

* Present-day Suzhou in Jiangsu Province.

# CHAPTER TWO

## Temple Fair

WALKING BY HER father through the streets of Guiji*, Hsi Shih could hear the noise of firecrackers everywhere. The capital city was permeated with a festive atmosphere in the wake of Yue's victory. She was barefooted, but had put on her holiday best, wearing a blouse of vivid azure, with a bright red ribbon on the upsweep of her hair and a pair of ruby-red anklets on her feet. Her father was clean-shaven, attired in a blue gown with a pair of black cloth shoes on his feet. Their destination was the Temple of King Yu.

King Yu was the ancestor of the Yue people and also the founder of China's first dynasty, Hsia. Legend says he spent eight years taming flood waters in the land. So devoted was he to his work, dredging waterways and digging canals, that he did not visit his

---

* Present-day Shaoxing in Zhejiang Province.

own home even though he walked past it three times during that long period. Therefore he was worshipped as a saint and a temple was built in his honor in the south of Guiji beside his mausoleum.

The square outside the temple was teeming with people. The local custom was such that most people walked barefoot, that many men were close-cropped and had their bodies tattooed. Even some of the women had their legs and feet tattooed. The women wore wide trousers adorned with three or four brightly colored belts at the waist, but their blouses were short—so short that the belly and navel were exposed. The word "navel" in the Yue dialect sounded like "money." Hence the locals believed that exposing the navel would be a way of courting wealth.

The temple fair was in full swing. Rows of snack stalls offered an array of enticing food, and rows of merchandise stalls were laden with goods ranging from toys to handicrafts, from clothes to housewares. At a lollipop stall the peddler was making birds, fish, animals and insects out of boiling sugar from a pot heated by charcoal.

There were also street entertainers such as jugglers, tumblers, magicians. Hsi Shih was attracted to the lion dance which drew the biggest crowd. Five lions, with fantastic heads and red, bulging eyes, were rollicking on an improvised stage, each played by two acrobats, one at the head and one at the tail. A third man wearing a clown-faced mask was teasing the beast with a big, red ball. As the lion tried to catch the ball, it leaped, pranced, rolled, and whirled. It changed its facial expression to the changing tunes of music by moving its eyeballs, ears and mouth, giving the spectators a good laugh.

Behind the cavorting lions, scores of men in colorful costume, with a red band around the forehead, danced to thunderous drumbeats and clashes of gongs and cymbals. The music was deafening. The locals believed the lion would bring good luck and dispel evil spirits, and evil spirits were afraid of loud noise.

Raised on a terrace surrounded by white marble balustrades, the Temple of King Yu was an impressive wood and brick structure with red doors and columns and window frames, its roof covered with glazed blue tiles animated with gold plated dragons and its walls festooned with red lanterns and colorful flags.

Stepping inside the temple, Hsi Shih found the courtyard swarmed with visitors whose attention was concentrated on the entrance to the main hall which was cordoned off by uniformed guards. Curious, she jostled her way to the front and saw a man clad in a resplendent yellow dragon robe just coming out, with his entourage in tow.

"Long live the king!" The crowd burst into a spontaneous cheer.

King Gou Jian had come here to thank his ancestors and to pray for their continued blessings. A smug smile on his face, he walked to the crowd, waving to them. The cheer became louder. The king's eyes, scanning the sea of faces, fell upon Hsi Shih. What a pretty girl! The king took a step closer. She had a broad forehead, a straight nose, small dimples, dark brows, long lashes and big, dewy eyes. And there was a fresh wholesomeness about her that was irresistibly appealing.

"Where are you from, little girl?" he looked at

her with a slitted gaze, his soft tone undercutting the boisterous chattering around.

Hsi Shih glanced up and smiled politely. Somehow the king's looks did not strike her as regal.

Her father, standing by her, was quick to reply. "Your Majesty, we are from Zhuluo Village in Zhuji County. She is my daughter. It's a great honor to meet you."

"What's your name?"

"Shih Cheng."

"What do you do?"

"I'm a fisherman."

"How far is Zhuluo Village?"

"It's about a hundred *li*\* from here."

"You and your daughter came all the way from your village to this temple?"

"Yes, Your Majesty. My wife is sick. We came to pray for her health."

"How old are you, little girl?" The king gently touched Hsi Shih's face.

Hsi Shih winced imperceptibly. With a child's intuition, she sensed there was something else in the king's keen gaze—something ulterior.

"My daughter is eight years old," her father answered for her again, "She's shy."

"She has a good sense of filial duty to come to pray for her mother," the king said. Suppressing another urge to stroke her face, he settled for patting her head instead. "I hope your wife would get well soon."

"Thank you very much, Your Majesty."

Shih Cheng bowed to the king and nudged Hsi Shih to do the same. The king then turned to talk to

---

\* One *li* is equivalent to one-third mile.

others in the crowd. A short while later His Majesty departed and the temple resumed its normal activities.

The statue of King Yu occupied the main hall of the temple; those of other gods were housed in smaller halls where visitors could choose from among half a dozen gods to worship. There were the god of wealth, god of fire, god of thunder, god of rain, god of moats and walls, god of Heaven—the Jade Emperor, and the most feared god of all, Lord Yan, whose ordained role was to judge the newly dead and decide what punishment to be meted out according to what they had done when they were alive.

Shih Cheng took his daughter straight to the main hall. They lit a few incense sticks, planted them in a bronze tripod in front of the statue of King Yu and knelt down to pray. Shih Cheng's wife had been suffering from chronic fatigue, dizziness and low appetite. The doctor said it was caused by anaemia, and deficiency in chi, the vital energy that flowed through the body, was at the root of the problem. To nourish blood and tonify *chi*, he prescribed a variety of herbs such as angelica dang gui, astragalus, licorice root, and ginseng to make decoction from. As these herbs were only available in drugstores in Guiji, Shih Cheng had to make regular trips to the town. Sometimes he took his daughter with him.

Hsi Shih liked touring Guiji. Crisscrossed with canals and narrow streets, Guiji was a picturesque town. Over the canals were elegantly shaped humpback bridges. Lining the canals were low, grey-tiled and whitewashed houses, with steps leading down to the water where women washed clothes—and vegetables and kitchen utensils. There were many boats in the canals. The few larger ones were rowed by boatmen with two oars in hand, but the numerous smaller ones were a sight, for the oarsman standing at the tail of the boat deftly paddled a single oar with one foot.

The drugstore Shih Cheng frequented was located at the other end of the town. Before going there, he and his daughter had lunch at a snack stall.

"Were you afraid of the king, Hsi Shih?" Shih Cheng asked as they sat down at the table.

Hsi Shih shook her head.

"Why didn't you answer the king's questions?"

"He ... he looks funny." Hsi Shih gave her father an impish smile.

"How so?"

"He looks like a ... a cormorant." Hsi Shih made a comical grimace. Her father used the cormorant to catch fish.

"What nonsense?"

"Did you notice, Papa, his eyes are as small and sharp as a cormorant's eyes, and his nose is as long and hooked like a cormorant's beak? His ears ... his ears stand out like a pig."

The analogy was so funny Shih Cheng found it hard to keep a straight face. But he managed to give his daughter a scolding glance. "Stop it, Hsi Shih. You must not talk about the king like that."

Hsi Shih giggled.

# CHAPTER THREE

## Battle of Guiji

KING GOU JIAN awarded General Fan Li a grand mansion and the aristocratic title of "Lord Fan Li" in recognition of his contribution in the battle of Zuili. Overnight Fan Li became one of the most respected ministers in the king's court and one of the most powerful men in the country. Fan Li had never expected fame and honor would descend upon him so soon, so easily. He was only twenty-six. Privately he did not think he deserved the laurels bestowed upon him. The king was much too generous.

The next two years saw no war between Yue and Wu. But Fan Li learned that Wu's new king Fu Chai was making intense preparations for a revengeful assault. The story went that Fu Chai made it a rule for the palace sentinels to challenge him with "Fu Chai! Have you forgotten Gou Jian killed your father?" each morning as he came to the palace to work. In response, Fu Chai would say, "No, I haven't, and I never will." The same challenge-and-password ritual was repeated in the evening when he left the palace to retire for the night. Whether it was true or not, the story told him of a man who was intent on avenging his father's death. But Fan Li had only twenty thousand men. So he asked the king to allow him to recruit another ten thousand. To his surprise, the king refused.

Usually it was easy for Fan Li to read a man's character, but King Gou Jian was difficult. Having worked with him for two years, Fan Li still could not figure out what kind of a man he was. At times, the king was so straight and predictable, that it amused him; at other times, the king was impulsive and suspicious, which made it difficult to work for him. The king seemed to trust him enough to often seek his advice. But he could not be sure what exactly the king thought of him. Beneath the king's amiable exterior, Fan Li sensed a hidden shrewdness, an unfathomable depth and an innate ruthlessness. But that would not diminish his loyalty. He was much too indebted to the king who had given him the responsibility that he normally could only hope to assume ten or fifteen years from now.

However, as Yue's chief general, he could not ignore the danger posed by Wu. So he told Prime Minister Wen Zhong about his concern. Wen Zhong, too, was baffled by the king's refusal. A man of neat features in his mid-forties, Wen Zhong had been Yue's prime minister for eight years. He was known for his patience, steadiness and sharp wit. King Gou Jian was definitely more complex than his father and less straightforward. Whatever his reason to turn down Fan

Li, it was unreasonable—even irresponsible. Wen Zhong felt obliged to intervene.

By the time the king granted Fan Li's request, it was too late. Barely had Fan Li finished recruiting when news came that Wu had launched an invasion. Wu's army of forty thousand met with only token opposition on its way and was soon deep inside Yue.

Fan Li knew he had a formidable adversary in Wu's commander, General Wu Yuan. He had long heard of Wu Yuan's reputation.

A native of Chu, Wu Yuan came from a distinguished family with a long tradition of military service. He fled to Wu after the king of Chu had wrongfully killed his father, brother, and many members of his family. Later he helped Prince Ho Lu remove a usurper from the throne. When Ho Lu became the king, Wu Yuan became his chief general. He also recommended his friend Sun Tzu to Ho Lu. By the time he and Sun Tzu led a successful expedition against Chu, the king of Chu had already died. All Wu Yuan could do was to dig out his corpse and give it three hundred lashes to vent his anger.

Over the years Wu Yuan had won many victories in the battlefield and his fame spread far and wide. Fan Li knew any mistake on his part would be ruthlessly exploited by his opponent. There was absolutely no margin for error. The circumstances dictated a defensive strategy. Without delay, he ordered that all able-bodied men and women in Guiji be mobilized in an effort to strengthen the fortifications of the capital, that those living within twenty *li* of Guiji be moved inside the city along with food and fodder, that all buildings within one *li* of Guiji be demolished and trees and bushes therein be cleared so as to deny the enemy any cover.

Wu's troops mounted several fierce assaults but were repulsed each time. The catapults and crossbows from the walls of Guiji were powerful deterrent. Those who got closer were hit by arrows, stones and lime pots. Those who managed to climb up the walls were attacked not only by lances, hooks, axes and clubs, but also boiling water, fiery wood, even urine and manure.

Ten days passed. The city of Guiji stood firm. Casualties among Wu's soldiers were rising. Another ten days passed during which there was no fighting. Word came that Wu's troops started pillaging the surrounding countryside.

"They must have run out of their supplies," Gou Jian said to Fan Li.

"No, they can't," Fan Li shook his head. "They should have plenty of provisions at this point."

"Why do they loot then?"

"To provoke us to attack them."

"So we should stick to our strategy?"

"We must. Wu's army came from afar. They undoubtedly prefer a speedy war. If we make the war a protracted one, they will have to worry about their supplies and will be forced to withdraw."

In Wu's camp, many soldiers got sick from drinking the water from the wells near their campsite and some had died. Earlier, Fan Li had most of the wells in the vicinity of Guiji filled up and the few remaining ones poisoned. After halting his attack Wu Yuan sent his troops to the countryside to plunder. However, five days of plundering had failed to lure Gou Jian out.

Fu Chai was getting anxious. "It seems that bastard of a Gou Jian won't be provoked."

"That means we have to take more drastic measures," Wu Yuan replied. He ordered his men to expand the area of their pillage and gave them permission to kill civilians.

Suddenly Wu's soldiers became ruthless. Anyone who resisted were beheaded on the spot; many houses were burned; and many livestock slaughtered. Gou Jian was disturbed at the news.

"We must stop them, my lords," he said to Fan Li and Wen Zhong at a meeting. "I can't bear the shame of shutting myself up inside when the enemy are butchering my people right under my nose."

He wanted to sally out but was dissuaded by both men who counselled him to hold off a little longer.

In the following days Wu's soldiers turned more brutal. More civilians were killed; women were raped; children and old people were beaten. Gou Jian's patience was running thin. "The longer we wait, the more civilians will they kill. They are a bunch of wild beasts."

"It is a sign of their desperation, Sire," said Fan Li. "It means our strategy is working."

"Working?" Gou Jian shot him an incredulous look.

"Yes. Our effective evacuation has forced them to travel a long way to pillage, but what they can seize is limited. Their real objective is to induce us to fight before their supplies run out. They cannot win the war by killing civilians."

Gou Jian was not convinced. "How many civilians have to die before we come to their rescue?"

"The death of civilians is disturbing. But much more is at stake. If we go into battle prematurely, we would lose. It would mean greater suffering. The execution of our strategy should not be dictated by civilian casualties."

Their conversation was interrupted by the arrival of General Ling Gufu whose pockmarked face looked very agitated.

"Your Majesty," he said gruffly, "the soldiers are anxious to fight. Many of their relatives are among the victims of Wu's brutalities. Why are we still waiting?"

Gou Jian turned to Fan Li.

"It is a difficult situation, General," said Fan Li calmly. "But the enemy is strong. We cannot afford to confront them. Our priority for now is to preserve our manpower and firepower because time is on our side."

"But I can't convince my soldiers. I don't know what to tell them. I don't know if I can control them for much longer. I ... "

"Can you control yourself?" Fan Li snapped.

" ... ... " Ling Gufu made a guttural sound.

"Our strategy calls for patience and forbearance," Fan Li continued. "No matter what happens, General, it is your duty to maintain discipline and wait for orders."

"Is it our strategy that we stand by and let the enemy slaughter our people?" Ling Gufu found his voice.

"It is a tough choice, but we have to wait for the right moment to attack if we are going to win."

"How long do we have to wait, pray?"

"No more waiting!" The king cut in before Fan Li could reply. "Tell the soldiers to get ready. Tomorrow we will teach the aggressors a lesson they won't forget."

There was no mistaking the finality in his tone.

The next morning a contingent of the Wu army was on its way to pillage yet another village when it encountered a large army of Yue. They were quickly surrounded and came under a hail of arrows which killed most of them. The few survivors fled back to alert General Wu Yuan. Shortly afterwards a major battle broke out on the outskirts of Guiji between the two sides.

King Fu Chai led his army into action amid rousing drumbeats and battle cries. Tall and dashing, the king cut a magnificent figure on horseback. Wielding a resplendent sword, he confronted Yue's General Ling Gufu, the man who had killed his father. Ling Gufu's stocky frame seemed surprisingly agile on horseback. He struck the first blow. Fu Chai nimbly swerved and raised his sword to strike back, but missed his target by the fraction of an inch. Ling Gufu struck again. Again Fu Chai dodged. Their swords swirled with blinding speed, and silvery arcs flashed in the air. Ling Gufu's sword work being flawless, Fu Chai could not prevail after some twenty rounds. So he feinted defeat and turned to flee. He ran up a slope to the left; Ling Gufu was behind him. He ran down the slope and back to level ground; Ling Gufu followed him there. Fu Chai let his opponent draw near. Just as Ling Gufu had caught up, he suddenly swung his horse around and hit him on the forehead. Ling Gufu staggered, nearly falling down. Another stroke from Fu Chai pierced him right between the eyes. Ling Gufu tumbled off his saddle and was killed instantly.

Wu's troops charged with irresistible force. Yue's troops, though outnumbered, put up a ferocious fight. In the heat of the battle, a messenger rushed over to report that Wu's army was raiding Yue's grain storehouse. Startled, Fan Li immediately took two thousand men and hastened to the scene, only to find that the storehouse was on fire, but raiders had already disappeared.

By then Wu's troops had gained the upper hand. They were better-trained and better-equipped and their morale ran high. Realizing that he was fighting a losing battle, Gou Jian ordered his men to retreat so as to avoid a complete annihilation. But the road to Guiji had been cut off. Gou Jian decided to head for the Guiji Mountains to the southeast of the capital. As he took his followers and escaped into a woody hill via a narrow valley, Fan Li emerged from the heavy woods to meet him. After failing to retrieve the grain from the enemy, he and his troops had been guarding the defile in anticipation of the king's arrival.

"Wu Yuan is after me," Gou Jian said breathlessly.

"Don't worry. If Wu Yuan comes after Your Majesty, he will pass this way, and I'm ready for him."

But Wu Yuan did not pursue. He simply summoned his troops to encircle the hill. He did not need to attack. He would starve the enemy now that he had increased provisions and Yue's remaining troops were cut off from supplies.

"What is Gou Jian now?" he said to Fu Chai. "Nothing more than a turtle kept in a jar."

Having served King Ho Lu faithfully for twenty years, Wu Yuan was as eager to avenge his death as Fu Chai. Ho Lu had appointed him to be Prince Fu Chai's mentor. After the death of Ho Lu's eldest son, Wu Yuan persuaded him to choose Fu Chai as his successor from among all the princes and promised to help his pupil be a good ruler. Now he looked forward to fulfilling King Ho Lu's unfinished cause—the conquest of Yue—together with Fu Chai.

# CHAPTER FOUR

## Peace Talks

OVERLOOKING HIS CAPITAL from his encampment on the Guiji Mountains, Gou Jian knew he was hopelessly trapped.

"I will never let them capture me," he bit out between his teeth. "I would rather die."

"Let's not talk of dying yet, Your Majesty," said Wen Zhong. "Let's do our best to preserve ourselves."

"Sire, let's strive to outlive the disaster," Fan Li echoed.

The moment Gou Jian cast aside his strategy and ordered an offensive against Wu's army, Fan Li knew the defeat of Yue was a foregone conclusion. The king's impatience had played right into the hands of his opponent. All he could do now was to help the king make the best of it.

"But how?" The king sighed, overwhelmed with

futility.

"Under the circumstances," said Wen Zhong, "it would be wise to seek a truce with Wu. Perhaps there's a chance to negotiate peace with them."

"I don't think Fu Chai would accept peace negotiation." Gou Jian shook his head despondently.

"If peace negotiation fails, we'll make him accept our surrender."

"Surrender? How can I degrade myself to such an extent as to beseech the mercy of my enemy? I'd rather kill myself."

"Please don't," pleaded Fan Li. "It is not just a matter of Your Majesty's life. The fate of our country is in your hands. If you kill yourself, all hopes will be lost. Yue will perish. The people of Yue will become slaves of Wu. Just think how your ancestors will regard you and how history will judge you."

These words had an immediate effect. Gou Jian became quiet. The enormity of his mistake had sunk in. He was in desperate straits precisely because he had refused the counsels of his ministers. He had ignored their plea not to respond to Wu's provocation. He had turned down Fan Li's request for expanding the army. He had suspected Fan Li of trying to expand his power by expanding the army, and he did not want anyone in his court to have too much power. He could not afford another mistake.

"It is humiliating to surrender, my king," Wen Zhong chimed in. "But to surrender is to play for time until events turn in our favor. Wu's Prime Minister Bo Pi is known for his greediness and his liking for the fair sex. We can work on him and ask him to intercede for us."

"I'm afraid Wu Yuan would not spare us." Gou Jian seemed to thaw a bit.

"But Bo Pi is known to be a smooth-tongued man," Fan Li said. "If he is willing to help us, Sire, we'll stand a good chance of survival. Then we will bide our time for our future victory."

Finally Gou Jian agreed to let Wen Zhong go to Bo Pi as his envoy to seek a peaceful settlement.

\* \* \*

Wen Zhong arrived at Wu's camp and petitioned for an audience with Prime Minister Bo Pi. His request was quickly granted.

Bo Pi was fifty-odd, a man of medium stature, with a roundish face, a flat nose and a pair of small, searching eyes. The visit of Yue's emissary was not unexpected given the desperate state Gou Jian was in.

"Your Excellency," Wen Zhong humbly went down on his knees when he entered Bo Pi's office, "my master, King Gou Jian, ordered me to bring this to you as an expression of his admiration for the good reputation Your Excellency enjoys among the nations."

He reverentially presented Bo Pi an exquisite gift-box made of carved boxwood. An attendant took the box from him and opened it for Bo Pi. Bo Pi's eyes lit up with sudden exultation at the sight of eight pairs of flawless white opals. As his assessing gaze rolled over these translucent stones, he knew they were the finest of their kind. *They must be worth a fortune.*

Knowledge of life told him that an emissary from a defeated enemy asking for an interview must have brought with him valuable gifts. But the magnificence of Wen Zhong's gift was beyond his expectation.

"Thank you very much, Lord Wen Zhong." Bo Pi accepted the gift with an air of arrogant condescension. "They look very precious."

"As a matter of fact, these gemstones are among the most treasured items in the collection of my king's family."

"I'm not surprised. But how did you get hold of them at this time?"

"They were smuggled into the Guiji Mountains," Wen Zhong answered sheepishly.

"I see," Bo Pi gave an understanding nod. "It's very kind of you, Lord Wen Zhong. What can I do for you?"

"Gou Jian's youth and ignorance have caused him to offend your great king. I am here to appeal to Your Excellency for help. I implore you to intercede with your king on behalf of my master."

"What does he want?"

"He wants to negotiate peace."

"To negotiate peace?" Smile faded from Bo Pi's face. He stared hard at Wen Zhong. "Gou Jian is out of his mind. His fate is in the hands of King Fu Chai who can exterminate him any moment he chooses."

"Your Excellency," pleaded Wen Zhong, "please help us. Please ask the great king to show mercy."

"Peace negotiation is completely out of the question." Bo Pi left his seat and began pacing the room, his hands clasped behind his back. "You know, King Fu Chai is bent on wiping out the State of Yue to avenge his father whom you people killed."

"My master is willing to surrender and offer his entire kingdom to be Wu's vassal state. Yue will send annual tributes to Wu."

"If that's the case," Bo Pi arched one brow, "I'll see what I can do. Be my honorable guest and stay for the night in my camp. I'll take you to see the king tomorrow."

\* \* \*

The next morning Wen Zhong's hope was dashed. As soon as he made a kowtow to King Fu Chai, the king spoke out.

"My prime minister has told me about your proposal. But I don't accept any settlement that would allow Gou Jian to live. The only way for me to withdraw my troops is for Gou Jian to kill himself. When I have received his head, I will take my troops and leave Yue. I want you to tell him if he does not kill himself, I will kill him. The debt of blood," he paused to underscore his message, "must be paid in blood."

Then, without giving Wen Zhong a chance to say a word, he motioned to the guards to usher him out. Wen Zhong asked to see the prime minister, but was told that Bo Pi was too busy and he was escorted out of Wu's camp unceremoniously.

The bad news brought back by Wen Zhong threw Gou Jian into a rage. He drew out his sword and slashed off a corner of the table.

"I will fight to the end," he growled. "We still have five thousand men. I'll make a last-ditch fight. I will not surrender."

"Your Majesty," Fan Li entreated, "please remember what we've agreed on. We must strive to survive."

"But that bastard won't let me."

"I believe there's still some hope for us." Fan Li was not surprised by Fu Chai's rejection and already thought of a new approach. He turned to Wen Zhong, "I think you need to go to Bo Pi a second time to reiterate our peaceful intention, and try to exploit the rivalry between him and Wu Yuan and sway him by self-interest."

"I'm contemplating the same thing," Wen Zhong concurred. "Bo Pi is jealous of the old general. I'll give him to understand that if he helps us this time, he can count on our friendship all his life."

Gou Jian signified his consent by silence.

* * *

Bringing with him another gift-box containing sixteen ingots of pure gold, Wen Zhong set out for Bo Pi's camp again a few days later.

"Your Excellency, my master Gou Jian is a grateful man. If you help him survive the disaster, he will serve you by all means should you ever need him. The annihilation of Yue may not be entirely in Your Excellency's best interest."

"Why?"

"Have you thought who would get the most credit if Yue is wiped out? Who would stand to gain most after ... "

Bo Pi raised a hand to stop Wen Zhong. He took the hint. He was a popular figure in King Fu Chai's court. Unlike Wu Yuan who tended to stroke the king the wrong way by his frequent remonstrations, he was witty and flattering. The king enjoyed his company.

Unlike Wu Yuan who often criticized officials for their negligence in their duties, he was ever-ready to pay little compliments to his subordinates—in the form of cheerful acquiescences or monetary gifts. But he did not have Wu Yuan's power and prestige. For this reason, he had long been jealous of the general. True Wu Yuan had performed meritorious service, but he was conceited. If Yue were wiped out, Bo Pi was sure the general would become more powerful, more prestigious—and more conceited. Fu Chai would come under his influence even more. Then what would become of himself? Wu Yuan never had a high opinion of him.

"Lord Wen Zhong," said Bo Pi in a cheery, big-hearted manner. "I will do my best to prevent your master from being killed. I was born with a kind heart, you know. Benevolence is my motto."

Wen Zhong fell on his knees immediately. "Thank you, Your Excellency. My master will deeply appreciate your kindness."

"But I'm afraid Gou Jian may have to be held captive—for a certain period of time."

"Please make it a short period, Your Excellency."

"It all depends, my lord. But I'll talk to the king again."

"Your Majesty," said Bo Pi to Fu Chai the following morning, "my unflinching loyalty to you prompts me to counsel that you accept Gou Jian's surrender. He offers to be your slave, to subjugate his entire realm to you, and to contribute all the valuables treasured in his palace to Your Majesty."

"I don't accept his surrender," Fu Chai said resolutely. "Gou Jian deserves death. His crime does not allow me to breathe the same air with him."

But Bo Pi was not deterred. "Sire, Marshal Sun Tzu said, 'A defeated enemy can still put up a formidable fight if they are pushed to desperation. Give them a way out.' At present, Gou Jian is surrendering in abject humility. If we refuse and insist on his destruction, he will become desperate. A desperate enemy can be very dangerous. Even if we have the power to destroy him, the cost can be very high. Moreover, we, as the victor, will be confronted with an angry populace in Yue burning with hatred for us."

"Yue deserves punishment."

"On the contrary," Bo Pi went on, "if you accept his surrender and spare his life, your good reputation will spread far and wide—your reputation as a magnanimous ruler worthy of Heavenly Mandate. Your mercy toward a defeated enemy will command respect from all the nobles of China and your wish to become the First Lord will undoubtedly be fulfilled. A ruler who is cruel toward a defeated nation is scorned by his peers."

Fu Chai remained silent. He felt there was some truth in Bo Pi's argument.

"Let me think about it," he said curtly before dismissing his prime minister.

News of Yue's emissary asking for peaceful surrender through Bo Pi's mediation quickly reached Wu Yuan. How could Fu Chai meet Gou Jian's envoy without letting him know? How could he only listen to Bo Pi? Had he forgotten his father's behest that he should consult his chief general on important matters? Wu Yuan knew Fu Chai could be muddle-headed but had not expected he would be so stupid as to consider accepting Gou Jian's surrender when total victory was in sight. He charged into the king's camp, his whole body shaking with rage.

"Fu Chai, stop this nonsense!" he snarled.

He was the only person who often addressed the king by name. Tall and sturdy, Wu Yuan had a rectangular face with a high-bridged nose, a prominent jaw, thick brows and big, piercing eyes. Although he was only in his late fifties, his hair and beard were as white as snow.

Fu Chai recoiled under the general's angry glare.

"Don't forget your father's dying words," Wu Yuan went on, "and the vow you made everyday in the past three years!"

"I haven't, my lord."

"Then you must not accept Gou Jian's surrender."

"Why?" The king was annoyed at the overbearing manner of the old general. He had been on the throne for three years. Regrettably his former teacher still treated him like a pupil.

"Because his surrender is meaningless. We are on the verge of wiping him out of existence. We will make the State of Yue a part of Wu."

"My lord, haven't you heard the saying that killing the subdued brings calamity not only to the killer, but also to his family?"

"What absurdity?" Wu Yuan sneered. "You must avenge your father. It's your duty. If you don't, you'll bring disgrace on yourself and your family. That would be real calamity."

Not knowing what to say, Fu Chai cast a hesitating glance toward Bo Pi.

"My lord," Bo Pi took the cue, cleared his throat,

and addressed the chief general, "we must have vision. Killing Gou Jian would give us immediate gratification, but it would be a very unwise thing to do. Wu is a great power. To show mercy to Yue will enhance our standing among the nobles of China. The king's decision is in the best interest of our country in the long run."

The king turned to the general, much relieved. "My respected general, the prime minister has a point. Gou Jian is in our hands. I can kill him any time. Please set your mind at ease."

Wu Yuan was incensed by Bo Pi's remark hinting that he lacked vision. He and Bo Pi used to be on good terms. But gradually they became estranged as he found Bo Pi to be a sly, greedy sycophant who lacked integrity and real talent. What Bo Pi was good at was to fawn his way to favor and advancement.

Wu Yuan controlled himself and continued to remonstrate with the young king. "My king, Yue has been Wu's bitter foe for generations. It would be foolish to throw away the chance of destroying it once and for all. Gou Jian is a dangerous man. Stamp him out right now is my advice."

"Your Excellency," Bo Pi cut in and said in a sarcastic tone, "please don't forget how *you yourself* spared *your* enemy, the king of Chu, when you had avenged your father. Why didn't you annihilate Chu when you were victorious? I suppose you wanted a good reputation for being lenient to a defeated enemy. Why should you now try to make the king bear a bad name among his peers?"

Wu Yuan knew Bo Pi had a glib tongue but had not expected that he would twist the facts in this manner. He was on that expedition too and knew very well that Wu could not have conquered Chu because Chu had obtained massive relief from Qin, a strong power in western China.

"You liar!" Wu Yuan roared and, in a fit of fury, he charged toward Bo Pi, but was stopped by Fu Chai.

Fu Chai was disappointed. His former mentor should have understood that his goal was greater than wreaking vengeance on Yue. Although he had never stated publicly, his dream was to become the First Lord of China, an honorable title given to a ruler who commanded respect from all other states. But Wu Yuan did not seem interested.

"No more arguing, my lords!" he ordered.

He turned to the chief general and said crisply, "I've decided to accept Gou Jian's surrender. But I appreciate your advice."

Speechless with wrath, Wu Yuan stormed out of the king's camp.

With Wu Yuan out of sight, Fu Chai asked Bo Pi to bring in Wen Zhong.

Wen Zhong entered, crawling on his knees. He humbly submitted a letter from Gou Jian stating his willingness to surrender to Wu without any condition.

"Is Gou Jian willing to come to my palace to do menial labor to prove his repentance?" asked Fu Chai.

"My master is most willing to be of service to Your Majesty."

"How soon can he come?"

"Please allow him enough time to go home to bring his wife with him."

"I'll give him a month's grace. Should Gou Jian fail to come, he will risk his own destruction."

# CHAPTER FIVE

## Surrender

KING GOU JIAN spent a month holding meetings with his ministers, assigning duties to each of them and preparing for the subdued nation's tribute to its conqueror. Fan Li offered to go with him to Wu. His sense of duty compelled him to go with king. He felt he was partially responsible for Yue's defeat and he owed the king a debt of gratitude ever since he had been promoted to be the chief general.

On the eve of Gou Jian's departure, all the ministers gathered in the audience hall to attend a farewell dinner for their king. At the head table sat King Gou Jian in a colorful silk gown, wearing a tall crown inlaid with gold, silver and precious stones, on top of which was a rectangular board with strings of jade beads hanging in the front as well as in the back. Sitting below were military officers on the right, headed by Fan Li, and civil administrators on the left, headed by Wen Zhong. They were all decorously dressed, Fan Li wearing a purplish red silk gown and a brass helmet with a tiger's face carved on it, and Wen Zhong a dark blue gown with a black silk hat.

The prime minister offered a toast. "On behalf of all of us here and the people of Yue, I wish Your Majesty great luck and a safe return."

Gou Jian rose and drank up the cup.

"My good lords, there is no knowing how long I am going to be held in captivity. I count on you all to preserve our nation. I don't have a son. If I am dead, please select a new king. I would be grateful if you could pay annual respects to my ancestors' temple."

In response, the ministers bowed low. Each, in turn, pledged their allegiance to the king and vowed to do their best to carry out their duties.

"I will do my best to run the country and see to it that the people live a decent life," pledged Wen Zhong.

"I will make sure that the weather forecasts are reliable and farmers sow and harvest in good time," said Ji Ni, Minister of Agriculture.

"I will promote understanding and strengthen friendship with other nations," said Yi Yong, Minister of Foreign Affairs.

"I will enforce the law and maintain good public order," said Ku Cheng, Minister of Justice.

Fan Li was the last to speak, "I will stand by my king. I will do my level best to shield him from danger and see that His Majesty return safe and sound."

Gou Jian and all the ministers stood up to give Fan Li a standing ovation.

Then the king took off his regal costume and had

his left ear lobe pierced so that he could wear an earring. This was to signify his subservience to his conqueror in much the same way as an ox wore a nose ring to be led by its master.

On the southern bank of Lake Tai Hu the next day, the king bade farewell to his family members, his ministers, and multitudes of civilians of whom many were tearful.

His boat set sail with the southerly wind.

"My good queen," he said to Lady Gou Jian as he sat by her in the cabin, "we are heading for an unknown destiny. I am the culprit, making you share my hard lot with me. I am so sorry."

A wry smile passed over Lady Gou Jian's face. She was tall and slender. Her features were attractive, but there was a hard look about her eyes. "Please don't say so, my good lord. With Lord Fan Li's erudition and resourcefulness, I'm sure we will be able to cope with any eventualities."

"Sire," said Fan Li, "the fact that we are going to Wu means we have already scored a victory over Wu."

"Victory?"

"Isn't it a victory that we have frustrated Wu's attempt to destroy us? Isn't it a victory that Yue has survived the worst disaster in its history? The road before us is tortuous for sure, but our future is bright."

But these words brought nothing more than a bitter smile to Gou Jian's grim face.

Compared with the king, Fan Li was remarkably calm and upbeat. Not long ago he was at what appeared to be the pinnacle of his career. Suddenly he was plunged into the abyss of failure. The reversal of fortune was brutally quick. But Fan Li was philosophical about it. Honestly his lofty position had come all too easily. Its foundation was shaky. Now he was going to pay a price for success. He recalled what his mentor had once said to him, "Wisdom and ability are forged in adversity. Before Heaven invests a man with great responsibilities, it will first try his resolve and test his endurance by putting him through a lot of pain, toil and sufferings, and by throwing obstacles in his way. Thus his mind will be sharpened, his abilities developed and his weaknesses overcome."

Fan Li was confident he would rise to the challenge. Not only would he survive the ordeal ahead, he would also help the king survive, and survival would mean victory.

\*　　\*　　\*

On the town bulletin board of Zhuji a notice was posted. It was King Gou Jian's last edict before his departure in which he announced that Prime Minister Wen Zhong would act on his behalf during his absence and he asked the people for cooperation.

News of Yue's defeat cast a pall over the town. In the marketplace the morning was as bustling as ever. The fruit, vegetable, meat, fish and grain stalls were crowded with customers jostling with each other, eager to lay their hands on the best items with the best prices before the goods were picked over. But the atmosphere was subdued and the din of the market tinctured with somberness.

At Shih Cheng's fish stall, customers were taking their pick from the variety of fresh-water fish—bass, bullhead, carp, cod, dace and perch—that were swimming in half a dozen wooden basins. Standing by his side was his daughter Hsi Shih who was now eleven years old.

Hsi Shih looked touchingly attractive in a scarlet blouse and black trousers. A scarlet ribbon adorned her warm, black hair blown loose about her face by the morning breeze. Around her waist were three belts of green, white and blue. Three matching anklets made of beads were set off nicely by the brown of her bare feet. Tinged with a light sun-tanned swarthiness, her pretty face and slim shape showed the innocent bloom of a young beauty.

Her eyes cast down, she was cleaning a carp for a woman who had just bought it from her father. Holding a scraper in one hand and pressing the fish with the other, she removed the scales from the tail to the head, sending scales flying as they came free, splashing her pretty face with tiny scales.

Next she lifted up the gill covers. A flick of the wrist and the gills were pulled out. Then she slit open the belly and pulled out the innards with a deft and forceful movement of her hand. It was a delicate job for she had to make sure the gall bladder was intact. The gall bladder had a very thin wall that could easily rupture. If the bile stored inside spilled out, its bitter taste would spoil the fish. Hsi Shih had never punctured a gall bladder.

After snipping the fins and tail with shears, she washed the fish clean and gave it to the woman with a swift smile. The woman put a few coins in her hand and left.

The next customer, an elderly woman with a wizened face, wanted to have her perch filleted. After scaling and removing the entrails, Hsi Shih turned the fish on its side. Using a sharp knife with a slender blade, she made one cut in front of the tail down to the bone and another cut near the head. Then turning the knife blade flat, she cut the flesh along the backbone and rib cage from head to tail, staying as close to the bone as possible. As she sliced down, she lifted away the fillet gently without tearing it. When one side was finished, she flipped the fish over to fillet the other side. Her fingers moved over the fish dexterously, their smooth rhythm broken only by the swing of her arm as she wiped off the drops of water that flew into her eyes.

As she stood watching, the old woman slid her glance from Hsi Shih's hands to her face, and a delightful sparkle entered her narrowed eyes.

"Your girl's on her way to being a great beauty," she remarked to Shih Cheng.

"No joking please, madam." Shih Cheng recognized the woman to be a well-known soothsayer in Zhuji.

"No, I am not. I couldn't say that to anyone but you. I predict some nobleman will come along one day and make a noble lady of your girl."

"Really?" Shih Cheng slanted her an incredulous glance.

"Your daughter is going to be a princess, a celebrity one day. Believe me," the soothsayer insisted.

Shih Cheng smiled. His daughter was his treasure. His wife being in delicate health, Hsi Shih not only did household chores but helped him sell fish every morning. Shih Cheng wanted his daughter to have a good life. But soothsayers always said such things to please people. Their words could not be taken seriously. Yet in a vague way, he felt the future of his daughter would be quite different from that of an ordinary country lass.

Now both sides of the fish were done, Hsi Shih removed the fillets, cut away some discolored portions and handed them to the woman.

"Thank you very much, girl. Mark my words. You will do very well," the soothsayer proclaimed cheerfully before she hobbled away without leaving a tip.

# CHAPTER SIX

# In Captivity

GOU JIAN, HIS wife and Fan Li walked humbly into the Gusu Palace under the escort of four guards. The newly decorated Gusu Palace was an imposing structure. Its gilded roof, red walls, colorful columns and carved balustrade formed a harmonious contrast with the rich green of the palace garden. In the foreground, royal guards in red, green, yellow, white and black uniforms stood in two lines armed with shining broad swords.

Gou Jian was stripped to the waist, wearing a pair of white pants fastened to the body with a jute rope. Lady Gou Jian was dressed in a black top over a white skirt and Fan Li wore a black top over white pants. All three of them were without stockings, only wearing shoes woven of jute, each having a long jute rope around the neck.

Slowly they climbed the steps leading to the Great Audience Hall. Fan Li scanned the hall from the corners of his eyes.

On the dais sat King Fu Chai in a luxurious yellow robe, embroidered with dragons. On his head was a six-inch-tall crown, inlaid with gold and precious stones. On top of the crown was a black rectangular board with jade beads hanging in the front as well as in the back. In his jade-studded belt was a sword with its hilt and scabbard richly embellished.

Below the dais stood two rows of his officials: military officers on the right with Wu Yuan at the head and civil officials on the left with Bo Pi at the head. Wu Yuan wore a red silk gown and a five-inch-tall coronet of deep mauve, on which spread out two long *Ho* bird plumes, the *Ho* bird signifying bravery because it would fight its enemy until death. Bo Pi was dressed in an exquisitely tailored dark gray silk gown with colorful hemming made of de luxe brocade and a five-inch-tall coronet made of white deer skin and studded with colored jade beads.

The three captives stopped in the middle of the hall, groveled before the king of Wu and kowtowed three times.

"My Sovereign Lord," said Gou Jian in a tremulous voice, "your unworthy slave, Gou Jian, is here to serve you."

Staring down at Gou Jian, Fu Chai could hardly sit still. His father's deathbed words ringing in his ears, a strong urge to kill rose in him. His heart beat fast. He wanted to chop off Gou Jian's head and spill his blood on the tomb of his father.

"Sire, this is Yue's tribute-sheet." Bo Pi made a deferential bow and handed Fu Chai a document detailing the amount of gold and silver bullion, gemstones and bolts of fine silk that Gou Jian had brought with him. But Fu Chai brushed him aside.

"Gou Jian, you deserve to die," he snarled.

"Yes, I deserve to die."

"Why didn't you kill yourself? You have no sense of shame!"

"I am at Your Majesty's mercy. Yue is at Your Majesty's mercy."

Fu Chai was amused to see the gold ring dangling from Gou Jian's ear catching the shaft of sunlight that came in through the latticed window. Gazing at Gou Jian's prostrate figure, he had never felt so powerful.

A long moment of silence passed. Bo Pi wiggled his toes uneasily. He was afraid Fu Chai might not spare Gou Jian, but decided to say nothing for the time being as he noticed that Fu Chai appeared to be savoring the pride and pleasure of the victor.

"Had I been really vindictive, Gou Jian," Fu Chai said with arrogance and contempt mixed in his tone, "you would have been a dead man already."

Bo Pi breathed a sigh of relief.

Gou Jian crawled a step forward and kowtowed again, "Thank you for sparing me my life, my Sovereign Lord. Thank you. As long as I live I will remember your magnanimity and be grateful. I will serve you all my life. I pledge my undying fidelity to Your Majesty and my lifelong allegiance to the State of Wu."

Fu Chai ordered his faithful aide-de-camp, General Wangsun Shong, to accommodate Gou Jian and his party in a stony shack at the foot of the Gusu Hill, twenty *li* southwest of the capital, where they were to tend forty horses in the royal stable.

*   *   *

Gou Jian and Fan Li worked hard. They would get up at cockcrow, cut the fodder, feed the horses, wash them, groom them, and clean the stables of dirt and dung. Lady Gou Jian would wash clothes and cook meals, often having to make do with rotten vegetables and stale meat that were given them.

While their captors would humiliate Gou Jian and order him about at will, Fan Li showed meticulous respect. When talking to Gou Jian, he would bow to him as though the stony shack were the royal court of Yue, and he, as the king's subject, always observed court decorum. He made a point of taking the heavier, dirtier job upon himself. At the meal table, he would not sit down until Gou Jian had taken his place at the head of the table.

Whenever King Fu Chai went out, Gou Jian was made to walk beside his horse-and-carriage to be paraded through the streets of Gusu. Pedestrians would point their fingers and jeer at him, knowing he was the former king of Yue and the present slave of King Fu Chai.

What Gou Jian witnessed in Wu convinced him that Wu was a rich and powerful country and that it was rather foolish for him to think Yue could have defeated Wu.

The splendor of Gusu—the symbol of Wu's wealth and culture—filled him with both envy and bitterness. Like Guiji, Gusu had more than a hundred bridges arching over a slim waterway, and many tree-lined lanes ran along its narrow, interlocking canals. But it also had glamorous shops, splendid restaurants and above all, famed gardens, that Guiji did not have. Masses of beautifully dressed people promenaded through the fashionable streets of Gusu. Unlike the bare-footed Yue natives, most people wore shoes. The women's dresses and shoes—with embroidered patterns of trees, flowers, birds and butterflies of various types—were eye-catching. The Wu dialect carried a pleasant accent and sounded especially charming when spoken by women.

*What a lovely city! I wish it were the capital of my country,* he thought in spite of himself.

Fu Chai often privately watched his captives from his balcony in the Gusu Tower, a vantage point that commanded a far-sighted view. The tower was originally built by his father as a summer palace on the top of the Gusu Hill.

"Our captives are doing a good job," he commented one day to General Wu Yuan. "The horses are well-fed, well-groomed and well-exercised, and the stable is clean."

"They'd better behave themselves."

"I do appreciate the way they behave to each other. No breach of etiquette even when they are living under such pitiful conditions."

"That young man Fan Li is a man of great talent," Wu Yuan remarked. "It'll be to our advantage if we could win him over. Use him or kill him is my advice."

"Kill him?" said Fu Chai. "That makes no sense. I'm going to make him serve me."

A few days later, Fu Chai summoned Fan Li for a private audience.

"My chief general Wu Yuan thinks highly of you, Lord Fan Li. They say a wise man doesn't serve a hopeless master. Would you consider working for me? I will offer you a high position and generous emoluments."

· It was not unusual at the time for an official of one state to serve in another to advance his career or for some other reason. For example, Wu Yuan fled to Wu to escape persecution in his own country. Naturally, Fan Li knew that. However, he was a captive of Wu. It would be utterly unconscionable to leave his own king, who had treated him very well, for a position in his captor's court. If he did so, he would forever be stigmatized as a shameless traitor.

"Your Majesty," Fan Li replied coolly, "I am grateful for your offer. But I am King Gou Jian's subject. I cannot desert my king when he is in distress. I don't think Your Majesty would appreciate a man who leaves his own master in the lurch for a high position in another country."

"Why do you talk like that?" Fu Chai said gruffly, "I can kill Gou Jian any time I choose. What good is it to serve somebody who has lost his country?"

Fan Li was unruffled. "Your Majesty, I always will be my king's subject."

"All right. Get out! Go back to feed my horses with your master."

Despite his disappointment, Fu Chai had to concede a certain grudging respect for his captive.

He mentioned this to Bo Pi a few days later.

"Fan Li is a man of only mediocre abilities," Bo Pi replied, ready to contradict Wu Yuan whenever he could. "He's given a high place because he's comparatively better than others in Gou Jian's court."

"Why did Wu Yuan recommend him?"

"Just imagine. Would Wu Yuan really recommend a talented man who could outshine himself? By calling Gou Jian a dangerous man and Fan Li a talent, he obviously wants Your Majesty to kill Gou Jian and annihilate Yue."

"Why is the general bent on wiping out Yue?"

"Well, he has his reasons."

"What reasons?"

Bo Pi pretended to hesitate.

"Speak up," Fu Chai urged.

"Your father-king had been grateful to Wu Yuan," Bo Pi said in a faltering voice. "When he was alive, he promised to share the kingdom with him. But your father-king died so suddenly that he was unable to keep his promise. At present, General Wu Yuan is the second most powerful man in the country, but that's not enough for him. If Yue is taken over, I'm sure he will ask Your Majesty to appoint him as the ruler of Yue."

An uneasy silence followed. Then Fu Chai motioned Bo Pi to leave the room.

\*   \*   \*

One evening Gou Jian, all covered with dirt and horse dung, was dead tired after a long day's work.

"I hate it!" he bellowed as he sat down at the supper table. "How disgusting! Befouling myself with horse dung day in and day out and eating what is fit only for a swine."

"Sire," Fan Li hastily interrupted, "please control yourself. Please keep your voice down. The guards are nearby."

"I don't care," Gou Jian spat on the ground, his

face contorted with hatred. "Tell me, how long must I live in this damned stony shack? How long must I stay in this accursed country? I don't know how much more of this I can stand."

One and half years had passed since they came to Wu. Fan Li had gotten used to Gou Jian's occasional tantrums. The hard life of a slave laborer had taken a toll on the king's emotional stability. Most of the time the king suffered the trials of his degradation patiently. However, he could be unexpectedly impulsive, which made him unpredictable, and unpredictable could make things dangerous for him. Whenever he had such outbursts, Fan Li and Lady Gou Jian would anxiously help him keep his temper.

"It's hard to say, Sire," Fan Li replied in a subdued voice. "Fu Chai has the whims of a cruel tyrant, but also the caprice of a kindly woman. With Bo Pi interceding with him in our behalf, and with Wu Yuan constantly urging him to get rid of us, there is no telling what is to become of us."

"What is to be done, then?"

"Your Majesty, I'm afraid that only by succumbing to playing the worm can we obtain freedom in spite of the general's obstruction."

"Playing the worm?"

"Exactly, because a worm is so small it can get into the depth of Fu Chai's heart."

"Hmm. I see your point," Gou Jian said with a wry smile.

"Sire, as you know, King Wen, founder of the Zhou Dynasty, was made to spend long years in jail. He was even made to eat the flesh of his own son who had been boiled in a pot by the order of King Zhou, the tyrant king of the Shang Dynasty. King Wen endured the unendurable, swallowed the unswallowable. But eventually he overthrew his enemy. He had crouched low enough for the final spring. His hard life in prison had prepared him for his eventual success. I believe Your Majesty's hard life is also a blessing in disguise."

A shaft of moonlight fell through the half-open door. For a long moment Gou Jian remained silent. He understood he had to endure, be patient, but sometimes it was very difficult to suppress his anger and despair. He marvelled how Fan Li could bear the ordeal with such equanimity.

"Thank you for your advice, my good lord." At last he broke the silence.

"My good lady," he turned to his wife, "thank you for the meal. I *must* eat. I *must* eat to live—and live on to have my revenge."

He swallowed down the meal without another word as though he were making a tremendous effort to swallow his pride. As a matter of fact, the dishes were quite edible thanks to Lady Gou Jian's cuisine skill, though they were nothing like what he used to have.

Thereafter the king rarely lost his temper. He became reticent. He seldom smiled and always seemed to be thinking, reflecting, calculating. But Fan Li could tell he was imbued with hatred. The king confided to him that his goals were not just wreak vengeance on Wu but eventually become the First Lord. The king was more ambitious than he had expected. But Fan Li could readily understand, and was encouraged. Such ambition would give the king the will to survive. It would energize him, motivate him, and enable him to endure the humiliation and hardships as Fu Chai's slave.

One day Bo Pi came to see them at meal time, with a servant in his wake. Gou Jian and his companions hastily knelt down to greet him.

"Please rise!" said Bo Pi. "How are you, my friends?"

"We are fine, Your Excellency," Gou Jian replied. "Thank you for asking."

"I have good news for you. As a result of the many efforts I made on your behalf and your own good behavior, King Fu Chai says he doesn't mind setting you people free. Says he'll make a decision soon."

"Thank you so very much, Your Excellency."

"I've brought some food and drink for you."

Bo Pi ordered his servant to present a few bottles of wine and some jars of delicacies.

"Oh, Your Excellency, how can we thank you enough!" said Lady Gou Jian.

Gou Jian's party knelt down again to express their gratitude.

\* \* \*

Gou Jian waited eagerly for the order of his release, but no good luck came his way. Bo Pi, however, was good enough to send food and drink to him every now and then.

One day Bo Pi told him that Fu Chai was ill.

"No wonder His Majesty has not used his carriage for nearly a month," said Gou Jian, for, as a rule, Fu Chai used his carriage six or seven times each month.

"What is the king's illness?" Fan Li asked.

"The doctor says the king has a liver condition. He has a fever, feels dizzy and his limbs are numb."

The news of Fu Chai's illness upset Gou Jian.

"If Fu Chai dies now," he said to Fan Li, "Wu Yuan would certainly have us killed."

"Fu Chai won't die," Fan Li assured him. "I have some medical knowledge," he explained. "Based on Bo Pi's description, Fu Chai seems to suffer from having too much *yang* in his liver. It takes time for *yin* and *yang* to regain balance. But I believe he will be fully recovered in ten to fifteen days because he has a strong constitution."

A few days later, Gou Jian walked to the palace to ask for an audience. At first, his request was turned down. But after he told Bo Pi that he had some medical knowledge which might be of use to the king, he was allowed to visit Fu Chai in the inner palace.

"It's awfully nice of you to come to see me, Gou Jian," murmured the bedridden king in a feeble voice. His face took on a dull, sallowish tinge and pouches hung listlessly beneath his lackluster eyes.

Gou Jian knelt before Fu Chai's bed. "I owe my life to Your Majesty. My soul and my mind will have no peace until I come to see and make sure that you are recovering."

"Thank you, Gou Jian."

Seized by a sudden urge, Fu Chai motioned to an attendant for a chamber pot. The attendant hastened to get one for him and waited till he had relieved himself. The attendant was just about to take away the pot when Gou Jian had a sudden inspiration. He knelt down by the pot, lifted the lid with one hand, dipped a finger of the other hand in the content, and licked. The offensive stench made all those in the room cover their noses.

"Congratulations! My Great Lord!" Gou Jian grinned obsequiously. "You will get better in a few days, and will be completely recovered by the beginning of the next month."

"Good heavens! How do you know that?"

"I studied medicine for a while in my younger days. I can tell from the taste of human excrement how soon a patient can recover. I just had a lick of your stool and it tasted a bit sour. The taste of human excrement varies with the season. If it goes with the season, the disease will soon be cured. If it goes against the season, the body will decline. Now the sour taste is in harmony with the season of early spring, it means that all is well, thank heavens."

"Gou Jian, it is very kind of you!" said Fu Chai, visibly moved.

"I only wish Your Majesty a speedy recovery."

Seeing Bo Pi standing at the bedside, Fu Chai asked, "My dear lord, would you do the same for me as Gou Jian did?"

Bo Pi flushed red with embarrassment.

"I don't blame you," Fu Chai cackled. "Not even my own son could be so filial to me."

"Gou Jian," he turned to his slave, greatly pleased with his manifest devotion. "The moment I get well, I will give you back your freedom."

Just as predicted by Gou Jian, Fu Chai was restored to perfect health by the beginning of the following month.

*   *   *

As soon as Wu Yuan heard about Fu Chai's intention of granting freedom to Gou Jian, he hastened to see the king in the inner palace, his face livid with anger.

"Fu Chai, you must not let the tiger break loose from his cage. Once you set it free, it will tear at you with its fierce claws."

"But Gou Jian is sincerely grateful to me for having spared his life," Fu Chai argued. "He is going to be our vassal."

"How can you trust a man like Gou Jian? Can't you see through his schemes?"

Irritated by Wu Yuan's insolent tone, Fu Chai decided not to be put down. "My respected general, can't yesterday's enemy become tomorrow's friend? If we treat him nicely, anyone can become our friend."

"My king, you are so naive. Gou Jian is a treacherous man. You're deceived by his appearance. If you grant pardons to him today, he will not grant pardons to you in future."

"Gou Jian is not that bad, my lord. I do appreciate his loyalty. You know he even licked my stool to diagnose my illness. Who else would do that?"

"Licking your stool to diagnose your illness? Pure nonsense! Ugh, how disgusting! Gou Jian is utterly shameless."

"Shameless?"

"Just think what man would degrade himself to such an extent."

"Eh? ... " Fu Chai did not know what to think.

"It only proves how crafty and dangerous he is," Wu Yuan warned sternly.

"I don't quite agree with you, my lord."

"Licking your stool is a prelude to sucking your blood and tearing out your heart, my king. If you set him free, you will bring ruin upon yourself. Gou Jian will make all of us his prisoners one day."

Fu Chai found Wu Yuan's reasoning ridiculous. "Please don't abuse a good man!" he said darkly. "I am setting him free. My mind is made up."

Fu Chai invited Gou Jian to a lavish banquet in his palace to announce his release. Gou Jian arrived in the company of Fan Li. Wearing his usual slave's outfit, he kowtowed to Fu Chai, his demeanor as humble as ever. Fu Chai stepped down from the dais to greet him and ordered an attendant to help him change into nobleman's costume.

As soon as Gou Jian re-entered the Great Audience Hall in his new attire, Fu Chai announced his pardon in the presence of all his ministers.

"King Gou Jian will soon return to his country. He and I agree that our two countries should bury the hatchet and live in peace. I am pleased to have him as the guest of honor. I hope every one of you will treat him as a friend. Please join me in a toast to his health and to the well-being of his country." Thus saying, he raised his goblet to his former slave, and his ministers followed suit.

The amicable atmosphere presented a suitable occasion for the signing of the peace treaty which stipulated that Yue was to be Wu's vassal state, that Gou Jian was to send annual tributes to Fu Chai, and that Yue was never again to commit a hostile act against Wu.

"Please read it and let me know if you have any question," Fu Chai told his guest.

Gou Jian readily signed his name on the document and reaffirmed his allegiance to his sovereign lord.

All these proceedings so irked Wu Yuan that he brushed his sleeves against the air and left the hall before the banquet started.

Goblets in hand, Gou Jian and Fan Li chanted a toast to the king:

*We wish you a long, long life;*
*We wish your realm forever thrive.*
*Benev'lence be your lasting aim,*
*And "Lord of Lords" your well-earn'd name.*

The banquet ended with everyone replete with good food and wine. The king was especially pleased to hear Gou Jian and Fan Li mentioning the title of "Lord of Lords" in their toast.

On the day of Gou Jian's departure, Fu Chai and all his court ministers, with the exception of Wu Yuan, accompanied the liberated king to the city gate of Gusu. General Wangsun Luo was ordered to escort Gou Jian's party to Lake Tai Hu that marked the border of the two countries.

"I hope you will let bygones be bygones," Fu Chai said to Gou Jian earnestly, "and always remember our present friendship."

"My Sovereign Lord," said Gou Jian, "your servant will forever be grateful to you. Had it not been for your kindness, I wouldn't have lived to this day."

Thus saying, he knelt down again, his eyes welling tears of thankfulness.

Confident of Gou Jian's gratitude and loyalty to him, Fu Chai waved good-bye to the vanishing chariot that carried Gou Jian and his company toward their freedom.

# CHAPTER SEVEN

## Homecoming

STANDING ON THE southern shore of Lake Tai Hu at the head of all the officials to greet the king were Prime Minister Wen Zhong and General Zhu Jicheng. Behind them were crowds of civilians eager to catch a glimpse of the royal countenance of their king.

Amidst the cheers of "Long Live the King!" a silver-haired elderly man stepped forward with a mug filled with wine and presented it to Gou Jian. Gou Jian took the mug and poured the libation onto the ground as a gesture of thanking Heaven and Earth for their blessings.

More shouts of "Long Live the King!" broke out as the king and queen waved to the greeting crowds and ascended a waiting coach.

The skies were a boundless blue, the rice fields luxuriant, the mountains robed in verdure and the rivers babbling joyfully.

"Ah—, I never dreamed that I would live to see this day." Gou Jian took a deep breath of the clean, fresh air. He was tanned, thinner but in high spirits.

Wen Zhong and Fan Li rode abreast on horseback.

"I've missed you a lot." Wen Zhong said, his eyes gleaming with joy. Absence had made the heart grow fonder. "The three arduous years seemed so long without you."

"I've missed you, too," said Fan Li, noticing Wen Zhong had changed little except his hair was greying.

"Thank heavens, all's over now."

"I'm afraid all's not over. The king wants to have his revenge on Fu Chai. By the way, do I smell like a horse, having messed myself with horse dung for three years?"

Wen Zhong pulled closer to Fan Li and sniffed him. "No, not at all," he chuckled. "You smell like a nobleman, my friend. Like a great soldier. You've lost some weight for sure, but you look as strong as a horse."

\* \* \*

To celebrate his homecoming, King Gou Jian held a banquet attended by all his ministers. The king did not wear his regal costume, but was dressed in a plain black robe. His ministers, all in splendid courtly costume, were caught by surprise.

"Please excuse me for not dressing up for the occasion," the king said, "but I feel more comfortable in this clothes. First, let me express my appreciation to each and every one of you for doing an excellent job during my absence, especially to Lord Wen Zhong for his leadership. I am deeply grateful. I would like all of you to join me to toast to Lord Wen Zhong."

He raised his goblet and drank it up. Wen Zhong bowed low as the king directed a commendatory glance toward him. He had managed to run the country well and the people were generally satisfied despite the hardships caused by the war. But, unbeknownst to him, his popularity had incurred jealousy in the king who believed nobody should enjoy more prestige in his kingdom than himself. Nevertheless, the king, ever so good at concealing his feelings, pasted a sincere smile on his face and made Wen Zhong feel appreciated.

Then the king turned to Fan Li. "Without Lord Fan Li's wisdom, without his faith and fortitude, I would not be here today. I owe Lord Fan Li my eternal gratitude. I want all of you to join me in saluting him."

With that, he raised his goblet again and drank it up. Fan Li made a respectful bow to the king from his seat.

"I've decided not to wear silk gown," the king continued, "and not sleep on soft mattress. Since my return I've been sleeping on a plank every night. I've also decided not to restore the imperial harem which I had disbanded before I went to Wu. And every morning I drink a cup of the bear bile. Do you know why?"

Before his ministers could answer, the king explained himself, "I drink it not because the bear bile has medicinal virtues, but because the taste of the bile will remind me of my bitter life in Wu."

The king's remark caused a stir in his audience.

"I want to work with all of you," he continued, "to turn our country into a strong, independent state. I want you to come up with ideas and suggestions. I was not very good at taking criticisms. But from now on I will welcome criticisms. I encourage you to remonstrate with me if I do something wrong."

Then he turned to Wen Zhong. "My dear prime minister, in your estimation how long will it take for us to catch up with Wu?"

"I think it will take ten years to build a rich and prosperous Yue."

"What about military strength? How long will it take for us to match Wu?" Gou Jian looked at Fan Li.

"I guess it will also take ten years."

"So we need twenty years."

"Not exactly, Sire," Fan Li said. "Military buildup can go in parallel with economic reconstruction. I reckon it will probably take fifteen years altogether to turn our country into a strong power."

"Very good. Let's make it our policy." The king motioned an attendant to bring a brush and some ink and wrote *Ten Years for Reconstruction* on one length of cloth and *Ten Years for Military Build-up* on another piece. Then the couplets were hung on the wall behind the head table.

"I shall hang them on my bedroom wall later," the king said, "and contemplate them everyday. Speaking of military build-up, we only have a few thousand ill-equipped men at present. It distresses me no end to see our troops in such a pitiable state. But we lack resources to build a strong army."

"We can start planning," Fan Li suggested.

"Quite so, my lord. For that purpose, I want you to go on an inspection tour around the country to get a better idea what needs to be done."

This was exactly what Fan Li had in mind. "Your

Majesty is most thoughtful," he said appreciatively.

"How long do you think the inspection will take?"

"Between six and nine months. I have a good mind to set up a training base in the mountainous area in the south."

"Not a bad idea but you have to be discreet. How long will that take?"

"Three or four months."

"That will make one full year. How old are you, my lord?"

"Thirty."

"And still single?"

Fan Li smiled self-consciously.

"You need to get married, young man," said the king solicitously.

"Duty comes before personal concerns, Your Majesty."

"I appreciate that. Never mind I've called on young people to get married before twenty. You need a good woman to look after you, my dear lord. Go and find a pretty girl to marry."

"Yes. I'll set out in a day or two. As soon as I get back, I will answer Your Majesty's call for population growth. I know our country needs more people."

His intention being distorted, Gou Jian gave Fan Li a reproving glance, and saw from the glint in his eyes that he was being mischievous. The ministers all chuckled.

"Let's drink a toast to Lord Fan Li's patriotic commitment," Gou Jian proposed jovially.

The ministers unanimously approved and the banquet began in a merry mood.

# CHAPTER EIGHT

## First Love

THE FIRST STOP on Fan Li's inspection tour was Zhuji, the seat of Zhuji County, about a hundred *li* to the south of Guiji. Centrally located, the town offered easy access to half a dozen counties that Fan Li planned to visit.

A welcoming dinner was given in his honor by the county leaders and village fathers in the Yellow Crane Tavern, the best restaurant in town. The tavern had a homely ambience, decorated in rustic simplicity with sprays of flowers and herbs and painted pottery, and furnished with tables and chairs of handy woodwork. A few wash paintings of landscape and pieces of calligraphy were hanging on the walls and the bamboo shades on the windows were let down to soften the light. In front of the building stood a tall oak tree from which hung a red-bordered white flag bearing the big characters *Yellow*

*Crane Tavern*, painted in black.

Thanks to the tavern, the townsfolk and villagers in the neighborhood were not at all ignorant of what was going on in the capital or in other parts of the country, for the tavern was an inexhaustible source of information where news and gossip passed from mouth to mouth.

"My respected elderly fathers," Fan Li addressed them after the introduction by the magistrate of Zhuji, "we are facing a difficult time. The king needs your cooperation in making our country strong and prosperous. His Majesty encourages early marriage. He has decreed that men over twenty and women over seventeen should get married. Otherwise their parents will be judged unpatriotic. Young widows are encouraged to break with the tradition and remarry."

"We'll visit every household in our villages to pair off young people," a village elder responded on behalf of all the elders present.

"Thank you, sir," Fan Li bowed to him. "His Majesty will grant a bottle of wine and a dog to a family for the arrival of a new baby-boy; and a bottle of wine and a pig for the arrival of a baby-girl. If a couple has two children, the state will pay for the expenses of raising one. If they have three children, the state will pay for the expenses of raising two."

The audience applauded.

"The king wants to promote economic growth," Fan Li continued. "Our granaries need to be filled to capacity. His Majesty understands the hardships you endured and has decreed to reduce the taxes by twenty percent. For families that have lost a member in the war, all taxes will be exempted."

The audience applauded again.

Another village elder stood up. "A number of young men are ready to join the army if you need them, Your Excellency."

"Thank you," Fan Li said, knowing he could not recruit openly yet. "But this is not His Majesty's priority at present. You need them to work in the field."

After his speech, he chatted informally with the audience, inquiring about their families, their livelihood as well as answering their questions about his experience in captivity. The dinner ended amidst toasts to the king's health when everybody lifted up his cup and drank off its contents.

*　*　*

Nestled in the fertile valley of the Guiji Mountains, the idyllic village of Zhuluo was a well-known scenic spot in Zhuji County. One day Fan Li decided to feast his eyes on the natural scenery after work. He changed into plain attire, dismissed his guards, and meandered down a broad boulevard along which was a stream lined with weeping willows. On the other side of the boulevard were heavily foliaged shrubs and multi-colored wild flowers, with well-kept farmhouses half-hidden from view.

It was late afternoon. Fan Li was sauntering aimlessly, inhaling the sweet-scented air and savoring a full sense of well-being. Gradually the road became narrower and the stream turned into a brook. All of a sudden he saw, to his delightful surprise, the image of a beautiful maiden on the unruffled surface of the brook. This must be a fantasy. He rubbed his eyes to see more clearly. But it was no fantasy. It was the full-length reflection of a heavenly beauty. His eyes quickly searched along the shore, and there, at the bend of the brook, he saw a beautiful damsel in a pale yellow blouse standing barefoot on a green-grass-carpeted mound, leaning against a rock, a basket of silk floss at her feet. Fan Li climbed up the mound for a closer look. The damsel heard his steps and turned her head, her hair adorned with a bow of pink ribbon, her eyes smiling.

She was a wonder to behold. She had a slender figure, a glowing complexion, a most lovely face with a pair of bright, watery eyes, crescent brows, cherry lips and charming dimples. Her whole being radiated an innate attraction, a natural warmth that very few women possessed.

Fan Li's heart missed a beat. She was more like a picture than a real person, he thought. But, no. No picture could be that beautiful.

Bracing himself up, he stepped forward and bowed. "Good afternoon, fair lady."

"Good afternoon," Hsi Shih responded, a most becoming smile flashing across her face.

Brought up in the milieu of Zhuluo Village where girls were simply girls, she felt flattered to be called "fair lady." She shot an inquiring glance at Fan Li. A tall, handsome young man with a noble bearing. A friendly smile curved his lips.

"You don't belong to this place, sir?" she asked.

"I come from Guiji, fair lady."

"Are you visiting somebody in Zhuluo?"

"I'm on a tour here."

"What can I do for you, sir?"

"Can you tell me where I can get some tea to drink?"

"Of course. There's a tea-house in the village. But it's half an hour's walk from here."

Seeing Fan Li a little hesitant, she added, guilelessly, "If you care to come to my humble cottage, sir, I'll make tea for you. My home is right ahead."

"Thank you," Fan Li's face brightened, "but I didn't mean to bother you, fair lady."

*Again ' fair lady.'* Hsi Shih felt a bit awkward to be addressed in this way.

"That's all right. I've just finished my work. I'm thirsty too."

"It's very kind of you, fair lady."

"My name is Shih. I am called Hsi Shih in the village. Please call me Hsi Shih too. What's your name, sir?"

"My name is Fan." Fan Li decided not to reveal his full name.

"Please follow me, Mr. Fan." Hsi Shih picked up her laundry basket and led the way.

Charmed by the back view of this village girl with shapely legs and lovely long hair braided in a thick queue swaying in cadence to her sprightly steps, Fan Li was suddenly possessed by an indescribable sense of inferiority, a feeling which he, as a senior officer of the king's court, had never before experienced. He felt something, something very precious, very vital, was missing in his life.

They soon arrived at a farmhouse. "Here we are, sir."

"Where are your parents, Hsi Shih?" Fan Li asked, looking around.

"Father's not at home. He's gone to help my aunt

in another village because she is sick and her husband is away."

"And your mother?"

At the mention of her mother, Hsi Shih knitted her brows and a melancholy expression appeared on her face. Her head tilted; her face turned pale. It looked as though she was going to faint, but she managed to stand still, bracing a hand on the table. Fan Li hastened to hold her in his arms.

"Hsi Shih," he called her name gently. "Are you all right?"

Her head was in a swim, but she was conscious of the smell of his masculine body, and could feel its warmth and muscularity. Nobody had ever held her like this except her father. It was embarrassing to be so close to a stranger, comforting as it was. Moments later, the spasm was over. She wriggled herself away from Fan Li, her beautiful face all in a flush.

"I'll get a doctor for you, Hsi Shih."

"No, there's no need," she said drily. "My mother passed away two years ago. My heart feels constricted when I think of her. I just can't help it."

As his own parents died when he was small, Fan Li was sensitive to grief in others. "I'm sorry, Hsi Shih," he said softly. "You must see a doctor."

"I did. The doctor says that's not really a disease, but—'a momentary reflection of the state of mind,'" Hsi Shih said, a wan smile twitching the corners of her mouth. "Please be seated. I'm going to the kitchen. I'll be right back."

Sitting on the chair, Fan Li took a quick survey of the room. It was furnished with a couple of tables made of wood and a few chairs made of bamboo. Simple, clean and tidy, the room was brightened up by the cheerful array of flowers in a wicker basket. On a smaller table lay a scroll of bamboo tablets. Curiosity prompted him to pace the room and examine the scroll. To his pleasant surprise, it was a collection of poems. He had expected the girl to do no more than just read and write.

"Here's your tea, sir," came Hsi Shih's sweet voice.

Fan Li took a sip. "Very tasty tea, Hsi Shih. I love it."

"Because it was infused with spring water."

"Because it was infused by Hsi Shih."

Hsi Shih lowered her glance; a blush climbed her cheeks.

Fan Li considered her closely. "You read poems, Hsi Shih?"

"Yes. I love to read."

"I'm very impressed. Have you been to school?"

"No. There is one in the county, but it takes a long walk to get there. My father cannot afford to send me to school anyway. But I study with a neighbor."

"A neighbor?"

"Yes, he is a teacher but he is kind enough to give me free lessons in his home."

"Free lessons?" Fan Li's attention was arrested.

"Yes. He is a knowledgeable man. I've learned a lot from him."

"Why's he so kind to you?"

"Because his daughter Zheng Dan and I are great friends. We study together and we help each other."

"I see." The information brought an unaccountable relief to Fan Li. "What is your father?"

"My father is a fisherman."

"You work too?"

"I wash silk floss to earn some extra income. I also breed silkworm and weave silk."

After they chatted for a while, Hsi Shih showed him her silkworm nursery next door. She talked about how she raised the silkworms, her big eyes twinkling warmly.

Basking in her presence, Fan Li did not want to leave. But he had to return to his inn before dark, or else his guards would form a search party to ensure the safety of their lord.

"Hsi Shih, thank you for the nice tea. Will you allow me to visit you again?"

"Certainly."

She saw him off to a crossroads and told him how to take a shortcut to the thoroughfare which would take him back to town. As he walked away, Fan Li was conscious that Hsi Shih's eyes—those bright, watery eyes—were fixed on him with a kind of lingering soft look that was curiously flattering.

*　*　*

Fan Li felt as though he were walking on air, his steps light as a feather. He began humming an ancient love ditty which he had learned as a teenager. He did not have a wink of sleep that night. The vision of Hsi Shih lingered: her beautiful face, her radiant smile, her sweet voice, the charm and naivety of a teenage girl on the threshold of womanhood. His heart yearned for her.

Two days later, he visited her again. Wearing a light grey skullcap and a deep blue silk gown with embroidered edgings in the fashion of the time, he trotted along toward Hsi Shih's house which was not difficult to find.

As he walked, the jade ornament hanging on his girdle gave out a melodious sound and the colorful tassel attached to it swayed with the rhythm. Jade ornaments were worn by many people at the time both as ornament and amulet. Most were discs or animal-shaped carvings strung with beads. Fan Li's was a work of art: a colorful combination of jade plaques and pendants of varying sizes strung together in such a way that when he walked, the jade pieces would clink pleasantly—giving a perfect expression to his mood that day.

He picked some roses, lilies, azaleas and sunflowers on his way and arranged them into a beautiful bouquet.

Hsi Shih gave him a brilliant smile as she opened the door and let out a cry of joy at the sight of the flowers. She had missed him in the last few days. This elegant, distinguished-looking young man was different from all the men she had met in the villages around here. He was a gentleman, a scholar, with a charming demeanor. Blushingly, she remembered feeling good in his arms. She had wondered if he would come again.

She was rejoiced to see him once more and invited him to have dinner with her. Fan Li offered to help her set the firewood burning and Hsi Shih prepared a tasty meal with shrimps, green peas, lilies and lotus roots.

After dinner, the two strolled along an unfrequented path, an area sprinkled with the shadows of tree branches. A soft summer breeze caressing their brows, their eyes met. A sweet warmth overtook Fan Li. His eyes were so tempting that Hsi Shih averted her gaze in embarrassment. She kept twirling the fringe of her waist band with her fingers. Fan Li held her in his arms and gently stroked her long, unbraided hair. His touch sent a rippling warmth down to the pit of her stomach. Hsi Shih trembled. Fan Li pressed her closer until her toes nearly left the ground. He kissed her forehead tenderly. Her face turned pale, her eyes closing and the long, dark lashes cast downward. The feel of her breast sent a quiver through him. His lips moved down till they reached hers. Then, in the moonlight, under a blossoming peach tree, the young couple kissed a long, sweet kiss in the joyful bliss of first love.

They met every night. The night was made for lovers. The two lovers would walk along the solitary path or along the banks of a pond where Hsi Shih, barefooted as usual, would step into the muddy water, stir the water with her feet, and grab, with her bare hands, a slippery eel or fish. Fan Li felt somewhat unreal about his encounter with this simple, trustful, pretty maiden, yet it was utterly natural that he should be with her. Her presence seemed to make him feel complete.

Fan Li tarried in Zhuji for some extra days until he could no longer extend his stay if his inspection tour was to be completed on schedule. It was time to leave. As usual Hsi Shih walked with him to the edge of the thoroughfare. They stopped by a pond. The water was calm and seemingly scattered with stars like the sky overhead. Nearby camphor trees grew in abundance, exuding a strong scent most soothing for the lungs. Hsi Shih leaned against a tree on the edge of the pond, stirring the water with her toes, sending a sudden ripple through its surface.

"Hsi Shih," Fan Li spoke in an earnest tone, "I have to go away for some time. But when my mission is completed, I will come to you again."

"You will always be welcome."

"I've been thinking of you all the time, Hsi Shih. The thought of you warms my heart."

A wash of color spread over her pretty face.

"I want to talk about many things with you when I come back."

Hsi Shih nodded.

"Will you wait for me, Hsi Shih?"

"Yes." Hsi Shih gave him a speculative stare, vaguely aware of the meaning of Fan Li's remark.

Fa Li lifted her hand and put it to his lips. "I love you, Hsi Shih."

A delightful silence followed. Hsi Shih stared into Fan Li's eyes. The deep, pure, faithful look in her eyes sent Fan Li's heart beating fast.

"Will you marry me, Hsi Shih?"

Hsi Shih went still, a breeze lightly lifting a lock of her hair off her forehead. She was not supposed to answer the question directly. But the joy on her face was easy to read.

"My father will be back tomorrow," she said softly, her lashes drooping. "He will answer for me."

"My dearest one, I'll be back to meet your father tomorrow."

*   *   *

As soon as Shih Cheng saw Fan Li the following evening, he recognized him.

"General Fan Li!" he bowed immediately, his mild face wreathed in surprise. "Welcome to our humble abode."

"What?" Hsi Shih was astonished. "You are ... "

"You've met General Fan Li?" Shih Cheng looked

perplexed.

"Why didn't you tell me who you are?" Hsi Shih demanded in an offended tone.

"I'm sorry, Hsi Shih," Fan Li said quietly, "I didn't think it necessary."

"Hsi Shih, be polite," Shih Cheng admonished his daughter.

"Please pardon me, Your Excellency," Hsi Shih bowed to Fan Li.

"What are you talking about, Hsi Shih?" Fan Li was flustered.

"If I knew who you are, I would not have treated Your Excellency so—so casually."

"Call me Fan Li please. I sincerely appreciate your hospitality, Hsi Shih."

Hsi Shih hung her head. Her mind swam dizzily. She was flattered by the attention of such a distinguished man but embarrassed by her own familiar way with him for last few days.

"Hsi Shih, it makes no difference what I do," Fan Li said eagerly. "We are equals."

Hsi Shih stared at him. A long moment passed before she turned into the kitchen and brought out a cup of tea for him without a word.

"Papa Shih," Fan Li bowed to Shih Cheng. "I've come here to ask for the hand of your daughter. Hsi Shih is the sweetest and most beautiful girl I have ever met."

A faint smile came to Shih Cheng's weather-beaten face. "Your Excellency, my daughter is just a naive, ordinary country girl. She does not deserve your attention."

"Papa Shih, Hsi Shih is an angel. Please let me marry her."

Shih Cheng fell silent. Hsi Shih was sixteen. Many young men in the village were her admirers. A few had proposed, but Shih Cheng, deeming them unworthy, had declined. General Fan Li must be the most eligible bachelor in the country. Shih Cheng recalled what the soothsayer in Zhuji had said about Hsi Shih years ago. Was Fan Li the nobleman she predicted? Was she correct after all? However, given Fan Li's exalted position, Shih Cheng could not be sure that it would be a good match. Fan Li was so busy, would he ...

"I love Hsi Shih," Fan Li's entreating voice interrupted his train of thought. "I promise to make her happy."

Shih Cheng turned around, looked at his daughter and Hsi Shih colored deeply. A fond look came over his face.

"Hsi Shih was a miracle to me and my wife," he said reminiscently. "On the eve of her birth, my wife had a dream. She saw a shaft of bright light blazing into her room through the roof. That's why Hsi Shih was named Yi Guang which means 'blissful light.'"

"Yi Guang?" Fan Li murmured.

"But the villagers prefer to called her Hsi Shih, 'the Shih Girl of the West Side,' to distinguish her from another girl about the same age whom they called Dong Shih, 'the Shih Girl of the East Side.' A number of the families in Zhuluo share the same name, you know."

"*Hsi Shih* sounds good," said Fan Li.

"I agree." Shih Cheng stared at him directly. "I believe you are sincere, General Fan Li. But you have a lot of responsibilities already. A wife, a family, will surely add to the load on your shoulders ... "

"I am prepared, Papa Shih. I will be kind to

Hsi Shih. I will cherish her, protect her, and provide whatever will please her, and I'm sure Hsi Shih will be my good helpmate."

"Yes," Shih Cheng seemed to find the words reassuring. "Hsi Shih has a pair of able hands, a kind heart and a strong sense of duty. She will make a good wife to you."

"You approved my proposal, Papa Shih?"

"Yes," Shih Cheng gave Fan Li an honest smile. "I give you my approval. You are a good man. I can see that. Her mother asked me to make sure that she would marry a man who would take care of her. I think she would be glad."

Fan Li turned his stare to Hsi Shih, and their gazes locked in an electric moment, their eyes glowing with happiness. As a ritual for betrothal, they knelt down side by side, and kowtowed three times to Heaven and Earth, three times to Shih Cheng and three times to each other. Fan Li took out of his pocket a gold necklace with a jade pendant and clasped it around Hsi Shih's neck.

"My mother gave it to me. I've been wearing it until now."

Hsi Shih held up the pendant to examine. It was a vividly carved unicorn. Her eyes sparkled with excitement. "It's priceless."

"It will bring you good luck," Fan Li said softly.

"How soon are you leaving?" Shih Cheng asked.

"Tomorrow morning, sir. As soon as I return, Hsi Shih and I will get married."

"Do you need to report this to the king?"

"Yes, but that's only a formality. I am sure the king will give us his blessing."

Shih Cheng turned to his daughter. "You'd

better keep your betrothal to yourself until a formal announcement comes from the king."

While Fan Li was talking with her father, Hsi Shih went into her room and came back with a silk handkerchief as a souvenir for Fan Li. Fan Li unfolded it and saw a hand-embroidered picture of two magpies perching on a flowering cherry tree.

"You made it yourself, Hsi Shih?" Fan Li brushed his fingertips over the design, admiring its delicate workmanship.

Hsi Shih nodded.

"Thank you, my sweet darling." His caressing gaze swept over her.

Shih Cheng took out a bottle of rice wine and gave it to Fan Li. "I don't have much to give you by way of a dowry. This is a token of my best wishes to you."

Zhuji was well-known for its rice-wine. The taste of wine improved with the years. So at the birth of a child, the local people would brew jars of wine and keep them in the cellar for use at a future date—on the eve of the imperial examination that a boy was going to take to wish him good luck or at a girl's wedding as part of her dowry.

Hsi Shih prepared a delicious silver carp stewed with green onion that evening, and the three of them enjoyed the meal heartily.

After bidding good-bye to Papa Shih, Fan Li took another stroll along the quiet path with Hsi Shih. It was a moonlit night, a perfect night for a walk outside. All around them was wonderful peace. Fan Li felt as though he were walking in a dream world. There seemed to be a mysterious charm in the atmosphere. The moon seemed brighter than ever; the night seemed more lovely and alive; the whole Zhuluo Village seemed to have become an enchanted spot because of Hsi Shih.

They walked on till they reached the edge of the thoroughfare. Neither tried to talk. At this moment silence felt sweeter than words. Hsi Shih stared at her hero. His face was beautiful and masculine, with vivid eyes, a well-shaped nose and a stern mouth that bespoke a tremendous willpower. A man of authority, with thousands of soldiers under his command, yet so sweet and so gentle to her, a simple village maiden. A mixed feeling of love and humble adoration rose in her. Fate must have guided him to her. Her heart swelled with gratitude and happiness.

"My lord, look at the moon. Tomorrow night we will be away from each other, but we will share the same moon."

"I'll miss you, Hsi Shih," Fan Li murmured.

"I'll miss you too." Hsi Shih threw her arms around his neck. Her heart beat against him; her lips quivered on his, her eyes moistening.

Silhouetted against silvery moonlight, the loving couple embraced so tightly as though their bodies were melting into one. At last they bade a tearful adieu in which joys and sorrows were intermingled.

*   *   *

Hsi Shih was washing silk floss by the brook the following day. Her friend Zheng Dan came to join her with some laundry. One year older than her, Zheng Dan was a vivacious, good-looking young lady, though not as well-proportioned as Hsi Shih. She was slightly taller and thinner, with a pair of big, passionate eyes on her sweet face.

"You're so quiet today, Hsi Shih," said she, staring at her friend questioningly. "Anything the matter with you?"

"No, no, nothing's the matter," said Hsi Shih, striving to conceal her excitement.

"They say a very important person has been visiting our county and the neighborhood."

"Who is he?"

"Chief General Fan Li. The king's right-hand man. He had meetings with all the village elders. My father and your father were there too."

"Yes?"

"They say he is a handsome young man."

"Really?"

"It's a pity we didn't meet him."

Hsi Shih nodded, her gaze fixed on her laundry.

With no brother or sister of her own, she regarded Zheng Dan as her elder sister. It was Zheng Dan who taught her how to swim, showed her how to catch frogs and field snails, and took her to the top of the Guiji Mountains for the first time. Without Zheng Dan, she would not have had any adventure. Both studied with Zheng Dan's father who taught at the county school. But Hsi Shih was a better student. She often helped Zheng Dan with her work. Without Hsi Shih, Zheng Dan would have gotten more scoldings from her father. As a result, the two girls were devoted to each other. They never kept any secret from each other.

However, this time Hsi Shih felt differently. She preferred to keep the secret to herself. Anyway, she was under orders to keep silent about her betrothal.

# CHAPTER NINE

## Beauty Selection

**B**EFORE SUNRISE, A few hundred young men were busy doing warm-up exercises, practicing somersault skills or wrestling in the clearing of a forest. They had been secretly recruited to form an elite force under the supervision of Fan Li. The training base was tucked away in a hilly area in the southernmost tip of Yue. As part of their training, they were learning archery from Master Chen Yin, the foremost archer of the land, and learning sword-fighting skills from the Virgin of the Southern Forest, the famous fencing master.

A short, soft-spoken, self-possessed man, Master Chen Yin began his class at dawn.

"Correct posture is a prerequisite for archery," he told his students, "and correct breathing is essential to good marksmanship. Now stand straight as if you were wearing a wooden jacket. Chin up and chest out. Step forward your left foot. Point your right foot to the right. Extend your left arm straight—imagine you are holding a tree in your hand. Bend your right arm—imagine you are holding a baby in it."

He paused to make sure that everybody was doing right.

"When you take aim at a target," he went on, "hold your breath and concentrate your attention. When you release the arrow, breathe out simultaneously. If you breathe steadily, your arrow will shoot steadily. To shoot with accuracy, you must coordinate every body movement correctly."

On the shooting range, targets were placed in a row for practice. Pointing at a big red circle painted on a wooden board, the master continued, "As a beginner, you will practice to shoot at this large target. Little by little you will learn to shoot at a smaller object. By the time you graduate, you will be able to shoot through a tree leaf hundreds of feet away."

There was a poplar tree about three hundred feet away. Master Chen Yin asked a student to choose three leaves of that tree and hang tiny red ribbons on them. Standing firm and erect, the master raised the bow until the arrow was about level with his eyes. With his chest fully extended and his shoulders thrust far apart, he pulled the bowstring to full draw. Holding the draw still, he fixed his gaze on the target. Twang! He released his hand with an exhalation of breath. The arrow shot through one of the chosen leaves. Then a second arrow, and a third. The shafts seemed to know where they should go. The trainees looked on in amazement.

"At first, the leaf seemed so small to me at such a distance," explained the master. "But after practicing for a while, the leaf grew in size to my eyes, and I found it easier to shoot. It's a matter of practice and perseverance."

On the neighboring drill ground, the Virgin of the Southern Forest was demonstrating fencing, with one of her students posing as her opponent.

Her opponent was the first to attack. His sword slashed up and down, left and right. But the Virgin cleverly dodged every thrust. Fixing her eyes on her opponent's right shoulder, she was able to anticipate each move of his right hand that was holding the sword. Catching a slight fault in the man's move, she lunged forward and counterattacked. Her opponent was forced to step back and their swords clashed. In the midst of sword play, the Virgin suddenly lifted her leg and kicked the man in the elbow. His sword dropped. The man turned to flee, but the Virgin was faster. Another sweep of her leg, and the man was tripped and fell to the ground. The next moment the sword of the Virgin was pointing at his throat, to the cheers of her students.

The Virgin proceeded to explain her tactics in the mock combat and instruct them to perform each individual move correctly.

Although slim and small, the Virgin was well-knit and good-looking. She had sensual lips, a small nose, and a pair of keen, deep-set eyes on her bronze-colored face, and there was a natural dignity about her. It was her father, a good hunter and fencing master, who had taught her how to play with the sword.

Once her father was struggling with a leopard on the top of a mountain. The leopard swept down on him so fiercely that while retreating he slipped and fell off the cliff and died. Since then the young daughter was determined to learn to surpass wild animals in her fighting skills. She observed how the monkeys swung from tree to tree, how the hawks swooped down on their prey, how the tigers and the leopards charged. By learning to apply such skills to the use of the sword, she became a better sword-fighter than her father. As her good name spread, many fencing masters asked to compete with her, but no one had excelled her in the competitions.

Both the Virgin and Master Chen Yin were recruited by Fan Li. In the past year, Fan Li had inspected all the important towns and counties in the country. He had built a shipyard in its crude form which, when completed, could build war vessels the size of Wu's biggest boat. Before returning to the capital, he stayed with the Virgin and Master Chen Yin for a while, taking care to see that the training was well on its way to perfection.

Lying on a bunk in the barracks, Fan Li could hear the noise outside. He was due to leave for Guiji that day. He planned to go back to Zhuluo Village as soon as he briefed the king on his inspection tour. He could hardly wait to marry the girl who had captured his heart. The thought of Hsi Shih accompanied him day and night. It engendered pleasurable heartbeats in him. It filled his mind with happy memories. He tried to envision the life after his marriage. His mansion should be large enough for the time being. It would take Hsi Shih some time to get used to the life in the city and feel comfortable moving among his circle of friends and colleagues. But she was educated. All she needed was some knowledge of court etiquette. Her beauty would make her the object of fantasy in many men's eyes. But he would not feel jealousy. After all, who would dare to mess about with the wife of the chief general?

* * *

Gou Jian was in conference with Wen Zhong in his private audience chamber. Spread out on the table were pictures of beautiful women painted on large squares of heavy cloth—the result of a nationwide beauty selection.

"Oh, they all look pretty," said the king as he thumbed through the pictures. "How did you select them?"

"As Your Majesty didn't want me to go about the assignment ostentatiously," said Wen Zhong, "I asked a dozen good painters to draw pictures of all beautiful girls in the realm below the age of twenty. They sent in more than two hundred pictures. Here are the twenty-four choicest ones for your examination."

A few months earlier, after learning that Fu Chai was rebuilding his Gusu Tower which had been used to keep his father's concubines, Gou Jian sent him fine wood and artisans to help the construction because he wanted to pamper Fu Chai's whims. Wen Zhong suggested that he might as well send some pretty girls too. Hopefully they would befuddle Fu Chai's mind and divert his attention from his duty. Gou Jian thought it was an excellent idea. But since all the women in his harem had been sent home, he asked Wen Zhong to find a few from among the general populace for the purpose.

"They are more beautiful than any of the women I used to have in my harem." Gou Jian said as he scanned the pictures, his lips frothing with saliva. "Get all the twenty-four of them here!"

"Yes. I'll see that they get proper training."

"How long will the training take?"

"About two years."

"Why so long?"

"Most of them are illiterate. Not only they need to learn how to sing and dance, but also how to read and write, and to familiarize themselves with court etiquette. That takes time."

"Why can't we send him illiterate beauties?"

"I've learned Fu Chai doesn't like illiterate girls. He'll expect us to train the girls before offering them to him if we are to have him believe in our sincerity."

"Ask Yi Yong to help you. Choose the intelligent ones and make them learn fast. Send them as the first batch. Make the illiterate ones study hard. They can go later."

"I'll do my best, Sire."

"What do you think of this one?" Gou Jian's attention was caught by one particular picture—it was that of Hsi Shih.

"Your Majesty has a most discerning eye. She is the most outstanding among the twenty four."

"Tell Yi Yong to personally escort the girl to the capital," the king said with unusual intensity.

"Here is another girl from the same village," Wen Zhong showed him the portrait of Zheng Dan.

"Good. Bring them here together. Girls like companions."

\* \* \*

The idea of escorting two beauties to the capital

pleased Lord Yi Yong. A rotund man in his early fifties, Yi Yong had an agreeable manner. He was bald-headed. But people did not notice his baldness thanks to the coronet he wore. Instead they were attracted to him by a pair of kindly eyes on his ruddy, round face.

As Lord Yi Yong came in a boat to take Hsi Shih and Zheng Dan, both Hsi Shih and her father thought it was the king's way of escorting her to the capital to meet General Fan Li. Still wanting to treat her betrothal as private, Hsi Shih chose not to ask Yi Yong anything about Fan Li. As for Zheng Dan, the king must know she was her friend and wanted her to meet some young nobleman whom he had his eye on.

Two days later they arrived in Guiji. Yi Yong lost no time in taking Hsi Shih to the king for an audience along with Zheng Dan. As they stepped into the audience hall, Gou Jian rose from his seat involuntarily. He was going to say something, but his voice died away. His gaze was fastened on Hsi Shih. What a divine beauty! She looked oddly familiar. He wondered where he had met her before. No, he would have remembered.

But Hsi Shih remembered him. The king had aged visibly and looked uglier. His gaze somehow gave her gooseflesh.

Gou Jian tried to conceal his excitement, but an urge to possess this young woman surged up within him. He wanted to pull her into his arms, strip her naked and grope her body. He wanted to make her his concubine and let her serve him until his desire was satisfied. He began debating with his own self.

*Why should I be so foolish as to contribute her to my enemy?*

*—For your revenge. Have you forgotten your*

*ignominious defeat?*

*But I would have lived in vain if I could not enjoy such a beauty.*

*—She would hold an irresistible power over Fu Chai. She would cause his dynasty house to fall.*

*But she is just too beautiful, too good to serve that bastard.*

*—Isn't this the very purpose of the beauty selection?*

His face twitched as his inner struggle continued. The ladies made an obeisance. But Gou Jian stood transfixed. There was an awkward silence. As Yi Yong had an itch in his throat, he could hardly suppress a cough. His cough helped restore the king to awareness.

"Welcome, ladies!" The king managed to smile quite agreeably. "I hope the journey was not too arduous."

"No, it was not, Your Majesty," Zheng Dan replied. "We were well taken care of by Lord Yi Yong."

"That's good."

"I'm going to show them around now," said Yi Yong.

"Very good. Beautiful ladies, I hope you will enjoy yourselves."

Gou Jian ended the audience abruptly. He had intended to have a longer meeting, but changed his mind: he was infuriated by his lack of self-control.

*I'm going to make Fu Chai pay for it—and pay dearly for it. Oh, Hsi Shih! Help me destroy Fu Chai with your charm!*

# CHAPTER TEN

## Choice

IT WAS AFTER midnight when Fan Li got home. As he was very tired after the long journey, he slept so soundly that he did not wake up till the late afternoon of the following day. He decided to call on Wen Zhong in his office which was in the immediate neighborhood of the royal palace.

"Your Excellency," the guard bowed to him, "the Prime Minister is not in. He may be in the New Beauties' Quarters."

"New Beauties' Quarters?"

"Yes, there!" the guard pointed a finger at an arched gateway about some five hundred feet to the west of the General Audience Hall.

Following the guard's finger, Fan Li saw the newly renovated stone wall which encircled a tree-shaded compound adjacent to the royal court. He recognized that the place used to house Gou Jian's concubines.

"Who are the new beauties?" he asked.

"I don't know, sir."

Fan Li quickly made for the New Beauties' Quarters. The moment he crossed the threshold of the arched gateway, he bumped into a young lady.

"Good God! It's you!"

The sweet voice was so familiar. Fan Li looked up. To his great astonishment, the young lady was none other than Hsi Shih. He could hardly recognize her. No longer the bare-footed country lass. No longer wearing her glossy black hair in a braid. Dressed in a flower-patterned silk blouse, adorned with jade bracelets and a gold necklace, and with jewels dangling from her aristocratic head-dress and a pair of embroidered shoes on her feet, Hsi Shih was a paragon of beauty and refinement.

"Oh, my darling! Fancy meeting you here!" Fan Li threw his arms around her and they hugged, kissed, heedlessly absorbed in each other until a rustling sound was heard. It was the gardener sweeping the courtyard. Hsi Shih took Fan Li by the hand and led the way to a bench in the shade of a tall elm tree.

"When did you come here?" asked Fan Li.

"About a month ago." Hsi Shih's eyes flashed a delightful smile.

"I didn't expect to meet you here, sweetheart. I was planning to go to Zhuluo Village. Tell me how come you are here."

"Lord Yi Yong brought me here. I thought you had told the king about our engagement."

"No, my sweetie, I haven't got around telling anyone about our engagement."

"Haven't you?" Hsi Shih's brow raised the fraction of an inch.

*I see.* A happy thought hit her. Now she understood. The king wanted to reward Fan Li for his meritorious services. That was why he had selected two dozen beautiful women for the yet unmarried general to choose a wife from.

"Tell me the whole story," said Fan Li. "I can't make head or tail of all this."

"A few months ago, a village father took a painter to where I was washing my silk floss. The painter asked me to pose for him. He also drew pictures of Zheng Dan and a few other girls. Then a month ago Lord Yi Yong came and took Zheng Dan and me to the king's palace. I was so happy."

Fan Li's expression turned contemplative. "Have you said anything about our engagement to anyone?"

"Not yet. I was waiting for you to come back."

"How many girls are living in the New Beauties' Quarters?"

"All together there are twenty-four of us from various parts of the country. Come with me to my place. I'll make tea for you."

Her suite was in one of those ivy-covered red-brick houses scattered inside the compound amidst tall, leafy trees. It was spacious, comfortable, and well-decorated. Hsi Shih changed into a casual blouse and brought out a tea set. The room was instantly filled with the aroma of fresh green tea.

Fan Li blew on the hot tea and took a sip. "My dear, what are you beauties doing here?" he asked.

"We are learning to become noble ladies. We study—under the supervision of Minister Yi Yong."

"What do you study?"

"Music, dance and court etiquette. And some history and literature, too. We had a class in etiquette today. That's why I was dressed up."

"Who teaches you etiquette?"

"Lord Yi Yong. Prime Minister Wen Zhong comes to give lectures once in a while. He was here this afternoon."

"What did he talk about?"

"Patriotism and ... " Hsi Shih paused as she noticed a shadow passing over Fan Li's expression. "What's the matter, my lord?"

"Nothing. Do you enjoy the class?"

"Yes. We also practice martial arts."

"Martial arts? What for?"

"It's part of our physical education."

"I see." Fan Li smiled quickly, brushing aside the dark shadow from his face.

He took Hsi Shih to his home to have dinner together. The chief general's residence was neat and tidy, the furnishings simple but comfortable, and it was tastefully decorated with calligraphy, paintings and antiques. Hsi Shih felt very much at home. At Fan Li's bidding, his chef prepared four delicious dishes and a soup, among them a silver carp stewed with green onion, to the delight of Hsi Shih.

After dinner, Fan Li presented her a diamond hair-pin. Her eyes widened at the sight of an exquisite dragon-and-phoenix design carved on it. The dragon and phoenix was the quintessential symbol for a married couple. A rush of warmth came over her.

"Put it on for me, my lord."

Fan Li fixed the pin on her hair dexterously, his

fingers tracing lovingly over the slender arch of her eyebrows and her lovely face.

She slid him an affectionate glance from beneath her lashes. "Shall we choose a lucky day for our wedding?"

"I'll look up in *The Book of Changes* and choose the nearest propitious day. Then I'll inform the king of our plan."

"Wonderful!" she exclaimed. "I knew I was sent here for a purpose."

Fan Li's smile faded; the dark shadow came back to his face.

"Sweetheart," he sighed, "you're too naive. I think you were sent here for a different purpose."

"What purpose?" Hsi Shih asked, perturbed. "I don't understand."

"I think you are being trained to carry out some assignment."

"What ... what assignment?" Hsi Shih asked apprehensively.

"You are probably meant to be sent to Wu, each one of you girls."

"To do what?"

"To serve the enemy king."

"Oh, no, no! Not me!" Hsi Shih was in utter consternation. "I don't want to go. I want to stay here —with you!" She clung to Fan Li's arms, struggling to keep her composure.

"Don't be afraid, my darling," Fan Li said. "You are going to be my wife. The wife of the chief general does not serve an enemy king."

"What are you going to do?"

"I will go and speak to the king about it—the

first thing tomorrow morning."

"I wish I had told Lord Yi Yong about our engagement," Hsi Shih mumbled, holding Fan Li tightly as though afraid that someone was going to tear her away from him.

* * *

Fan Li called on Wen Zhong early next morning when Wen Zhong was having breakfast with his wife, a genial, intelligent, young woman.

"Hey, how are you, my good friend?" Wen Zhong greeted him cheerily. "When did you get back?"

"I came back yesterday. I want to talk to you." Fan Li looked dead serious.

Sensing something unusual in the atmosphere, Lady Wen Zhong was ready to leave the breakfast table on an improvised excuse. But Fan Li stopped her. "Please stay, Lady Wen Zhong. I want you to know."

"Let's have breakfast together and then talk," Wen Zhong suggested.

"Thank you." Fan Li sat down at the breakfast table. "I'm going to be married. I sincerely request the honor of your presence at my wedding ceremony."

"Who is the bride-to-be?"

"Hsi Shih—one of your students in the New Beauties' Quarters. I met her in Zhuluo Village on my inspection tour, and we are engaged to be married as soon as I get back."

"Congratulations!" Wen Zhong beamed on his friend, but his expression changed instantly. "Why didn't you tell me earlier?"

"Earlier?" Fan Li's face fell. "Did I have a chance

to talk to you? What difference does it make—earlier or later?"

"It makes a world of difference, my friend."

"Why?"

"If you had told me earlier, I wouldn't have selected Hsi Shih for the king."

"What does the king intend to do with her?"

"The king has already decided to present her to Fu Chai. I'm afraid it might be too late for a change."

"How can you talk like that, my friend? Hsi Shih is going to be my wife. How can you expect my wife to serve the enemy king?"

"My lord," Lady Wen Zhong broke in, "you must help Lord Fan Li."

"Don't be agitated, my friend," said Wen Zhong. "Let's put our heads together and see if there is a way out."

"I'm going to appeal directly to the king. You must help me."

\* \* \*

Breakfast over, Fan Li and Wen Zhong rode to the king's court and were heartily received by the king who was very pleased with Fan Li's report about his inspection tour, the shipyard construction and the training base in the southern hilly area.

"I do appreciate your effort, my favored lord. Now you need a good rest. Take a few days off. Take a vacation."

"I want to get married now, Your Majesty." Fan Li came straight to the point and told the king about his plan.

"Good for you! It's high time that you got married. Congratulations!"

"Thank you."

"Who is the lucky lady? I want to drink a toast to you and the future Lady Fan Li."

"She is Hsi Shih from Zhuluo Village."

"What? Is there more than one Hsi Shih in Zhuluo Village?"

"No. Hsi Shih is now living in the New Beauties' Quarters."

"My Chief General, I marvel at your quick work. When did you meet her?"

"It's not quick work, Your Majesty. We've known each other for more than a year now. We were betrothed and we planned to get married the moment I returned from my travels."

An awkward moment followed. A mirthless smile played on Gou Jian's thin lips.

"Hsi Shih will make a good wife for the chief general." Wen Zhong suggested tactfully.

"Your Majesty!" Fan Li knelt down before the king. "I beseech thee not to send my betrothed to the enemy king."

Gou Jian kept silent, a stony look on his face.

"Sire, have mercy on me," Fan Li heard himself saying, "Hsi Shih is my wife. Hsi Shih is my life."

Suddenly the king threw himself on his knees before Fan Li. "I ... I am an unworthy ruler," he wailed.

Fan Li was caught off guard by the king's debasing gesture. Not knowing what to do, Wen Zhong, too, dropped on his knees.

"I am an unworthy ruler," repeated Gou Jian, beating his chest with both hands, his eyes flooding with tears. "I am a worthless man, having to enlist the help of beautiful women to achieve our goals. It is all because Wu is too strong for us."

"But what has it to do with Hsi Shih?" Fan Li protested desperately. "Why on earth was she chosen? Aren't there other women around?"

"Sire, we can send another girl to Wu. There are plenty of beautiful ones." Wen Zhong pleaded on behalf of his friend.

A torrent of eloquence rolled off the king's tongue.

"My good lord, you have shared so much woe with me. I've privately learned that Fu Chai tempted you with money and status to leave me and work for him, but you scorned to be bought by gold. I am very grateful for your loyalty. Now I am asking you to give up your betrothed. I know I am asking too much of you. I'm ashamed of myself."

Gou Jian bowed to the ground before Fan Li and continued.

"But Hsi Shih is the beauty of beauties. Only she can destroy Fu Chai with her charm. I will be forever grateful to you for your sacrifice; my people will be forever grateful to you. My lord, on the day when we defeat Wu, the first thing I promise to do will be to bring Hsi Shih back to your arms. I need your help now, my good lord."

Thus saying, the king bowed again, his forehead knocking on the floor with a dull thud.

"Please don't." Fan Li was shocked, confused, perplexed.

Tears were streaming down Gou Jian's face. "Will you help me, my lord?" he entreated as he kowtowed repeatedly to Fan Li.

Mesmerized, Fan Li responded curtly, "Yes."

He was so devastated tears fell from his eyes. Wen Zhong wept, too.

\* \* \*

In the inner palace, the queen was entertaining Hsi Shih with lotus-seed tea. It had been arranged that she was to give Hsi Shih an audience that day after the girls' morning class and the king was to join her to have a few words with Hsi Shih as well. It was her first face-to-face meeting with this young woman. She had heard about how attractive she was. Now that she saw the girl with her own eyes, a twinge of jealousy arose in her heart. She welcomed her visitor with a smiling nod, though the smile never quite reached her eyes.

"Miss Hsi Shih, you are very beautiful. I have never in my life seen anyone like you."

The words were complimentary, but Hsi Shih sensed the deep reluctance beneath them.

"The king places great hopes on you," the queen continued. "You know, our country is a vassal of Wu. The king of Wu is bleeding our people dry by demanding tributes from us."

As the queen's gaze raked over her, Hsi Shih flinched.

"We can't live under bondage forever. Miss Hsi Shih, the king and I need your cooperation to help our country regain freedom. Can we have your promise?"

The queen giving her no choice, Hsi Shih nodded in confusion.

"Even though we are working hard," the queen

went on, "to build Yue into a strong country, we still have a long way to go before we can catch up with Wu. Miss Hsi Shih, we want you to use your charm as the sword to conquer the conqueror, to weaken the enemy state from within. It is your patriotic duty."

The queen's words sounded ominous. Hsi Shih wanted to tell her that she was going to be the chief general's wife. But Fan Li was meeting the king and the king would certainly agree to their wedding. She decided to keep quiet.

"Do you agree, Miss Hsi Shih?" came the queen's high-pitched voice, pressing her for an answer.

"I'll do my best." Hsi Shih heard herself mumbling.

It was at this point that the king, accompanied by Fan Li, appeared at the door. Hsi Shih was greatly relieved at the sight of her betrothed. At this moment, she wanted to be in his arms more than anything she had ever wanted in the world.

"Ah, nice to see you, fair lady," the king made a half-bow. "Lord Fan Li is here to escort you back to your quarters. You will have a lot to say to each other, I believe."

The king and queen saw the young couple to the gate of the inner palace.

"Why dismiss the girl so soon?" asked the queen as they walked back. "I thought you intended to say a few encouraging words to her."

"Yes, I did. But it's better to let Fan Li do the persuasion."

The king went on to explain how Fan Li had pleaded to marry Hsi Shih and how he had persuaded the young man to yield his personal consideration in favor of the interest of the nation.

"How cruel of you to separate the couple!" Lady Gou Jian chided her husband. "Poor girl, she didn't say a word about their romance, but I did detect melancholy in her pretty face."

"That's why I left Fan Li to talk to her."

\* \* \*

Having left the inner palace, Fan Li and Hsi Shih took a quiet tree-shaded path back to the New Beauties' Quarters.

"What's the news, my dear?" Hsi Shih asked. For a moment she tensed with hope. But Fan Li hung his head without a word.

"What did the king say?" she repeated. But Fan Li was maddeningly silent. Hsi Shih held breath as she saw his expression change, a dark color creeping up his face.

"What happened?" she pressed anxiously.

"Sweetheart," Fan Li struggled to speak. "The king begged me on his knees to put the interest of the nation before our own."

"What did you say?" Hsi Shih was panic-stricken.

Fan Li choked up and started sobbing. Hsi Shih had never seen him sobbing. Immediately she realized things had gone wrong. A fit of dizziness seized her, and she fell unconscious into Fan Li's arms. When she came to, she saw Fan Li still sobbing.

"Let's talk to the king again," she said weakly. "I don't want to go."

Fan Li shook his head. "It's too late. I've given the king my word."

Hsi Shih broke down at once and cried. Then she jerked away from him and ran off. Fan Li hastened his steps after her until she stopped in front of a pavilion in the depth of the garden. He went down on his knees.

"I'm sorry," he said, his face twisted by pain. "I'm so sorry."

"Go away," Hsi Shih said tonelessly, without turning around.

"Please forgive me, Hsi Shih," he implored. "Please."

Hsi Shih stood motionless for a moment and suddenly sank to her knees. Fan Li swiftly reached her and pulled her into his arms.

"I'm scared," she muttered between whimpers.

"Don't be scared, darling—" He stopped abruptly. Any word of comfort from him would sound like mockery when he, the chief general of the country, could not protect his betrothed. Shame swept over him, his cheeks burning with anger, guilt, self-reproach. Still he felt compelled to say, "Let's stick together. Let's overcome the difficulties together." Yet he knew his words were empty, powerless.

They spent the night together in Hsi Shih's suite. She changed into a comfortable night gown, the shining cascade of her soft, silken hair now released from the restraint of her elaborate head-dress.

"My lord, I am yours. Yours only." Snuggling against his body, she felt the smooth muscle of his chest and the steady rhythm of his heart.

Fan Li's fingers sifted through her rippling, sweet-smelling hair. "You are mine—now and forever," he said softly.

He bent to cover her lips with kisses. The hot kisses went on until Hsi Shih cooed, "My lord, ... " She unbuckled the belt of his official costume. Then she boldly slipped off from her own night gown.

He made her sit on his lap and ran his tongue gently around the hardening peaks of her breasts while his fingers wandered from her shoulders to her thighs. Hsi Shih purred and twisted as his touch sent a delicious sensation through her body.

"My lord, take my body—and my soul ... " She writhed uncontrollably, pressing her warm, satin-smooth body against his solid torso. Her wanton groans drove his senses to a smoldering heat.

Desire exploded inside him. Breathing hard, he could no longer hold his control. His maleness rose in throbbing eagerness. Suddenly he realized he had gone too far. Hsi Shih's chastity was to be the price of Yue's victory over Wu. His body stiffened at the thought. It was through sheer will-power that he managed to jerk himself away. But it was agony. His muscles trembled with the effort of holding back.

Then Hsi Shih realized what Fan Li was doing, or rather, was not doing. She, too, remembered that she was to be presented to the demon king of the enemy state as a supreme sacrifice on the altar of patriotism. He certainly expected her to be a virgin—intact, untainted. Her body did not belong to herself. She had wanted to be a dutiful wife and mother. She had hoped to live a happy, peaceful life. Now she was to be used as human bait to ensnare the enemy.

Overwhelmed by a sense of utter helplessness, she buried her head in Fan Li's lap and burst into tears. Her body ached with unspent passion. The pain of unsatisfied desire was maddening. It hurt like nothing she had ever experienced, and there was no remedy. Patriotic duty sounded hollow to her. Only the agony in her body— and her heart was real.

Fan Li was weeping, too. His tears drenched her naked shoulder. At last Hsi Shih calmed down. Exhaustion overtook pain. She stumbled to her bed, and fell asleep. But she did not sleep well, for she was harassed by dreams of a gargantuan monster reaching for her with its out-stretched claws.

Sleepless, Fan Li lay beside Hsi Shih, holding her in his arms and reliving every moment of that fateful day. What would have happened he had sent a message to Wen Zhong earlier? Wen Zhong would have withheld Hsi Shih and Gou Jian would have chosen another girl. "The very person to seduce Fu Chai," he would say. But what's the good of thinking about might-have-been's?

Looking up at the full moon through the dark limbs of the tree outside the latticed window, he sighed a deep, sorrowful sigh. The bliss of his first nuptial night could only exist in fantasy. *Fate is too cruel*, he protested silently, *too cruel*.

# CHAPTER ELEVEN

# Mission

FROM AMONG THE twenty-four girls, Hsi Shih, Zheng Dan and six others were selected as the first batch of girls to be presented to Fu Chai. Gou Jian made his astrologer decide on a propitious day in early summer for the beauties to set out for Wu.

On the eve of their departure, the king invited them to a dinner party in his palace.

"Fair ladies," he addressed them in a slow, solemn tone. "I would like to express my sincere appreciation for what you are going to do for our country. You all know that we were defeated by Wu. As the king of a subdued nation, I'm compelled to offer you to the king of Wu to serve in his palace. To do this is against my own will, but I have no choice.

"King Fu Chai may place you in his harem or in the song and dance troupe of his court or make you his servants. Please obey him. Remember he is your master and you are his slaves. Do whatever he asks of you and you will be doing a great service to our nation. I will take good care of your families in Yue. And when our country becomes stronger, I'll make Fu Chai send you back. You will be richly rewarded. But for now you must endure."

The king's words casting a pall over the party, nobody had much appetite for the fine food on the table. The ladies consumed the dinner in silence, pondering what the future had in store for them.

Dinner over, Hsi Shih and Zheng Dan were asked to stay behind for a special audience with the king. Wen Zhong, Fan Li and Yi Yong were also present.

"I place great hopes on you, just the two of you." The king's voice assumed a conspiratorial tone. "You have two tasks. The first is to corrupt the enemy king. That you already know."

"Miss Hsi Shih," the king stared intently at her. "I believe you stand a very good chance of becoming Fu Chai's consort. Fu Chai is forty years old. He lost his wife two years ago. Even though you are his slave, you can make him fall in love with you and marry you."

Hsi Shih drooped her head under the king's gaze which then turned to Zheng Dan.

"Your job is to help Hsi Shih achieve her goal," the king said. "When she becomes Fu Chai's wife, offer to be her maid so that the two of you can work together. Your role is different, but it is no less important."

Zheng Dan nodded primly.

"The second task for the two of you," the king's tone turned grave, "is to gather enemy intelligence and pass it on to us. This is a secret mission. Don't divulge it to anyone."

He paused to let the two girls absorb his message which took them rather by surprise.

"You will be Yue's agents working in the inner court of the enemy king. I will make Lord Yi Yong your liaison officer who will give you specific assignments. You must be discreet and resourceful in carrying out your task. Remember you and all of us here are working toward one and the same goal. Your intelligence work is vital to our victory. When Yue defeats Wu, ladies, I will personally welcome you home and honor you as our national heroes. Do you have any questions?"

Hsi Shih and Zheng Dan were so tense that they did not know what questions to ask. At the end of the meeting, they stood up and made a solemn pledge of secrecy and their life-long loyalty to the king and the nation.


Fan Li accompanied Hsi Shih back to her residence. He presented her a pair of gold rope chain anklets inlaid with gemstones crafted by the best goldsmith in the country.

"I meant to give these to you as wedding gift. Now our wedding is postponed, I still want you to have them."

"They're lovely," Hsi Shih said absent-mindedly. The intricate patterns of anklets escaped her notice. "I'll keep them for our wedding."

Fan Li had expected her to be a bit more enthusiastic. "I want you to wear them now, darling."

Making her sit on a chair, he knelt down and put them on her.

"I'll wear them everyday," Hsi Shih murmured,

still thinking about her new role of a spy.

"Let's go for a walk, sweetheart," Fan Li suggested.

The night life of Gusu centered round the square outside the Temple of King Yu. The temple was still open. They went in to pray together—for the success of her mission, for their mutual well-being, and for their future.

Then, hand in hand, the two lovers strolled along the zigzag canals where hundreds of lights glimmered from the boats on the water.

"So on top of being a seductress I am going to be a spy," Hsi Shih muttered, her voice edged with misgivings. "But I haven't got any training. I don't have any skill to do the job."

"Don't worry, sweetheart. Once you set your mind to it, I believe you can do a competent job."

"But I don't have the qualities of a spy," Hsi Shih grumbled.

"Yes, you do." Fan Li said breezily.

"I do?"

"You are intelligent, articulate, discreet and loyal to your motherland. These are the qualities of a successful spy."

Fan Li's words rang a bit hollow to her. "I wonder if I can gain Fu Chai's trust just by—pleasing him."

"Fu Chai is a stupid man," Fan Li assured her. "A little flirtation, and you can wrap him around your fingers."

Hsi Shih was not pleased by the compliment. Seducing a man with deceit might be natural to some women, but it went against the grain with her. Fan Li should have known that.

"I doubt it would be that easy," she pouted.

"Of course, you have to make sacrifices. But what you give up is only your body. Not your soul or your spirit."

*Only* her body? Hsi Shih was disappointed, even a little offended, by his reply.

"It's a leap in the dark, my lord." A wry smile pulled up her lips. "I may get caught."

Fan Li gave her a forbidding frown. "Sweetheart," he squeezed her hand hard, "I don't want you to do anything dangerous. Rather you don't complete an assignment than risk your own safety. Do you understand?"

Hsi Shih nodded.

"The most important thing is," he met her eyes and made his tone as serious as possible, "to protect yourself."

Hsi Shih said no more.

In the past months, she and Fan Li had met frequently. But they had avoided talking about her mission in Wu as though it were a forbidden topic. They talked fondly about the remembered moments of their past—and their reunion in the future. How they would go travelling and see places in the land of China after they were wedded. How they would have a big family with many children. Fan Li spoke about his interest in getting into business after retiring from office. But Hsi Shih felt these were empty talks. The biggest concern on her mind was how to deal with the daunting challenge that was awaiting her in Wu.

Now the role of a spy would add danger to her mission. She had an ominous feeling that once she entered the Wu palace, everything would change. All their plans about the future would come to naught. What if Fu Chai just treated her as a sex object? What if she was found out? What if she had a baby?

These were her concerns. Obviously. She wanted to talk about them. Fan Li should have thought of them too. But he was not as sensitive as she had hoped. Not wanting to spoil their time together, she kept her uneasy thoughts to herself. She did not want to worry him. It was no use raising them, anyway.

Right now she just wanted to be with him, to savor the last golden moment together. Only later did it occur to her that it was odd they were unable to talk about what was most important to her, to both of them.

It was approaching midnight when they returned to the New Beauties' Quarters. All was quiet in the garden. A gentle breeze set the trees whispering. It was the same silvery moonlight and the same star-studded sky like the night when she bade good-bye to Fan Li in Zhuluo Village. A surge of loving tenderness rose in her. Hsi Shih threw her arms around Fan Li, encircling him with all her strength. Lowering his mouth to hers, Fan Li kissed her sweetly. His lips, warm and intense, was on her cheek, her ear, her neck, her throat, while his hands stole beneath the rustling layers of her gown. Quivers of delight vibrated through her, igniting her craving. Hsi Shih pressed harder, deeper until she nearly lost herself in his arms. Their bodies crushed deliciously against each other, Fan Li felt he was approaching a flash point beyond which the pleasure would become disaster. With a tortured groan he wriggled himself away.

"Fan Li—" Hsi Shih tried to pull him closer, but he resisted.

"I don't know when we shall meet again," he whispered breathlessly, with a mixture of love and anguished passion on his face. "But meet again we shall, sweetheart."

"My lord, my heart is with you—always," Hsi Shih said, her voice quavering with emotion.

"Sweetheart," Fan Li lifted her chin and looked into her glistening eyes. "I will wait for you till the mountains rot, till the sea dries up."

"So will I, my lord. Till the mountains rot, till the sea dries up." Hsi Shih struggled to hold back the tears that threatened to flow down her cheeks.

Reaching her arms around his neck, she crushed her lips to his in a long, caressing kiss, and then she went inside.

Fan Li stood motionless in the shadow long after the sound of her footsteps had faded.

# CHAPTER TWELVE

## King's Favorite

THE EIGHT BEAUTIES from Yue, chaperoned by Yi Yong, stepped timorously into the Gusu Tower shortly after their arrival in Wu. They were dressed in fine silk gowns, each having chosen her own colors, the color of the gown matching perfectly the color of the sash around the waist as well as the color of the silk shoes, complete with matching jewels glittering on their head-dresses.

"Great King of Wu," Yi Yong addressed Fu Chai as he and the ladies fell on their knees, "Your Majesty's humble servant, King Gou Jian of Yue, has empowered me to pay his tribute to you and present these ladies to be your slaves. They will serve you in whatever capacity you see fit."

The sight of Hsi Shih swept Fu Chai off his feet. He was overwhelmed by a mixed feeling of wonder and excitement. He had seen hundreds of attractive women, but never such a fairy-like being whose beauty defied description. He riveted his gaze on her, entranced.

A long moment passed before he recovered himself. "How's Gou Jian? I trust he is in good health?"

"Yes, he is. King Gou Jian also wants to reassure Your Majesty of his life-long fidelity as your obedient vassal."

"I appreciate that," Fu Chai said, immensely pleased. "Tell him I'll take good care of these ladies. Their presence will serve as a reminder of his good will."

"Your Majesty is very kind." Yi Yong bowed deferentially.

"Their accommodation is ready. You can accompany them there, and have some rest yourself." He ordered an attendant to escort Yi Yong and the girls to retire.

Hsi Shih stole a fleeting glance at the specter sitting on the dais before she left and was startled by the impression she got. He was huge, his massive shoulders and wide chest bulging beneath his magnificent robe and a pair of blazing eyes on his face. He did not look demonic. Not at all.

Hsi Shih could easily tell that the Gusu Tower excelled Gou Jian's palace in splendor by far, but had not expected her suite to be so luxurious. It was adorned with gorgeous draperies and screens, decorated with exotic plants, and pieces of shellwork and ivory sculpture, and commanded a full view of Gusu as well as the pastoral scenery of the surrounding countryside. But she was too fatigued with the journey to enjoy the view. She slept the afternoon away.

In the evening she and the other girls, together with Wen Zhong, were invited to a lavish banquet. The girls of Yue were greatly amused by the king's debonair manners. Much of their apprehension had vaporized. They were treated to performances by the dance ensemble of the Wu court who seemed very professional and smooth, but Hsi Shih felt they were lacking in verve and gusto.

She had expected Fu Chai to be like the monster she had seen in her dreams. But this morning she got an entirely different impression. She was not sure. Now that she saw him again, she realized he was definitely not a monster. He was not at all what she had expected. He was handsome, much as she hated to admit it. He was tall, well-built, with manly looks, robust physique, baritone voice and amiable demeanor. He might not be as handsome as Fan Li, but much more gentlemanly-looking than King Gou Jian. It was a disquieting discovery.

Two days later the girls of Yue gave a performance for the king who invited all his ministers to attend. It was meant to be an opportunity for the king to evaluate each of them and decide what their respective role would be in his palace.

They danced to the sound of Yue's drum music, each with a band of flowers around the forehead, the neck, the wrist and the ankle, their navels exposed above the grass skirts they wore. Like native Hawaiian dancers, they danced barefoot, their buttocks swinging, their bodies rocking and twisting, their arms swaying in the air to the rhythm of the music. It was a sensual performance well-choreographed.

At the king's instance, Hsi Shih danced a solo. She changed her costume and appeared in a neatly fitted bodice over a varicolored, pleated skirt. Her headdress resembled a peacock's crown. Barefooted and wearing the jewelled anklets Fan Li had given her, she gracefully entered the dancing floor in striding steps and a big jump.

Balancing her body on one leg, she stretched the other away from the center of her body while her torso, arms and head were artfully held in harmony to her legs. Then she slipped smoothly into a lunge, first arched backward, and then folded, downcast and arched forward, displaying her beautifully proportioned form to the audience.

She danced with both softness and passion. Her body seemed buoyant as she moved lithely across the floor. Her gliding and darting were mixed with pirouettes and spins. The flapping of her rippling arms were accompanied by tiny, swift steps that were as smooth as a string of pearls. Every motion was a spontaneous expression of beauty, every posture a perfect form of artistry.

At the end of her performance, she swung herself in circles, her pleated colorful skirt fanning out like a peacock's tail. A storm of applause followed. Hsi Shih smiled her sweetest as she bowed to the spellbound audience who had never been treated with such a visual feast before. Suddenly she had a tickling feeling on her forehead. She glanced upward and met the king's eye. His stare was so intense it made her uneasy, almost frightened.

It had been a long time since Fu Chai had been so strongly attracted to a woman. Hsi Shih had ignited a passion inside him. He felt an infinite yearning to possess the prima donna. Lurid thoughts flooded his mind. He wanted to savor her charms, to possess her body, to claim her soul. He could hardly control himself.

The following night he summoned Hsi Shih to his bed chamber. As she entered the opulent bed chamber, she saw a huge bed with carved bedposts, draped in rich yellow satin brocade and silk curtains, had been prepared for dual occupancy. She winced inwardly as she went down to her knees to greet the king.

"You may rise, Hsi Shih," the king said softly.

Hsi Shih rose but her head hung.

"How are you?" the king asked as he approached her.

Hsi Shih recoiled and the king stopped in his tracks.

"I enjoyed your dance very much," he said. "It was the best performance I've ever seen."

"Thank you." Hsi Shih's voice was nearly inaudible.

"How long have you been dancing?"

"A year."

"Very good. I hope you would feel at home here."

There was no reaction from Hsi Shih as though she had not heard him.

"Would you like some tea?"

Hsi Shih shook her head.

"What about some refreshments?"

No. She felt like a lamb waiting to be pounced on by a wolf. But she refused to succumb to the beast.

Fu Chai paused. She was apparently too frightened, or too shy, or both, but her icy manner was a trifle irritating.

"Look at me!" came his deep, raspy voice.

Startled, Hsi Shih raised her face to him. A mixture of fear and defiance swept over her and sudden perspiration lent her skin a faint shimmer.

Fu Chai stared at her steadily. She was so dazzlingly pretty that his heart ached. And she possessed a quality which surpassed her physical beauty. She was graceful and effortlessly sensual, with a hint of passion concealed beneath her delicate exterior. As his gaze snared hers, he detected a flicker of resentment and some other unfathomable emotion in her eyes. Hsi Shih was shocked. No man had looked at her that way, as though he could eat her with his gaze. Her body stiffened. Her breath quickened. Her face flamed with excruciating self-consciousness.

After a long moment, Fu Chai spoke brusquely. "Go back to your own chamber."

Hsi Shih was surprised, but patently relieved. She had expected the king to be angry. As she left she could feel the heat of his gaze on her back.

A few days later Fu Chai took Hsi Shih and Zheng Dan for a sightseeing tour in Gusu. Having learned they were friends from the same village, he thought Hsi Shih might feel less anxious if Zheng Dan was with her. She needed to be broken in gently.

Zheng Dan had noticed the king's interest in Hsi Shih from the beginning. The look in his eyes when he watched her dancing was telltale: Hsi Shih was his favorite among the eight, just as Gou Jian and everyone else had predicted. The target had risen to the bait. But Hsi Shih was not playing her part. Not at all. During the ride, she kept her gaze glued to the window of the carriage and herself at a distance from the king. The severe look on her face and the reserve of her manner discouraged any attempt by the king to have a conversation with her. Worse still, she cringed when the king edged a little closer to her in the carriage. The king kept a pleasant countenance, but Zheng Dan could sense the tension in the air. Fortunately it was a short journey.

They alighted in the center of Gusu for a walking tour. There were gardens in nearly every main street. Hsi Shih had heard of the beauty of Gusu gardens, but they were more marvelous than she had imagined. Each garden had its unique elements. Plants, pools, bridges, walkways, pavilions, pebble mosaics, mock mountains, houses with whitewashed walls and decorative windows, stones carved with poems and literary quotations were so arranged that they would create a series of delightful views rather than a single vista. Hsi Shih felt as though she was walking in a picture. However, her enjoyment was marred by the king's relentless attention which she was determined to ignore.

Witnessing Hsi Shih's aloof attitude, Zheng Dan decided to step in to remedy the situation.

"Sire," she said with a sunny smile on her face, "now I understand why Gusu is called a paradise on earth. These gardens are so fantastic they must have been designed by master architects. But where did they find so many curiously shaped rocks and colored stones?"

"From Lake Tai Hu, my lady. That is the one advantage they have."

"So the architects must also be rock connoisseurs."

Her comment drew a short laugh from Fu Chai.

"Precisely. The garden artist sees himself as a master painter who does not allow a single dead stroke and a master writer who does not permit a single inharmonious sentence. He fuses landscape painting and literary composition to create an art of its own in his garden."

"I guess that's why each garden has distinct features."

"Exactly. Each garden artist has his own style just like a painter."

As they wandered through a maze of connected pools and islands in one of the gardens, Zheng Dan was disoriented. "Sire, it's impossible to tell where the water begins and where it ends. It's so confusing."

Fu Chai chuckled. "It's meant to confuse you, my lady. You see, the maze is an illusion because there is only one, long, meandering lake. But the artist created the illusion by dividing the space into distinct segments and presenting a new vista at every turn."

"I see. I guess I need several visits before I can really appreciate its wonder."

"Quite true, my lady. Gusu gardens are not meant to be visited in a hurry. You need a little patience, and then an entirely new vision will open up."

Fu Chai seemed to enjoy talking with Zheng Dan who was pleasant, relaxed and quick of comprehension. For the rest of the day, he did not spare Hsi Shih a single glance, totally ignoring her. Hsi Shih cast furtive glances at him. Beneath the king's cool veneer, she sensed something tightly reined and threatening.

A virile man, Fu Chai enjoyed the company of beautiful women in his imperial harem, but when it came to having a more enduring relationship, he was very fastidious. He had to care for the woman seriously before he married her. Two years after the death of his wife, he had not found such a woman until he set eyes on Hsi Shih whose presence had stirred up something deep inside him. But he did not want to coerce her. He did not want to force himself upon her by means of his authority as the ruler of the victor state. To claim her peremptorily like a conqueror would cause her to feel bitter, and he did not want her to be embittered. Precisely because she was in such a vulnerable position, he wanted to win her heart by the art of gentle persuasion. He wanted to *earn* her affection. Perhaps he should see what she would want for herself.

"Apparently Hsi Shih doesn't like it here." The king told Zheng Dan as he summoned her for a private audience.

Zheng Dan stared at him blankly.

"Tell me the truth, Lady Zheng Dan, does she resent being sent here?"

"I don't think so," Zheng Dan had to lie. "She understands what her duty is."

"Does she have a boyfriend at home?"

"Not that I know of." She had to lie again.

"Well, I'm sick of her martyred air and her melancholy look. I won't force her to stay if she wants to leave."

The king's words took her by surprise.

"Go tell Hsi Shih she can go home if that is what she wants."

Zheng Dan felt a leap of pleasure at the king's suggestion. If Hsi Shih was gone, she could have his attention. Fu Chai was an attractive man. Seducing him for the sake of her country would be a tantalizing venture. She would not mind doing that at all. But she instantly dismissed the idea. Fu Chai was interested in Hsi Shih, not her. If Hsi Shih was sent home, it would mean the failure of their mission. It would disrupt King Gou Jian's plan and delay Yue's victory. Much as she sympathized with Hsi Shih, her sense of duty quickly prevailed and she became alarmed. No, Hsi Shih must not go home. She must perform her duties. She must serve the enemy king willy-nilly. Zheng Dan decided to talk some sense into her.

"Hsi Shih is just shy, Your Majesty," she said apologetically. "Please be patient with her."

"I will. But she has to make up her mind. Tell her I won't keep her against her will."

"I'll talk to her," Zheng Dan assured the king. "Please give her some more time."

Directly she went to see Hsi Shih in her chamber. "Hsi Shih, I want to talk to you." Her tone was serious.

"What's the matter, Zheng Dan?"

"The matter is: you have to decide—stay here or go back."

"What?"

"Fu Chai says if you were unhappy here, he would send you home."

Hsi Shih could not believe her ears.

"He says he wouldn't force you to stay here if you are reluctant to be his companion."

"Fine. I'll go home then. I belong to my lord Fan Li anyway."

"My dear sister, it is also Lord Fan Li's wish that you sacrifice your personal interest in the interest of the nation. You have pledged to do your bit for the country.

Just think what Lord Fan Li would say if you go home now. You would be a disgrace to Yue—and to Lord Fan Li."

Hsi Shih did not respond.

"Think of the consequences, Hsi Shih," Zheng Dan warned her. "Fu Chai is not as terrible as you think," she added.

In the still watches of the night, Hsi Shih was lying awake. Zheng Dan's message hit her with brutal clarity. She realized there was no way out for her except to bow to reality, to come to terms with her mission. She had made her promise. She would not disappoint Fan Li.

A few days later, a maid was heading for Fu Chai's bed chamber with a bronze wash basin to wash his feet when Hsi Shih stopped her in the corridor.

"Let me do it tonight," she said softly, taking over the basin from the maid. When she entered, Fu Chai was reclining on a coach in a night gown, his eyes closed, a wine cup placed on the teakwood table by the coach. Hsi Shih quietly knelt down and gave him the footbath.

After drying his feet with a towel, she held his foot in her hands and began a long, slow stroking motion with her thumbs, starting at the tip of the toe all the way to the ankle, and then she stroked the bottom of the foot from the base of the toe all the way to the heel. It was followed by ankle rotations. Then with one hand grasping the foot beneath the arch, and with the other hand, she pulled, rolled and squeezed every toe, her fingers sliding into the tender creases between the toes, sending shivers of pleasure, deliciously erotic pleasure, up Fu Chai's spine.

Fu Chai opened his eyes. There, to his stunning

surprise, was Hsi Shih kneeling in front of him.

"Hsi Shih!" he choked.

Hsi Shih glanced up at him. The glint of defiance in her eyes was gone. In its place was a look of resignation. "Please let me be your slave, Your Majesty," she supplicated in a sweet, meek tone. "Please let me serve you." She found herself bending down and touched his toes with her lips.

Fu Chai was overjoyed, not a little puzzled by the quick turnabout in her attitude. He also felt an odd sense of disappointment that she had succumbed so quickly. "You do excellent foot massage, Hsi Shih. Where did you learn it?"

"I used to do it for my father."

Fu Chai scrutinized her. She was dressed in a black silk gown with a scarlet scarf around her neck, her dark, springing hair loosened on her bare shoulders in a wild, silky disarray. Her lush breasts seemed ready to spill from her low-necklined gown, and her feet were bare.

"Would you like some wine?" he asked.

Hsi Shih crawled a step forward. Fu Chai let her drink from his cup. Hsi Shih gulped it all down.

"Do you want some more?"

She nodded. Fu Chai watched with obvious satisfaction as she drank deeply from the wine cup he held to her lips. She drank four cups altogether as though she wanted to get drunk.

"Why do you want to be a slave? Is that what Gou Jian told you?" His question caught her off guard. Seeing her perplexing expression, he added, "I guess he sent you girls here because he wanted to demonstrate his loyalty. But I've got plenty of women in the palace. I never asked him for girls."

This was a new revelation to Hsi Shih who had been given to understand that female slaves were part of the bargain Gou Jian struck with Fu Chai and that he was forced to deliver them to him.

"If I did," Fu Chai continued good-naturedly, "General Wu Yuan would have objected. Anyway, I'm very pleased you are here. I don't see you as a slave. If I wanted a slave, I would have taken you by force any time these last days."

Hsi Shih knew that. At the hands of a less chivalrous master she would have suffered a far worse fate. She would have already been brutally subdued.

"However, I *am* in need of a companion," he said in a soft voice, "and I want you to be that person. I want to marry you. I suspect that is also what Gou Jian really wanted when he sent you here. He seemed to understand my matrimonial need. You'll find life far more enjoyable as my wife than as my slave. You'll have nothing to fear or worry about. Would you consider my proposal, Hsi Shih?"

Hsi Shih hesitated an endless moment, knowing she had no choice. Then, staring up at his handsome, earnest face, she nodded. An inaudible sigh of relief escaped her. In a way, Fu Chai had made things easier for her, for he spared her the need to "seduce" him as Gou Jian had bid her to.

Fu Chai lifted her into his arms. His lips descended to hers in a tender kiss. He marvelled at her soft, flawless body, her scent sweet as honey, her translucent skin smooth as the lotus petals in the pond. His fingers stroked her face, curving over her cheeks, brushing the corner of her mouth. And he kissed her again, his lips warm and light. Hsi Shih realized he was trying to reassure her.

Slowly his hands pulled at her gown. Clasping his shoulders to steady herself, she wriggled to help him strip it down her legs. His fingers came to her breasts and gently squeezed them, sending an exquisite sensation through her body. Gradually he increased the intensity of his fondling. Hsi Shih writhed in surrender. She tilted her head back to let him know that she was in his power, that he could fondle her to his heart's content. Pleased with her willingness, he became more aggressive.

He kissed her more fervently, hungering for the sweet taste of her. Her breast swelled; her nipples stood out like dark red grapes. So carnal and compelling were his lips that she could not help responding. She could not help wanting more kisses and caresses from the man she was supposed to hate.

An endless moment of radiant delight, and he carried her in his arms to the bed. They tangled together, rolling on the huge bed, their legs wrapping and twining around each other. Hsi Shih groaned in pleasure. Delicious quiver of energy running up and down her body, and a current of throbbing excitement rose from deep inside.

They made love all night, spurred on by a strong mutual desire to discover each other. Fu Chai was sweet and wild, smooth and rough at once. Acting like a perfect slave, Hsi Shih yielded her body to please him in a way he had never known before. She struggled to remember he was the enemy king, but his body was warm and soothing, his scent intoxicating, and his lovemaking filled her with pleasure. Her thoughts scattered. *Why, there is nothing repulsive about the man—not at all.*

She was ashamed that she was unable to control her own treacherous body.

She tried to tell her outraged conscience that she was sacrificing herself for her country, she was doing something noble. But her sacrifice was a delicious experience, her martyrdom a paradise of delight.

* * *

Hsi Shih was made the king's consort. She would be called "Lady Hsi Shih." She could not be the queen, for only the king's first wife could be called queen. When the queen died, the title died with her. However, a legal consort, in reality, enjoyed the same rights and privileges as the queen. She appointed Zheng Dan as her lady-in-waiting and two other Yue girls, Ding Hong and Gao Lan, as her maids.

The wedding ceremony was an extravagant dream. The king's merry mood was contagious. The entire court was immersed in a festival atmosphere. All the ministers were invited to share the gaieties at the dining table.

"A toast to the king and his bride!" Bo Pi took the lead to offer congratulations, his face flushed with self-importance as he raised his goblet high in the air.

"There never was a prettier bride. I wish you happiness!" General Wangsun Shong exclaimed.

"May the gods bless you!" General Wangsun Luo echoed.

One after another, the ministers rose from their seats to toast to the newly weds. Even Wu Yuan was compelled to chime in.

Apart from sumptuous repasts, the banqueters

were entertained by the song-and-dance troupe of the court to which the remaining four girls of Yue were assigned to join. Fu Chai introduced his fourteen-year-old son, Prince Yiou, to her. The prince had an elegant physique and the good looks of his father. He said little at the banquet but stole frequent glances at her.

The prince lived in his own palace but joined his father for dinner several times a week. When he came to the king's residence two days later, he found only Hsi Shih at home. The boy was shy at first, but his curiosity asserted itself after the maids had gone.

"Are you angry with my father, Lady Hsi Shih?" he asked.

The question caught her by surprise. "Why should I be angry?"

"Because you were forced to marry him." He stared at her directly.

A faint smile came to her face, her thoughts hidden behind a mask. "No, I'm not angry," was the only answer she could give.

"Um, you don't look angry," the boy seemed to agree with her. "Do you like him?"

Another outrageous question.

"It's my duty to serve the king." Hsi Shih said defensively.

"But do you *like* him?" He met her eyes without blinking.

Hsi Shih did not want to tell an outright lie. "I ... I don't know the king well enough to form an opinion yet."

"Well, I hope you would be happy," the boy said wistfully. "I've never seen my father so happy since my mother passed away."

"How did your mother die?"

"She died when she was giving birth to her second child. They both died. Father was distraught and has been lonely for a long time."

"Lonely? But there are so many ... "

"Yes," he cut her short. "But none of them could make him genuinely happy until you came along. I can see that."

Hsi Shih was at a loss what to say.

"I called you Lady Hsi Shih. Actually I'm not supposed to. I don't know what to call you. You're not old enough to be my mother. Don't you agree?"

Being only five years older than the prince, Hsi Shih could not but agree. "What would you like to call me?" she asked with amused interest.

"Of course, you should call Lady Hsi Shih *Mother*." The reply came from Fu Chai who had just stepped into the room. "That is the only proper form of address for you."

"Yes, Father."

Hsi Shih and Prince Yiou struck up an easy rapport. The boy was both precocious and innocent. His questions were probing but Hsi Shih did not found them offensive. She knew he did not ask them to embarrass her but out of his sincere concern for her. His friendship brought her comfort, but it made her a little uneasy.

# CHAPTER THIRTEEN

# A Woman's Charm

FU CHAI WOULD have dallied away more time in the company of Hsi Shih had it not been for the intervention of General Wu Yuan. The king's merrymaking irked him.

"You must be careful of the trap laid by Gou Jian." Wu Yuan warned Fu Chai portentously.

"What trap?"

"These pretty women have the ability to ruin a country. Gou Jian has an ulterior motive sending them over."

"He has *no* ulterior motive. He is grateful to me because I spared his life."

"He wants you to indulge yourself and neglect your duty, my king."

"The women from Yue won't interfere with my duty. They are here to sing and dance for us. How can singing and dancing ruin a strong power like ours?"

Wu Yuan did not mention Hsi Shih by name, but Fu Chai knew he was insinuating that she was a bad influence, and he was not amused at all.

Hsi Shih had filled his life with sweetness and sunshine. She seemed to devote every effort to making him happy. She was instinctively able to anticipate his desires and knew how to please him. She was better at this than even his first wife. Fu Chai's contentment was boundless—so much so that he did not feel the need to explain to Wu Yuan. He could not imagine a more ideal wife than Hsi Shih. He found himself thinking of her most of the time when she was not with him. He could not stop himself. She had become the source of all pleasure to him. There was no temptation more intense than what he felt with her.

Like his father, Fu Chai spent summer time in the Gusu Tower and the rest of the year in the Gusu Palace in the city proper. As autumn came, he moved back to Gusu.

Hsi Shih did not mind returning to Gusu at all. She had taken a fancy to the lovely city ever since her first visit. During the day, she took exercise, read books, practiced dancing or horseback riding, or played sports such as ball games or chess games with other court ladies. In the evening, she often attended parties or courtly entertainments with the king. Sometimes she danced at the king's request. She had a special program of her own and her performance never failed to drive him into rapture.

The king often took her for a walk in the palace courtyard after dinner, where the lawns were meticulously manicured and the footpaths spotless. As this developed into a habit, Hsi Shih would go for a stroll by herself, or with Zheng Dan, when the king was too tired to join her. At such times, they would change into casual clothes and take off their shoes, feeling free and comfortable, just the way they were in Zhuluo Village. The guards at the gates would greet them with a bow and marvel at their beauty.

They would go sightseeing or shopping together. The gardens of Gusu never ceased to fascinate them. The embroidery shops in the marketplace were well worth visiting again. Hsi Shih had never seen such perfect needlecraft. The most stunning was the double-sided embroidery on a canvas of thin silk gauze with two different images stitched on the front and the reverse side.

"The double-sides are the most prized items," said the shop owner. "It takes one artist three years to stitch a piece."

Hsi Shih would buy a few every time and have them mounted on elegantly carved frames.

There were also the fan shops. The sandalwood fan, with patterns of cats, fish, birds, flowers or the calligraphy of a poem carved on it, was Gusu's traditional handicraft.

"The sandalwood fan would keep its fragrance for years to come," the shop-owner informed her patron. "The locals use it as a multi-purpose gift."

Hsi Shih bought many such fans to send to her relatives and friends in Yue.

"You are wonderful, Hsi Shih," Zheng Dan said one day when they were walking around in the market. "You act so well that people would think you are genuinely in love with Fu Chai."

Noting the ring of jealousy in Zheng Dan's voice, Hsi Shih slid a reproving glance at her and said tersely. "It's my job, isn't it?"

In any case she was pleased that her effort was taking effect. But she was definitely not in love with Fu Chai. Of course not. However, she was finding it difficult to ignore a softening in her heart toward the man she was supposed to hate.

Unlike Gou Jian who was obsessed with taking his revenge on Wu, Fu Chai did not seem to harbor a lasting malice against Yue. He never mentioned the past feud between Wu and Yue to her. Perhaps out of consideration for her sensibilities. More likely, he was the kind of man who would have the entire matter off his mind once the conflict was over. In her opinion, this might explain why Fu Chai seemed much happier than Gou Jian.

Fu Chai never treated her as a trophy from a conquered nation. She was cherished as a wife and honored as a queen. In fact she was being pampered as she had never been in her life. In addition to Zheng Dan and the two maids from Yue, twelve maids from the Wu palace waited upon her day and night.

Compared with Fan Li, Fu Chai was less serious and far more apt to tease and laugh, which she found quite charming. He was a sensual, sensitive lover, and his lovemaking invariably left her very fulfilled. But the most seductive quality about the man was his sincerity. His single-minded love unnerved her. And there was an intensity about it that she had not discovered even in Fan Li. It was very unsettling.

According to the arrangement made with Minister

Yi Yong, King Gou Jian's liaison, Hsi Shih and Zheng Dan were supposed to meet with him within six months after their arrival in Wu. Their first assignment was to report on General Wu Yuan's barracks. As the deadline was drawing near, they became anxious.

"That's no easy job for us, I'm afraid," said Hsi Shih. "I feel it in my bones that the general does not like us."

"He is an honorable man. But he is Yue's worst enemy."

"True."

"Hsi Shih, you have to coax Fu Chai to take us to his barracks. I believe he will say yes to your request."

"I'll see what I can do. Fu Chai would never suspect me of anything in the nature of ... of ... espionage."

As Fu Chai went regularly to Wu Yuan's army barracks to review military exercises, he was only too pleased to oblige when Hsi Shih asked to accompany him along with Zheng Dan.

\*   \*   \*

In the army barracks on the outskirts of Gusu, Prince Yiou was studying *The Art of War* by Sun Tzu under Wu Yuan's guidance after practicing martial arts in early morning. Despite the age gap, they were bosom friends. The prince admired the general for his uprightness and loyalty and the general treated the prince like his own son.

After two hours of lessons, Wu Yuan suggested a break as usual. An attendant brought some refreshments to the table.

"Sir, last night Lady Hsi Shih treated me to dinner in the palace," Prince Yiou told the general. "I've never had such tasty snails—and chestnut cakes which you would surely have liked."

"How do you like Lady Hsi Shih?" The general was curious.

"Very much. She is so beautiful, and so nice to me."

"Aha! The charmer has cast a spell on the youngster."

"Oh, no. What do you mean?"

"My dear prince, you must be wary of beautiful women."

"Why?"

"Because such women are dangerous. They can bring disasters to us. Do you know that both the Hsia and Shang dynasties were brought down by evil beauties?"

"No, I don't."

The prince took literature and history lessons with Bo Pi, but Bo Pi had not told him about any of the evil women who had played a role in the destruction of these former dynasties. Wu Yuan regarded it as a gross omission. Suspicions about Hsi Shih lurking in his mind, he felt it was necessary to warn the prince. His first story was about Mo Shi.

"When the last king of Hsia, King Jie, defeated a tribe called Yiou Shi, the Yiou Shi chieftain offered his daughter Mo Shi to be the king's slave. She was extremely beautiful. King Jie adored her. Whatever pleased her pleased the king; whatever amused her amused the king. Having led a wild life in her born days, she was often dressed like a man, wearing a man's hat and carrying a man's sword.

"Mo Shi enjoyed watching performances by magicians, jugglers and pygmies, and the king recruited such entertainers by the hundreds and often sat Mo Shi on his lap to watch their show.

"Mo Shi liked to hear the swishing sound that came from tearing silk, and the king ordered the royal warehouse keeper to have hundreds of bolts of silk brought to the palace and court maids of tough build to tear the silk for her amusement.

"Mo Shi fancied human flesh, and the king ordered the royal kitchen to butcher selected slaves for the table.

"Mo Shi loved wine, and the king ordered to have a wine pool dug for her. The pool was big enough for swimming and was filled with wine. He made some slaves crawl around the pool with ropes on their necks held in the hands of other slaves who were ordered to whip them. Then he made the drummers beat the drums. At each drumbeat, the slaves were ordered to stretch their necks and drink the wine from the pool. The drummers kept on beating the drums and the slaves kept on drinking until they became so drunk that they fell into the pool and drowned. Mo Shi found the game singularly entertaining.

"Acting upon Mo Shi's whim, one day the king ordered a tiger to be released into a crowded marketplace. As the tiger suddenly appeared before them, people were panic-stricken and stampeded. Stalls were knocked over. Many were trampled to death as they ran for their lives. Watching from a platform nearby, Mo Shi found the scene of chaos great fun.

"When a loyal minister warned the king that his depravity would cost him his dynasty, he retorted, 'I'm the Sun. Can the Sun perish? When the Sun perishes, I will perish with Him.'

"A few years later, the king attacked another tribe called Yiou Min. To save his tribe from doom, the Yiou Min chieftain offered him two pretty girls. The girls soon won the favor of King Jie at the expense of Mo Shi. Mo Shi was so jealous that she became a vicious spy. She secretly collaborated with the king's enemies and gathered intelligence for them. In the end they defeated the king's army and King Jie died in exile. His dynasty ended in disgrace."

"King Jie and Mo Shi were both evil people," the prince commented.

"True. But Mo Shi was the more wicked of the two, in my view." Wu Yuan said before he moved on to his next cautionary tale.

"The fall of the Shang Dynasty was somewhat similar. The last king of Shang, King Zhou, was a debauched ruler. Having learnt that the Yiou Su tribe chieftain had a most beautiful daughter named Da Ji, he ordered the chieftain to send her to his harem. But the chieftain ignored his order. King Zhou threatened to use force to crush his tribe. The chieftain wailed, cursing himself for having a beautiful daughter. Da Ji persuaded her father to let her sacrifice herself in order to save the tribe and the family. So, she was presented to King Zhou.

"King Zhou was enamored of her. He built luxurious houses for her; he collected exotic animals to fill the royal zoo to amuse her; he gave frequent parties in the palace to please her and, while eating and drinking, he made naked young men and women dance to lascivious music to entertain her.

"Some ministers remonstrated with the king about his misconduct. Thereupon the king devised a fire pit as a torture instrument. A brass pillar, smeared with grease, was laid horizontally above a fire pit heated up with charcoal. Whoever dared to remonstrate again would be forced to walk on the pillar. As the pillar was so slippery, in no time the victim would lose his footing, fall into the fire pit and be scorched to death. Da Ji enjoyed watching people die this way.

"When the king's uncle admonished him not to be so cruel and so dissolute, the king flew into a fury. Da Ji said, 'Your uncle talks like a sage. I heard that the heart of a sage is different from that of normal people. Is that true?' Whereupon the king had his uncle executed and took out his heart for Da Ji to examine.

"It was not difficult to understand that Da Ji's heart was with her father. She provoked the king into killing many of his loyal ministers. Eventually a rebel force led by a nobleman, King Wen, overthrew his regime. King Zhou committed suicide by burning himself. Da Ji was beheaded. Her head was hung on top of a white flag to show that she was responsible for the fall of the Shang Dynasty."

"How terrible!" Prince Yiou was abhorred.

"You see, these women were all beautiful but all black-hearted."

The prince nodded. The general's obvious insinuation was not lost on him.

Wu Yuan went on to tell him the story of Bao Shi, another beautiful woman in history, who had caused the present Zhou dynasty, the third dynasty of China after the Hsia and Shang, to be so weak and powerless.

\* \* \*

"About three hundred years ago, King You of Zhou was the ruler of China. The king was fond of women and wine, and merry-making was his first concern of life. Believing that a king was entitled to have many beautiful wives, he dispatched officials to various parts of the country to search for pretty women.

"When Minister Bao Shiang remonstrated with him, the king was so irritated he threw him into prison. Three years went by and Bao Shiang remained a prisoner. His worried family began to look out for a pretty woman as the price to buy his pardon. They found a beautiful girl in the countryside and offered her parents a large sum of money for their daughter. The girl was unwilling, but her parents were too poor to resist the offer. So she came to join the Bao family and was renamed Bao Shi.

"The Bao family presented her to King You in exchange for the release of Bao Shiang. Stupefied at the sight of such a beauty, the king immediately set the minister free.

"From that moment on, the king shut himself up in his inner palace with Bao Shi, seldom attended to his duties, and ignored his queen completely.

"The queen's father, the Duke of Shen, tried more than once to remonstrate with him, but the king turned a deaf ear to him. The duke was so hurt he resigned from his office as the king's counsellor and returned to his own fief, the State of Shen.

"In the course of time, a deep rancor developed between the queen and Bao Shi, for Bao Shi had an arrogant demeanor and spurned the queen to a frightful extent.

"Crown Prince Yi Jiu hated her to the marrow of his bones. One day, when the king was holding his court, he charged into the dwelling place of Bao Shi and gave her a sound beating. This rash act threw his father-king into a rage. The king ordered to have the prince banished.

"After Bao Shi gave birth to a son, the king nullified the title of crown prince conferred upon Yi Jiu, and made Bao Shi's child his successor. He also forced the queen to abdicate in favor of Bao Shi because only the mother of a crown prince was entitled to be the queen.

"The king heaped all his favors on Bao Shi, but she never smiled.

"'My treasured sweet baby,' the king pleaded, 'you know how pretty you are. If only you could smile.'

"'My lord,' said Bao Shi. 'I am, by nature, not easily amused. I have never been in the habit of smiling.'

"To win a smile from Bao Shi, the king ordered his court musicians to play all kinds of music, and summoned the singers and dancers of the palace to perform. But none of these entertainments could elicit a smile from the queen.

"'My pretty little thing,' said the king anxiously, 'is there any kind of music that you'd like to hear?'

"'Nothing in particular, my lord,' said Bao Shi. 'I really don't know.

"The king was at his wits' end. He issued an injunction to reward a thousand ounces of gold to anyone, within the court or without, who could contrive a way to bring a smile to Bao Shi's pretty face.

"Lord Guo, a sycophant-minister, came up with a stunning idea. He proposed that beacon fires be lighted to provoke the queen to a smile. The Zhou Dynasty had adopted a feudal system. Many members of the royal family were made to be the king's vassals and given fiefs to rule. In the event of barbarian invasion they were duty-bound to defend the royal domain. For the purpose of speedy communication, more than twenty beacon-towers had been built on the Li Mountain near the Zhou capital, Haojing*. It was agreed that if the capital was in danger, beacon-fires would be lit as a signal to summon all the nearby fief rulers to come to the king's aid.

"'Your Majesty,' said Lord Guo. 'The kingdom is enjoying peace under your wise rule. There is little use for the beacon-fires. May I suggest that Your Majesty and the queen set your table for a drink on the city wall? We can light the beacon-fires to summon the fief rulers. It will be a spectacular scene which, I believe, will be amusing enough to make the queen laugh.'

"This ingenious idea appealed to the king. The following evening drums were sounded and the beacon-fires on the Li Mountain were lit. As beams of flame rose into the air and sparks soaring with a deafening splutter like fireworks, the night sky turned into a beautiful sight, but also a frightful one.

"At the sight of the fire and the sound of drums, the king's vassals thought that the royal domain was in danger. They hurriedly gathered their troops, set out in full armor and raced to the king's rescue. The drumbeats rumbling like thunderbolt, the horse hoofs kicking

---

* Near present-day Xi'an, Shaanxi Province.

up the dust, the soldiers shouting battle cries, but, to their astonishment, the nobles found no enemy when they reached the capital. Instead they saw a banquet in progress on the city walls amid festive music playing. The king came out to greet his vassals, chanting merrily, 'Good my lords! Dear my lords! Thank you. I appreciate your effort. But we have no invaders. Ha! ha! No invaders.'

"Bao Shi was really amused this time as she leaned out over the railing to watch the bustle and stir down below. The king's extravaganza so titillated her that she clapped her hands and giggled.

"This was a numbing shock to the lords who realized they had been made fools of by the debauched king for the amusement of his concubine. Since then the king was held in utter contempt.

"'My sweetheart baby, you are so charming.' The king was elated. 'One smile of yours is worth a hundred beauties put together.'

"Lord Guo was rewarded a thousand ounces of gold. The king's foolish act provoked the Duke of Shen, father of the abdicated queen, to send in a petition which read:

> 'Your Majesty has come under the pernicious influence of a demon. Unless you abolish Bao Shi right away, revoke your decrees of renouncing the legitimate queen and the crown prince and stop trifling with national defense, you will put the House of Zhou at risk. I earnestly urge you to refrain from treading on the same ruinous path that the last kings of Hsia and Shang trod. Otherwise our kingdom will crumble and you will lose your

*throne.'*

"'It's as clear as crystal that the duke is bent on rebellion against Your Majesty,' Lord Guo said when the king showed him the petition.

"'What are we going to do then?' the king asked in apprehension.

"'Strike him down before he takes action against us.'

"A royal edict was immediately dispatched to deprive the duke of his title, and Lord Guo was made the commander to lead an army to his fief and take him prisoner.

"The Duke of Shen was worried.

'Ours is a small principality,' he said to his advisors. 'How can we confront the king's troops?'

"'We are in grave danger,' said one advisor. 'If we don't take the initiative, we'll be subdued and taken prisoners. The nomadic tribe on the western frontier has a well-trained cavalry force. The only way to save us is to appeal to the nomad chieftain for temporary use of his troops.'

"The proposal was adopted and the nomad chieftain was only too willing to oblige as the duke promised to reward him with free access to the treasury in the royal palace.

"King You was alarmed when he learned that the combined forces of the Duke of Shen and the nomadic horsemen were advancing toward the capital even before Lord Guo readied his force.

"Beacon fires were lit up to summon aid from nearby nobles, but not a single soul came to the king's rescue. The king was desperate. He ordered Lord Guo to engage the nomads in combat. But the lord was a poor fighter. Within days his army was put to rout and he was killed. The defense of the capital broke down. The king put Bao Shi and the young prince in a carriage with himself and tried to sneak out of the city in the chaos. But his regal costume betrayed him. He and his young prince were hacked to death by the nomads, and Bao Shi was taken to the nomad chieftain. She was forced to serve him as a sex slave.

"When the nobles finally learned what had happened, they hastened to gather their forces and chased the nomadic barbarians out of the capital. Left behind by the nomads in their flight, Bao Shi hanged herself as she could not bring herself to face the victors.

"Crown Prince Yi Jiu was enthroned as the king. But the royal palace was in ruin, with all the treasures looted by the nomads. The new king decided to move his capital from Haojing in the west of China to Luoyang in the east. This marked the end of the Western Zhou Dynasty and the beginning of the present Eastern Zhou Dynasty."

# CHAPTER FOURTEEN

## Army Barracks

**P**RINCE YIOU WAS not convinced that all pretty women were bad, least of all Hsi Shih. "But Lady Hsi Shih is not like any of them," he contended. "She is beautiful because she can't help it. Aren't your own concubines also beautiful, sir?"

"My boy, Lady Hsi Shih comes from our enemy state. Gou Jian presented her to your father as tribute. No matter how nice she is, Gou Jian is her real master. She may have been sent here to spy on us, you know."

"I don't believe she is a spy. I don't think it's in her."

"What if she is?"

The prince was at a loss what to day: the supposition was too unreal to contemplate.

"Anyway it doesn't hurt to be vigilant, my boy."

The prince was not firmly persuaded, but did

not want to argue with his mentor. Just when he was leaving, an attendant announced that King Fu Chai had arrived along with Hsi Shih and Zheng Dan. Wu Yuan hastily took the prince to the gate to greet them.

"My general," the king sounded more cheerful than usual. "These two ladies have heard of your high reputation and would like to pay their respects to you. I thought your training exercises would be quite a spectacle for them to see."

*What do these women want? What business have they got to visit me in my barracks?* Wu Yuan wondered. He was certain that this was more than an innocuous tour. He had a strong suspicion that they were going to report to Gou Jian what they saw there. Very good. He might as well take this as an opportunity to show them that Wu's troops were combat-ready, and that Gou Jian had better remain an obedient vassal and not make any trouble.

"You are most welcome, Honored Ladies," he greeted them grudgingly. "You've come at a good time. A drill is scheduled today for new recruits."

Prince Yiou felt awkward in the presence of the two beautiful women who might be enemy spies. "Please excuse me. I have to attend other classes now."

But Wu Yuan stopped him. "Your Highness, before you leave, show our guests what you've learned in archery."

The prince ordered an attendant to fetch his bow and arrows, and then invited the visitors to a shooting range next to the barracks where a row of targets stood. But Wu Yuan had a different idea when he saw a wild goose in the sky.

"See that bird flying? Shoot!" he challenged.

The prince notched an arrow, took aim and

released the bow string. The arrow whizzed, and down fell the wild goose. The king looked on with a great degree of pride. The ladies were very impressed and lost no time in complimenting the young man on his marksmanship.

The prince having left, Wu Yuan asked his visitors to have a cup of tea in his office. Hsi Shih noticed the office was furnished simply. Apart from a few desks and chairs, there were a variety of weapons laid on the iron racks and a number of books, in the form of rolls of bamboo strips bound up by thongs, placed on the wooden shelves. Nothing in the big room marked the occupant as a high-ranking nobleman whose official position was second only to the king.

Zheng Dan nudged her at the sight of a map on the wall. Rough as it seemed, it was a military map, with rivers and hills and locations of army barracks marked in colored ink—army barracks in all key points in the country. The two exchanged meaningful glances. When Wu Yuan went out to speak with an officer who came to report on some assignment, they took the opportunity to examine the map, pretending they were trying to locate Guiji, and made a mental note of the important details of the map.

After tea, the general took his guests to the platform of the training ground. He ordered his men to sound the bugle. Instantly six hundred armor-clad young men rushed out of their barracks, weapon in hand, and organized themselves into neat columns and rows.

A round of drumbeats, and the foot soldiers charged toward their imaginary foes. All Hsi Shih could see were glittering arcs of the swords, spears, battle-axes and halberds moving rapidly in mid-air. Then came the sound of the gongs, and the soldiers reorganized themselves into retreating columns in perfect order. Next came a show of archers shooting at distant targets, with most shafts hitting the bull's eye. It was followed by a mock hand-to-hand combat and finally there was an exercise by the mounted unit.

The drill in Wu Yuan's army barracks made a deep effect on Hsi Shih and Zheng Dan. Both felt disheartened. Both wondered how long it would take for Yue to match Wu in military strength.

On their way back, the king waxed expansive. "The old general is not only a superb commander, but also an excellent trainer. You know he's a good friend of Marshall Sun Tzu. Have you have heard of Sun Tzu?"

"Yes," said Zheng Dan. "Sun Tzu is a famous general."

"I'm glad you know that. Sun Tzu is a genius. He used to work for my father. He wrote *The Art of War* and dedicated it to my father."

"So Your Majesty is holding the book now?" Hsi Shih asked, thinking of getting hold of the well-known book and having it copied for Fan Li.

"No, my father decided to leave the book with General Wu Yuan and have him teach me."

Hsi Shih's heart sank.

The king kept on talking. "When this round of training is finished, the general will pick the good ones and place them in Pingwang and Fujiao where his elite troops are stationed. Some soldiers there will be called back for training. The general has a rotating program to train his men. He believes it is the best way to maintain a superior fighting capacity."

The two ladies expressed their admiration for the general while committing to memory what the king had divulged. Upon their return they wrote a report of what they had seen in Wu Yuan's camp and what they had heard from Fu Chai. They also drew a map from memory indicating the locations of major army barracks in Wu.

*　*　*

A few days later, Hsi Shih feigned illness. Lying in bed, she complained of a headache, her eyes closed, her brows knitted, and her hands rubbing her temples. The royal physician could not diagnose what was wrong with her; Fu Chai was anxious.

Zheng Dan saw her chance. "Your Majesty, Lady Hsi Shih had the same trouble when we were in Yue's palace. One day she was seized by a sudden dizziness. No physician could cure her until King Gou Jian sent for the court acupuncturist. He used a little needle treatment, and all was well with her."

But there was no acupuncturist in Fu Chai's palace. A courier was dispatched to Yue immediately and the acupuncturist arrived on the morning of the third day. With a wig on his head and a medical bag over his shoulder, he was none other than Lord Yi Yong, well-disguised. In fact Yi Yong knew in advance that Hsi Shih would pretend to be sick so as to have an excuse for summoning a doctor from Yue.

He examined his patient, felt her pulse, looked at her tongue, and then inserted one needle into her wrist and another into the crook of her arm. The acupuncture therapy worked miraculously. Hsi Shih's headache was gone in no time. The king asked the acupuncturist to stay in the palace overnight to make sure that her condition was stable.

The next day when Yi Yong departed, Fu Chai gave him in recompense for his service a heavy bag of gold coins—an amount Yi Yong had never received in his life.

Zheng Dan offered to see the physician to the palace gate. She had already placed their report and the map within the lining of Yi Yong's medical bag.

As they ambled along a quiet path, she briefed Yi Yong on their visit to Wu Yuan's barracks.

"You did a wonderful job," Yi Yong was very pleased. "You were quite resourceful."

"We were really scared."

"The first time is the hardest. Your next assignment is to find out whether Wu Yuan has spies in Yue. And if he does, find out their identities."

"How do we find out?"

"The starting point would be to search his correspondence file."

"So we have to ransack his office?"

"Yes, you need to be bold but cautious. The king also wants Hsi Shih to play on Fu Chai's vanity. You know, Fu Chai covets the title of the First Lord. But to be recognized as the First Lord, he will have to use military force to coerce the northern lords. That'll be good for Yue."

"Why?"

"Because fighting in a distant land will wear down Wu's strength and expend its resources."

"I understand."

"I've bought a drug store in the center of Gusu,"

Yi Yong informed her. "A trusted aide of mine is in charge of the store. I will come over on the sixteenth day of every other month to meet you. There are so many shops in the marketplace; you can easily find an excuse to come out. I leave it to you to decide whether one or both of you should come. In case you have an urgent message, just ask the apothecary to get in touch with me."

They were stopped by the guards at the gate.

"Pardon us, Lady Zheng Dan." The head guard bowed politely. "We must check on the physician before we let him pass."

"Don't you know this gentleman was sent for by the king?"

"It makes no difference."

"Since when do visitors have to be searched?"

"It's General Wu Yuan's new order. All visitors must be searched before they are let in and before they are let out."

Zheng Dan wanted to protest but Yi Yong motioned her to be quiet. The guards searched his medical bag, his garment—and his sleeves. All gentlefolks wore garments with very broad sleeves in those days. Except for the gold coins and a few acupuncture needles, nothing was found. The head guard apologized, saying they were only doing their duty.

Hsi Shih was relieved that all had gone well, but the whole episode left her exhausted, mentally. She felt acutely uncomfortable for the deceit and trickery she had used to accomplish her task. She had always been honest, and now she was forced to resort to deceit. Although her cause was worthy, the means employed by her was not. Her pride had been assaulted.

# CHAPTER FIFTEEN

## Interrogation

HSI SHIH AND Zheng Dan worked out an action plan for their next task. Fortunately the guards were posted at the entrance of the palace and the gates to the king's family quarters, but not in the official area.

One morning Hsi Shih was sitting at her dressing table before a brass mirror, busy fixing up jewelry onto her delicately swept-up coiffure when a tap at the door announced the arrival of the king. That day he was to take her for a tour of his court. Pleased with Hsi Shih for her recent interest in his official duties, Fu Chai decided to show her what various official chambers were like.

It was only a short horse-ride from the royal family quarters which were in the rear of the palace complex, separated from the official area by a big garden. On their way to the court, the king talked about his ambition.

"I've been on the throne for eight years. It is my long-cherished dream to make Wu the Lord State ... "

" ... and its king the First Lord," Hsi Shih finished the sentence.

Fu Chai smiled.

"Who is the present First Lord?" asked Hsi Shih.

"The Duke of Jin. But Jin is actually in a declining state."

"How can the duke still hold on to the title? Isn't Wu more powerful?"

"Things are not as simple as they seem. The Duke of Jin has the support of the Duke of Chi. Unless Chi is subdued, it would be difficult to make the Duke of Jin relinquish his title."

"What are you going to do then?"

"I have to wait for a good opportunity."

"I hope it won't be too long," Hsi Shih said, reminding herself to play on the king's vanity. "This honorable title should belong to you, my lord."

A grunt of approval escaped the king at her remark.

Presently they arrived at the king's court. The Great Audience Hall was in the middle. There were a few smaller halls on both sides of it. To the west was General Wu Yuan's office; not far to the south was Prime Minister Bo Pi's office. Both offices were characteristic of their occupants. Bo Pi's office was ornate; Wu Yuan's office had an austere look just like the one in his army barracks. The prime minister's welcome was enthusiastic, but the chief general's welcome was lukewarm.

Then Hsi Shih visited the royal library where thousands and thousands of rolls of bamboo-strip-bound books were kept. Realizing the library contained vital information about Wu which she could pass on to Yi Yong, she expressed her interest to visit it often and Fu Chai readily granted her free access. Her final stop was Prince Yiou's study-room. The prince greeted her with only distant civility. His affability had disappeared. Hsi Shih wondered what could have caused the change in the prince's manner. In recent days, he had been noticeably reticent when he came to have dinner. He almost ignored her. Something had definitely come between them. But what could it be?

* * *

General Wu Yuan worked hard. It was his habit to leave his office after everybody else had gone home. Sometimes he would return after dinner to check up on the day's work. That very night he was heading toward his office to work on some unfinished document when suddenly he discerned a flash of light inside.

Who could it be? A burglar? An arsonist? He tiptoed to the building and stopped, motionless and noiseless, at the door to his office and hid himself in the shadow. To his surprise, the intruder was a woman, her back toward him. Holding a candle in her hand, she was examining the room as though looking for something. The woman was slim but not bony. Having fumbled for a while among the documents on one of the desks and obviously not finding anything of interest, she turned around and walked to another desk. In the candlelight, Wu Yuan recognized her to be none other than Hsi Shih. One more glance, and his breath was caught.

Out of a general aversion of anything from Yue,

Wu Yuan had never looked at Hsi Shih closely, though he realized she was very pretty. But now he understood why the muddle-headed king was so bewitched by this dangerous woman spy. He himself had more than a dozen beautiful young concubines, but not one of them was her match. Barefoot and wearing a thin dress, Hsi Shih appeared even more alluring.

*She is Mo Shi reincarnate. She is Da Ji reborn. She is the woman who will destroy Fu Chai and his kingdom.* Wu Yuan shuddered at the thought.

In the shade of a giant pine tree not far from Wu Yuan's office, Zheng Dan was keeping a lookout for Hsi Shih. As soon as she saw a shadow approaching the general's office, she mimicked the mewing of the cat. It was supposed to serve a warning signal to Hsi Shih. But Hsi Shih was so absorbed in her work that she forgot what the mewing was intended for. By the time she was roused to awareness, it was too late. General Wu Yuan was already at the doorstep.

"Stop your snooping, woman!"

Hsi Shih whirled around in panic. The first thought that came to her mind was to run for her life. Throwing the candle onto the ground, she dashed to the door. But Wu Yuan was quick enough to block her way. Fondly hoping that the martial arts training she had received in Yue would come in handy, she backed off a few steps, charged toward the rock-like figure of the lord general, and raised a leg to throw a front kick. Wu Yuan dodged it by a narrow margin. Hsi Shih followed with a side kick, but missed Wu Yuan who moved just a few inches beyond. When she tried to hit him with another kick, Wu Yuan shot out his arm and grabbed her leg.

"B-e-a-u-t-y!" he hissed between his teeth,

throwing her to the floor. His foot landed on her back, and Hsi Shih could no longer move. "Don't you know my office is a forbidden area? You are under arrest!"

"Guardsmen!" he shouted. "Come here. I've seized a spy!"

"Let me go!" Hsi Shih screamed.

The general did not waste a word with her.

Moments later four uniformed guards arrived.

"This woman is a spy," Wu Yuan snarled. "Strip her clothes and search her!"

Hsi Shih reeled in the midst of noise and bright light of torches. All her clothes were ripped off, her nerves shattering. The guards recognized the culprit to be Hsi Shih and were frightened.

"Your Excellency, I'm afraid you have seized the king's consort," said a guard.

"The king's consort was caught red-handed poking around my office," the general bellowed.

Nothing incriminating was found on the prisoner. The general ordered to have Hsi Shih tied to a pillar in the room to be interrogated.

"What were you trying to steal?" he demanded.

"Nothing," Hsi Shih answered. Her chest rose and fell in frightened spasms as her hands and feet were being bound with a heavy cord.

"What were you up to, then?"

Hsi Shih stared at the floor and kept silent.

"Talk!" Wu Yuan yelled coarsely. "Are you sent by Gou Jian to spy on us?"

Hsi Shih writhed in her helpless nudity, but refused to say a word.

"Are you going to talk?"

Hsi Shih hung her head but remained stonily

silent.

"I'll make you talk."

Stepping forward, Wu Yuan grabbed her by the hair, and gave her a sharp slap in the face. Hsi Shih dropped her head and groaned. Then came another slap.

"Woman, you are guilty of espionage. Tell the truth, or you'll die for it."

Still there was no response from Hsi Shih. The general motioned a guard to whip her with a riding crop. Biting lashes came down on the arms, the thighs, and the front. Hsi Shih squirmed in agony. Too proud to cry, she gritted her teeth, steeling herself to endure.

Never in her life had she been whipped, and whipped so harshly. Tears of pain sprang to her eyes. She began to moan. The whipping continued for half an hour, leaving welts all over her body. Thinking she was going to be beaten to death, Hsi Shih prayed silently for the strength to accept her fate.

As the noise wafted from Wu Yuan's office to where Zheng Dan was hiding, she listened in anguished horror, not knowing what to do.

"Stop!" A man's voice rang out. All turned around and saw Bo Pi on the threshold.


Bo Pi had been spending the evening in the chamber of Lady Lin, one of his concubines—a plump, voluptuous woman. They were drinking tea after the evening meal.

"Where is my diamond necklace, my lord?" asked the lady.

"It's in my office, darling."

"Why did you leave it there? You promised to

give me today."

"Sorry I forgot. Wu Yuan was in my office and we left together. I'll bring it to you tomorrow. I kept it in a shiny lacquered box."

Lady Lin moved over and perched on Bo Pi's lap. "To-morrow?" she cooed. "Tomorrow you will give it to somebody else. Last time you promised me an emerald bracelet. But you gave it to somebody else. Please go and bring back the necklace. I want it now." She tickled the nape of his neck. "I'll make you very happy tonight, my lord."

"All right, all right."

Bo Pi rode to his office to fetch the box. He was ready to return when he heard a commotion in Wu Yuan's office across the courtyard. He went over to find out what was going on and was shocked to see Hsi Shih, trussed up like a sacrificial animal, being flogged like a criminal.

"My general, what are you doing?" he exclaimed.

"I caught her in my office."

"What was she doing in your office?"

"She was trying to steal my documents. She is a spy."

"Then you should hand her over to the king. Don't beat her."

"I won't let her go until she has confessed."

Bo Pi took a step forward, directed a furtive glance toward Hsi Shih's attractive, naked body and bowed. "Your Ladyship, don't worry. I'll be right back."

He dashed out, mounted his horse, and galloped away.

Wu Yuan felt thirsty and told a guard to fetch

some water. Seeing the prisoner sweating all over, he gave her a drink. Then the interrogation started again.

Again he urged Hsi Shih to make a clean breast of her guilt, but she remained stubbornly mute. He was about to have her whipped again—with a rattan cane—when Fu Chai barged in, with Bo Pi behind him.

"Fu Chai, this woman is a spy. You must send her to jail," Wu Yuan demanded angrily.

The king had already learned from Bo Pi that Wu Yuan caught Hsi Shih in his office.

"Why are you in the general's office?" he asked mildly.

"I ... I was looking for something."

"What were you looking for?"

By then His Shih had already thought up a pretext for being there. "My hairpin," she replied quietly. "I might have dropped it here when we visited the general's office this morning."

"Have you found it?"

"Yes." Her hair was tousled, but the gold hairpin was hanging onto it.

"Did you take anything from the general's office?"

Hsi Shih shook her head.

The king hastened to unfasten her, picked up her torn clothes from the floor and helped her to dress. He was agonized at the sight of the thong-cuts on her body, but found his favored consort peculiarly beautiful in her tortured state.

"My king, she is lying!" Wu Yuan bellowed furiously.

"Have you found anything on her, General?" demanded the king coldly, his voice strained with the effort to keep himself from shouting back.

"Fu Chai, you must open your eyes. Gou Jian sent her to spy on us, to take your mind away from your duties, to beguile you away from good sense, to bring your kingdom to ruin. She is Mo Shi! She is Da Ji!"

"This is outrageous!" Fu Chai gnarled, his face twisted with wrath. "Don't you dare to compare my lady to evil women!"

"Fu Chai, you must wake up now!"

"You old blasphemer! I've had enough of you!" Fu Chai's voice was edged with savagery. His trembling hand opened and closed on the hilt of his sword.

"My lord!" Hsi Shih suddenly knelt down before Fu Chai, "please don't lose your temper. I plead guilty for trespassing by mistake. General Wu Yuan is right to be vigilant."

This act of altruism on the part of Hsi Shih caught everyone by surprise. The uproar subsided; the room became as silent as a graveyard.

A long moment passed before Fu Chai said softly, "Let's go home."

Carrying Hsi Shih in his arms, he strode out. They rode back on his horse. The cool night air gave Hsi Shih a soothing sensation. Sitting behind Fu Chai with her arms wrapping around him and her cheek pressed to his back, she felt safe, protected. He was Yue's enemy, she reminded herself. But for the moment, that did not matter nearly as much. She was grateful that he had come to her rescue.

# CHAPTER SIXTEEN

## Bear-Paw Feast

THE CORPORAL PUNISHMENT she received after breaking into Wu Yuan's office was a humiliating experience to Hsi Shih. Strangely, she did not hate the general. She venerated him.

But that was not the reason she begged Fu Chai not to lose temper for fear he might have killed the general. She did it out of instinct to protect herself. She was afraid that if Fu Chai killed the old general in a fit of anger, he would surely regret when he sobered up. Then he would surely turn against her. The consequences would be dreadful to contemplate. Moreover, it was not in her nature to hurt anyone. The thought of being the cause of anybody's death frightened her, revolted her, instinctively.

She had sustained only superficial wound, yet Fu Chai insisted on taking turns with Zheng Dan and the other maids to wait upon her, changing plasters on her sores, helping her bathe and dress. Hsi Shih was so touched by his attentiveness she felt embarrassed for what she had done. After all, wasn't she caught when she tried to find information that would have been used by Gou Jian to do him harm? The very thought jarred her soul. Compared with Gou Jian, Fu Chai was a much more likable man. Gou Jian never inspired any respect in her. On the contrary, he struck her as hypocritical and hard-hearted. She felt that she had been coerced by him into doing something against her will. But he was the king of Yue. She had to obey him. Besides, she was doing it for Fan Li. If it were not for Fan Li, she wouldn't carry out her mission here.

She expected Fu Chai to blame her for her indiscreet action, however, not once had he uttered a word of reproach, not once had he mentioned the incident again.

\* \* \*

The marks on her body soon disappeared. But Hsi Shih could still feel the hostility of General Wu Yuan. It seemed all too palpable. Even though she did not think Wu Yuan would do anything underhand to hurt her, she felt insecure. She did not know what he might do to her next since he took her for an evil woman like Mo Shi, like Da Ji. Strangely, she felt like a little girl who had been punished by her father after she had done something foolish. She wanted to do something to ease off the general's hostility, to make herself less afraid of him.

One week later, she appeared at the doorstep of

the general's office, with a case of freshly baked chestnut cakes in her hand.

"Your Excellency," Hsi Shih said with a deep curtsy. "I came here to apologize for having caused a most disturbing scene. It was my fault, and my fault alone. I could not feel easy without coming here to say 'I'm sorry.'"

Wu Yuan was quite thrown off his balance. He asked Hsi Shih to be seated and hastily ordered his attendant to bring some refreshments and herbal tea.

"Are you all right now, my honored lady?" The general felt somewhat stiff before this beautiful woman.

"Yes, Your Excellency. I've brought some chestnut cakes that I made. I knew you like them."

"Thank you very much." Wu Yuan poured some hot tea for his visitor. He did like chestnut cakes and was surprised that Hsi Shih knew about it. "Your Ladyship, it is very kind of you to come here. I should like to take this opportunity to say a few words for your benefit, if you have no objection. You will please excuse my bluntness."

Hsi Shih slanted him a speculative glance and nodded. Wu Yuan began to pace the room, trying to find appropriate words to use.

"Your Ladyship, you are a most beautiful woman. I don't know the real reason you were sent to our country. But please compare Gou Jian with Fu Chai. Gou Jian is devious, Fu Chai is honest; Gou Jian is treacherous, Fu Chai is straightforward; Fu Chai loves you with all his heart, Gou Jian makes you his *pawn*."

"I am not his pawn," Hsi Shih said, though she could not quite understand the word.

"Use your brains and think, my honored lady,"

Wu Yuan stared her in the face. "Be a good helpmate to Fu Chai, and you will have a lifetime to enjoy with him! But if you act as Gou Jian's spy and try to ruin him, you will only ruin yourself!"

Hsi Shih fixed her gaze on the floor. "I am not Gou Jian's spy, Your Excellency."

The general did not heed her denial. "Your Ladyship, Gou Jian is the kind of man who would do anything, sacrifice anybody, in order to attain his goal. It's foolish to be his pawn."

A pregnant pause followed. Hsi Shih saw in her mind's eye Gou Jian kneeling before Fan Li begging him to give up his betrothed for his country. In the depth of her heart, she knew there was some truth in the general's remarks. She had never liked Gou Jian, anyway.

"Your Excellency, I have to go now. I sincerely hope you have accepted my apology. I wish you every success!" She stood up and made an obeisance.

Wu Yuan saw her to the door and sighed softly as he watched her walk away. Hsi Shih's visit was totally unexpected, but somehow it pleased him. *No, she is not Mo Shi; she is not Da Ji. She is very unusual. I just can't make her out.* The general still had a lingering suspicion of Hsi Shih, but enmity dissipated.

\* \* \*

Having learned how Hsi Shih had intervened when his father's hot temper might have hurt or even killed his revered master, Prince Yiou hastened to the Gusu Palace to pay his respects. Out of respect for his mentor, he had distanced himself from Hsi Shih recently. But in his heart of hearts he had always believed she was a good woman.

"Mother, I've brought you a gift." The prince showed her a beautiful Persian cat in the basket he was holding. "Mao Mao is six-month-old. He is a delightful animal. His mother is a pedigreed cat."

Mao Mao's body was covered with a soft, silky dense fur that was as white as snow. His eyes were big, curious. His face had a sweet expression. As Hsi Shih took him into her arms, he moved his ears forward and raised his tail affectionately to her. She took an immediate fancy to the kitten.

"How's everything?" she asked. "How's your study?"

The prince ignored her question. "You must hate General Wu Yuan," he blurted out. "I would understand."

Hsi Shih was caught off guard by his remark.

"The general has a temper," he added.

"I don't hate Lord Wu Yuan. I blame myself for what happened." There was not a trace of resentment in her tone.

"The general is too suspicious."

"The general is a loyal minister. He's entitled to his opinion."

"It's very kind of you to say that, Mother, but he's wrong about you. Sooner or later he'll realize his mistake. Please be patient with him."

"I will. I have a great respect for the general."

Hsi Shih was greatly pleased that Prince Yiou and her were friends again. It was the year for the royal family to celebrate the prince's fifteenth birthday. She proposed a bear-paw party for the occasion, and her idea met with Fu Chai's hearty approval.

During her training in Yue's palace, Hsi Shih had studied cuisine and the master chef had taught her how to prepare the bear-paw soup, among other things. So she took it upon herself to supervise the process.

The bear-paw soup was a rare delicacy. It was difficult to procure bear paws, for bears live in the mountains in the north. Hunters sold bear paws to merchants, and merchants sold them at exorbitant prices for the rich man's table.

Long hours were needed to immerse the paws in boiling water. Then the hair was plucked from the skin; the major bones, extracted; and the grease and dirt, removed. Another way to eliminate the hair was to have the paws wrapped up in yellow soil and baked in a native-styled oven. The hair was removed, together with the hardened soil after baking. After that, the paws were washed in clean water, boiled for a while, and kept simmering on a low flame until they were soft enough to be processed, as the remaining hair had to be cleaned and the tough skin at the bottom had to be removed. The paws had to be washed again. Together with green onions, ginger, wine, paprika and some water, they were put in a pot to be steamed until they were eighty percent done. Then the toes were slit to have the small bones removed, but the original shapes were to remain intact. The water in the pot was changed again, and new spices and threaded ham or other delicious bits of meat were added. When the remaining twenty percent of cooking was completed, the bear-paws were ready to be served, their aroma tantalizing.

Knowing Hsi Shih was to host the grand party, Wu Yuan could not make up his mind whether or not he should go.

"Sir, are you coming to my birthday party?" asked the prince.

"Hmm. You know, I don't trust Hsi Shih. She may be a spy."

"I know she is not, sir," the prince said impatiently. "She can't be. I'll be unhappy if you don't come to the party."

"All right, young man, I'll come."

Hsi Shih, the gracious hostess of the party, won the admiration of all the guests. The bear-paw soup was such a luxurious gourmet that everyone considered it a great gastronomical experience worth boasting to friends and relatives about. The guests also enjoyed the performance of the palace dance ensemble. Even Wu Yuan found the party entertaining.

*If only Hsi Shih were not from Yue!* he sighed.

*     *     *

Before she knew it, Hsi Shih had already been in Wu for a year. Summer came again, and she moved to the Gusu Tower with Fu Chai. Around her chamber was a balcony that gave a panoramic view of the beautiful city of Gusu. But she was not in the frame of mind to enjoy the beautiful scenery. Leaning against the railings of the balcony, she reflected upon her relationship with Fu Chai and Prince Yiou. Both adored her, trusting her as a member of their family. Yet the more they treated her this way, the more uneasy she felt. For the first time, she had doubts about her mission.

Gou Jian had bid her to subvert Fu Chai with her charm. But Fu Chai was making it increasingly difficult for her. He was not a mean man. Not at all. She understood she had to put aside her personal feelings to do her job, but the nature of her assignment was more demanding than she had anticipated. She could not bring herself to hate him—a man who genuinely loved her.

After the mishap in Wu Yuan's office, Yi Yong did not give Zheng Dan and her any risky assignment. He just asked them to regularly report what they had seen and heard inside the Wu palace. Their task was to preserve themselves and familiarize themselves with everything in Wu and wait since it would be some time before Yue acquired the capability to invade Wu.

Her role required her to be a liar, a double-dealer, a back-stabber. Belatedly, she came to realize that she was not cut out for the job. But what about her duty to her country? What about her promise to King Gou Jian? To Fan Li? ...

Thoughts like this clashed within her and she was bothered by them.

One day the king found her in an unusually pensive mood. "What has upset my precious dear?" the king asked. "Are you all right?"

"I am all right, my lord. I just miss Zhuluo Village, my old home," said Hsi Shih, quick to improvise a reason for herself.

The king regarded her musingly and said, "I can understand."

A few days later, he took Hsi Shih for a tour in the Lingyan Hill, about thirty *li* west of Gusu. The scenery delighted Hsi Shih. The valleys were strewn with flowers and the hills clad with trees and bamboo groves. Ducks and geese floated on the ponds and lakes that crisscrossed lush rice field, and the rivers teemed with fish. Hsi Shih had never been here before. Yet there was something familiar about the surroundings.

"Do you like this place, my sweet?" the king asked.

"Yes, very much."

"I've looked at a few places," the king said. "This site seems the most ideal."

"Ideal for what?"

"If it pleases you, sweetheart, I will build your home village here. If you don't like this place, there are other places to consider."

Hsi Shih could not reply. She was stunned at the king's extravagant idea—to build a village for her. It sounded so fanciful that she found it difficult to comprehend at first.

"No, no," she said breathlessly. "Of course I like this place. It reminds me of Zhuluo Village. But.... "

"Very good!" The king said, his eyes sparkling. "I think it should be a replica of the best part of Zhuluo, but much more fantastic. Of course, your suggestions will be very important."

"But I ... I don't need it. It is just too ... too costly." Hsi Shih murmured, realizing the king was serious.

Fu Chai looked amused. "It *is* worth it, darling. I want you to be happy. I want you to feel at home. I thought about its name. I think I'll call it 'The Beauty's Palace.' Do you like this name?"

Hsi Shih nodded, feeling a lump in her throat.

"Very good!" The king grinned. "I'll put Bo Pi in charge of the project."

"Thank you, my lord," Hsi Shih smiled, her teeth shining like polished alabaster.

# CHAPTER SEVENTEEN

## Magic of Speech

Q UFU, THE CAPITAL of the State of Lu, was a small walled town about one thousand and two hundred *li* to the north of Gusu. Charming, clean and tranquil, it had remarkably courteous and literate residents. Hotels, hostels, tea houses and restaurants were often filled with scholars and students from other states who travelled to Qufu to listen to Confucius' lectures.

Confucius lived in a time of political upheavals and internal strife in China. Although the dynasty house of Zhou was the sovereign ruler, the kings of Zhou held only the vain title of the "Son of Heaven" and the capital city of Luoyang was the only place they could exercise any control. The "divine right" which they claimed to be theirs had long been ignored by the rulers of their numerous vassal states—hereditary nobles whose ancestors had been kinsmen to the royal house of Zhou.

In the course of time, these hereditary nobles had established their own armies and governments in their principalities. Some of them even called themselves kings. As a rule, one state at a time was recognized as the "Lord State" and its ruler designated as the "First Lord." The Lord State was supposed to support the royal house of Zhou, defend it against barbarian invasion, and assist weak and needy states. In return, it would receive annual tributes from other states and its ruler would become the most prestigious figure in China next to the king of Zhou. The arrangement seemed reasonable, but craving for this honorable title had turned into open strife for supremacy among contending feudal lords of various states.

As Confucius said, there was no just war during that period. It was against this background that he began his crusade for a better government based on benevolence, virtue and universal education.

Earlier that year, he came back to his native land after an absence of fourteen years, during which time, he wandered from state to state, fondly hoping to advance his ideals. The rulers of various countries treated him with respect but no one adopted his proposals. At the age of sixty-eight, Confucius decided to give up his political ambition and returned to Lu when inter-state strife for supremacy was at its height.

As a politician, Confucius was a failure, but as a teacher, he was a great success. With his profound knowledge of statecraft, history, philosophy, poetry and music, he spent his remaining years giving lectures and writing books for the benefit of future generations.

His residence was located in the northeastern

part of Qufu. Its main gate was painted black with red borders and had shiny brass knockers and a pair of calligraphy inscriptions reading *Never Be Bored of Learning*, and *Never Be Tired of Teaching*. A pair of stone lions stood at both sides. Inside the gate was a wide grassy courtyard filled with trees of all sorts. A stream spanned by three stone bridges ran through the courtyard.

Beyond the bridges was what could be described as Confucius' college, consisting of a front hall, a lecture hall spacious enough to hold more than a hundred people, a dining hall, a kitchen and a few offices. The roofs were green-tiled, the pillars red-painted, the walls carved with pictures and poems. Confucius and his family lived in the secluded rear part of the yard behind a gated garden. A tangible atmosphere of serenity pervaded the entire place.

Confucius was compiling *The Annals of Spring and Autumn*, a book of Chinese history covering a period of two and half centuries up to his time, when one of his disciples, who had just returned from a trip to the State of Chi, came with the news that Chi's troops were being stationed by the Wen River at the Chi/Lu border, ready to make war on Lu. That Chi's prime minister Chen Heng was the chief plotter. The bad news shocked Confucius, for Lu was the weaker of the two states that had always been at feud with each other.

*Alas!* Confucius thought, *Lu is my birthplace. I must save my fatherland from disaster.*

He posed a question to his class, "Which one among you can save our country?"

"I can," said Tzu Lu, a burly-set young man known for his foolhardiness. "I'll go to Chi and murder

Chen Heng."

Confucius chuckled. "Do you think it's that easy? Your courage is commendable, but this mission requires more than just bravery."

Then Tzu Zhang offered to go. "Master, I believe I can talk Chen Heng into withdrawing his troops."

The whole class laughed at his statement, knowing that Tzu Zhang, though having a facile tongue, was a bluffer.

"Talking big won't help, my boy," said Confucius. "Chen Heng is a tough customer to deal with."

"Master, could I be honored with this assignment?" asked Tzu Gong who was the brightest of the class, well-rounded and a man of great depth, though his good looks and easy manners belied his profundity.

Confucius beamed. "Yes, you are the very man for the task. Come and see me after class. There's no time to lose."

Tzu Gong had not only impressed his mentor with his knowledge of history and his grasp of the political dynamics in China but also his social skill and eloquence. These qualities, Confucius believed, would stand him in good stead in his dealing with the rulers of various states. The two men put their heads together and quickly worked out a strategy.

\* \* \*

When Tzu Gong arrived at Linzi\*, the capital of Chi, and asked for an interview with Prime Minister Chen Heng, no warm welcome was evinced. Knowing

---

\* Present-day Zibo, Shandong Province.

that Tzu Gong was Confucius' disciple coming from Lu, Chen Heng was determined not to be dissuaded from his plan of action. A plain-looking man in his forties, Chen Heng achieved his rise through cunning, discreetness and hard work, and would not scruple to use trickery in his own interest.

"Sir, you intend to use your clever tongue to persuade me to withdraw my troops, I guess?" he greeted Tzu Gong bluntly.

"No," responded Tzu Gong. "I've come here for *your* benefit, Your Lordship."

"That's interesting."

"I'm here to advise you to give up your attempt of attacking Lu," Tzu Gong said flatly, "because if you do, you will lose. I advise you to attack Wu, because if you do, you will win."

Tzu Gong had done his homework. He knew there was a power struggle between the prime minister, who had newly assumed the reins of government, and some senior military officers. To weaken his opponents, Chen Heng had persuaded the Duke of Chi to commission them to launch an attack on Lu in the hope that the war might wear down the military.

"What are you talking about?" Chen Heng snorted. "What absurdity!"

"You will lose if you attack Lu," Tzu Gong said positively, "because its ruler is incompetent, its army inexperienced, its walls of defense thin and the moat narrow and shallow. You will win if you attack Wu because its ruler is capable, its army well-trained, its walls of defense thick and the moat wide and deep."

Chen Heng was perplexed. "My lord, you are talking in riddles."

"I heard that the Duke of Chi has proposed for three times to grant you a noble title, together with a fief, but you still haven't got it."

"No, not yet."

"Why haven't you?"

"Do you know why?"

"Because your opponents are against it. I guess Your Lordship's exalted position has caused jealousy in certain circles who are seeking to undermine your influence."

Chen Heng signified his agreement by silence.

"If you let them attack a weak country like Lu," Tzu Gong continued, "they are bound to win. They will return victorious and their battlefield merits will outshine your domestic achievements. They will grow so powerful that they can threaten Your Lordship's position. On the contrary, if you let them attack a strong country like Wu, they are bound to lose and your influence will be enhanced. Consequently Your Lordship will hold sway in the government. Isn't it obvious that if they win, you will lose; and if they lose, you will win?"

Chen Heng found Tzu Gong's argument potent. "My honored sir, your point is well-taken. Yet there is still one difficult issue. Our troops are already garrisoned at the Wen River. I could not very well call them back and ask them to attack Wu."

"There is no need for a recall because you will have a good reason to attack Wu."

"I don't see how."

"Wu and Lu are friends. King Fu Chai wants to be seen as a ruler who supports the weak. I can go and persuade him to dispatch his troops to Lu's rescue. Then you can ask your troops not to attack Lu, but to continue staying at the Wen River to guard against the advance of Wu's troops. Tell them to first defeat Wu's forces and then go on to subdue Lu. Your opponents may lose because Wu's forces are strong. But even if they win, they are bound to pay a high price for their victory. Win or lose, by the time the war ends, your opponents in the military will need a long time to recover. By then, Your Lordship's position will have been as secure as Mt. Tai."

"My friend," Chen Heng was brimming with warmth, his face wreathed in smiles, "your words are like brilliant light that floods in upon my darkness. I'm much obliged."

When Tzu Gong took his departure, the prime minister saw him off to the gate of the palace and offered him gold and silver which Tzu Gong thankfully accepted.

Shortly afterwards the Duke of Chi informed the military of a likely Wu invasion and asked them to suspend their planned attack on Lu for the time being.

\*     \*     \*

In Wu, King Fu Chai's court was in session. General Wu Yuan had some grave news to report after sending his spies to collect information in Yue.

"We've all heard the names of Chen Yin and the Virgin of the Southern Forest. Both of them have now been hired by Gou Jian. It is obvious he is plotting a revengeful attack on us."

Bo Pi disagreed. "Hiring them does not necessary mean Gou Jian is plotting against us. Gou Jian could be training guards for internal security."

"If Gou Jian wants to train some guards," said Fu Chai, "why does he need the best master of archery and best master of fencing? The only reason he hired them is to train professional soldiers, but he is bound by treaty not to raise an army against us."

"Precisely," Wu Yuan concurred. "If he has nothing to hide from us, he would not have set up the training base in a remote mountain."

"I guess Gou Jian is trying to make trouble and hamper my effort to become the First Lord," said Fu Chai irritably.

"Before you devote yourself to becoming the First Lord, my king, the threat posed by Gou Jian must be eliminated."

"I agree. I will not allow him to sabotage my goal. I think we should stop his war effort by launching a preemptive strike."

"It would be a wise move, my king," Wu Yuan was gratified that Fu Chai took Yue's threat seriously. "I'll draw up a plan for actions."

Tzu Gong arrived in Wu when preparations for war were in full swing.

"Your Majesty," he said to Fu Chai. "I have come here with bad news. Lu is in dire danger: it is on the verge of being conquered by Chi's force. It needs your help."

"Chi is a bully indeed."

"Your Majesty certainly remembers how Wu joined forces with Lu to beat back Chi's invasion a few years ago. Now Chi is coming again. After subduing Lu, Chi may even sweep down to the south to attack Wu."

Fu Chai did not agree with Tzu Gong's assessment

but did not wish to argue with him.

"Would Your Majesty come to Lu's rescue?"

Fu Chai did not respond.

"If Your Majesty helps Lu confront Chi, your prestige will be tremendously boosted, and you'll send a powerful message to all fief rulers in China. If Chi is crushed, Jin will have to succumb. And the recognition of Your Majesty as the First Lord will be a settled thing."

"I understand. But it's not the right time for me to get involved in the north. I have trouble at home."

"May I know what that is?"

"Gou Jian, the ruler of my vassal state Yue, is secretly training his army and plotting a revenge against us. I have to nip his attempt in the bud."

"Your Majesty wants to punish Yue first, and then turn to Chi?"

"Quite so."

"I'm afraid it will be too late. Lu will already have been annexed by Chi by that time. Your Majesty, just imagine what other rulers would think if you avoid confronting a big power like Chi because you fear a small country like Yue."

Fu Chai frowned.

"It will be a manifestation of *cowardice* if you don't help Lu," Tzu Gong went on, "and it will show a *lack of wisdom* on your part if you let go an opportunity of demonstrating Wu's power. Isn't it your goal to become the First Lord? Well, *cowardice* and *lack of wisdom* are not exactly in keeping with the qualities of a First Lord."

Fu Chai looked at his guest sullenly.

"As for Gou Jian," Tzu Gong continued, "a small country like Yue can never surpass a powerful country like Wu. If Your Majesty has misgivings, I will make a trip to Yue and ask Gou Jian to join you in fighting Chi under your command. That will test his loyalty to you."

"That sounds a good idea." Fu Chai grinned. "You could help clarifying Gou Jian's intent. I'll wait until I hear from you."

\*     \*     \*

Gou Jian had just received an urgent report from Hsi Shih and Zheng Dan that General Wu Yuan had found out his secret training and Fu Chai had decided to invade Yue. The message came like a thunderbolt. He was about to convene a meeting with his ministers when he learned that Tzu Gong was coming from Wu. Gou Jian ordered his protocol officials to greet the Confucius' disciple as far as thirty *li* outside the capital. The thoroughfares of Guiji were swept extremely clean to welcome the honorable guest.

"Your visit to our humble state is a great honor to us," said Gou Jian respectfully as he received Tzu Gong in his palace.

"Your Majesty, I have bad news for you."

"What bad news?"

"I'm afraid Yue is faced with imminent disaster. I've just been in Wu to urge Fu Chai to help Lu against Chi's impending invasion. But Fu Chai intends to crush Yue first, because he suspects Your Majesty of clandestine war preparations against his country."

Now Tzu Gong had confirmed the information from Hsi Shih and Zheng Dan, Gou Jian became so upset that his face turned white.

"Your Majesty," said Tzu Gong, "it will be *unwise* if you make your opponent suspect you of harboring ill intentions when you are *not*. It will be *suicidal* if you make your opponent suspect you of harboring ill intentions if you really *are*."

"My honored advisor, the fact that you honored us with your visit means you can help us head off the disaster. Am I right?"

"Your Majesty is a smart man," Tzu Gong smiled benignly, "but you don't have many options. To dispel Fu Chai's suspicion, the wise thing to do is to take a few thousand men with you, place yourself under his command, and go to war with him as his loyal vassal."

Tzu Gong's proposal took Gou Jian by surprise.

"Should Your Majesty be willing to consider my advice," Tzu Gong continued, "I will go back to Wu and persuade Fu Chai to accept your offer."

"But ... "

"Of course, I'll try to persuade Fu Chai not to let you go to the front personally. After all, it's a risky thing to fight Chi."

"I'll be much obliged."

"Your Majesty, fighting a powerful state like Chi is a costly endeavor. If Fu Chai loses, Wu will be weakened and Yue will have a good chance."

"That's true. But what if he wins?"

"Yue will also have a good chance."

"How can that be possible?"

"Because victory will swell Fu Chai with pride. I have no doubt he will go on to contend with his remaining rival, the Duke of Jin. He may embark on another expedition. If that happens, wouldn't it be a good opportunity for Your Majesty?"

Gou Jian bowed to Tzu Gong. "My honored sir, your words are truly enlightening. You have saved me!"

He presented the Confucius' disciple two thousand ounces of gold and two thoroughbred horses as a token of his gratitude.

\* \* \*

Night fell when Tzu Gong arrived at Gusu. Fu Chai received him without delay.

"Gou Jian was grieved to learn that he had aroused Your Majesty's suspicion," Tzu Gong reported to the king. "He says he is loyal to you. He is sending an envoy here to explain."

Fu Chai asked Tzu Gong to stay in Gusu and wait to meet with Yue's envoy. Five days later, Yue's prime minister Wen Zhong arrived.

"My master sent me here," he bowed humbly to Fu Chai, "to reiterate his allegiance to Your Majesty and to dispel the concern you have regarding the police force we are organizing."

"Police force? I heard you've been training an army behind my back."

"It is not an army, Your Majesty. Just a police force of a few thousand for maintaining law and order. "

"If so, why did you find it necessary to hire a master archer and master swordsman to train them?"

"Because bandits have been harassing our southern border. We need an adequate force to deal with them. But now as my master heard that Your Majesty is ready to wage war against a strong power in defense of a weak nation, he wants to support your righteous cause by offering his service at your disposal."

"What does he propose to do?"

"He asks Your Majesty permission to let him

take three thousand men to join you and fight under your command. Wu's enemy is Yue's enemy. No fear of death can shake my master's unwavering fidelity to his sovereign lord."

Fu Chai's face lit up. He turned to Tzu Gong and said, "Gou Jian is indeed a man of his word. My honored sir, should I accept his offer?"

"Of course. Accept the services of the three thousand men but dismiss their king."

"Why should I not let Gou Jian come?"

"Because it would be improper. The king of a vassal state is still a king. Showing consideration for him would earn you a good name."

Fu Chai took Tzu Gong's advice, pleased that his troops were to be expanded by three thousand men.

Wu Yuan was caught by total surprise when Fu Chai revoked his decision to attack Yue and chose to embark on a northern expedition against Chi instead.

"My king, you are being misled by Tzu Gong!" he protested in exasperation. "It is absolutely foolish to go on an expedition so far away while the real threat comes from next door."

"My lord, I agree we must first eliminate the threat from next door. But the fact is there is no threat from next door. You've raised a false alarm."

"No, I haven't. My king, it is you who is being deceived by Gou Jian's cunning."

A taunting laugh broke from Fu Chai.

"All along you've been harping on the same old tune, general. Why? Don't you see that our victory over Chi will establish me as the First Lord and Wu as the Lord State? The prime minister looks forward to it. Other ministers feel the same way. Even Hsi Shih is happy for me. You alone predict disaster."

"Lady Hsi Shih could be in the employ of Gou Jian."

"What impudence!" Bo Pi cut in. "Why do you vilify Lady Hsi Shih? What proof do you have to support your allegations, General?"

"You are imagining things, General," Fu Chai sneered. "You've served our country well. But you are getting old. Your judgment no longer holds true."

"The northern expedition will be a grave mistake, my king. What is Chi compared to Yue? Chi is like a skin rash: its harm is only skin-deep. Yue is like a cancer: its poisonous growth is life-threatening. Remove it now. Don't wait till it is too late!"

"I'm not going to argue with you any more, General," the king said. "My mind is set. The northern expedition is on our agenda."

With that, he dismissed Wu Yuan.

# CHAPTER EIGHTEEN

## Interpretation of a Dream

FU CHAI DECIDED to send an emissary to Chi to ask the Duke of Chi to either withdraw his troops from the Wen River or be ready for a confrontation with Wu. Having turned over the matter in his mind, he decided that General Wu Yuan was the most suitable person for the mission. Wu Yuan's reputation as a renowned war hero might threaten the Duke of Chi into calling back his troops and thus have the matter settled without a fight.

"My lord," he said to Wu Yuan, "I know you are opposed to war with Chi. If you can make the Duke of Chi withdraw his troops, then there will be no war."

Wu Yuan was only too glad to accept the mission. He had sent his teenage son Wu Feng to advance his studies in Chi six years ago, Chi being the most culturally advanced state in China at the time. There he had a good friend and old schoolmate, Lord Bao Mu, a warm-hearted, wealthy aristocrat, with whom he had entrusted Wu Feng. Wu Yuan had not had a chance to visit his son since. Now this mission was a good opportunity. He needed a heart-to-heart talk with him and his guardian.

Upon arriving in Chi after a journey of one thousand and five hundred *li*, Wu Yuan went straight to Lord Bao Mu's residence which was located in a quiet section of the capital. It was an imposing edifice of red brick. A row of Chinese parasol trees led the way to the magnificent entrance fronted by a huge lawn. Lord Bao Mu, a scholarly-looking grey-haired man, and Wu Feng, now a strapping youth, came out to welcome him. Wu Yuan hugged both of them in a tearful embrace.

"How is Wu Feng doing?" he asked Lord Bao Mu as he was ushered into the drawing room.

"You should be proud of your son, my friend," Bao Mu gave him an infectious smile. "Wu Feng is an all-round good student. He excels in all subjects."

"I'm glad to hear it. Wu Feng is getting the best possible education a young man can get. If he doesn't work hard, don't spare the rod!"

"Wu Feng is a conscientious young man. He is studying under a very strict tutor. Of course, I regularly check on his work myself."

"Thank you so much, my good friend!"

"Father, are you coming to take me home?" asked Wu Feng.

"No, I'm not," Wu Yuan said solemnly, "I'm on an errand."

Then he turned to Lord Bao Mu and asked, "Would you please be my son's foster-father and take care of him if anything happens to me? I want him to settle down in Chi."

"Of course, my friend. But why did you say that?"

"I have my reasons, my good friend."

He told Lord Bao Mu that Fu Chai was so duped by Gou Jian's fake subservience that he had dropped all vigilance against Yue and so consumed with vanity that he wanted to earn the title of the First Lord at all costs.

"No remonstration could make him mend his ways," he sighed.

"My friend," urged Lord Bao Mu, "don't make a pest of yourself by remonstrating with the dupe of a stupid king. Please stay here and don't return. Your talent will be appreciated by the Duke of Chi. Lady Wu Yuan can join you here. In fact, your absence will please Fu Chai as much as it will please Bo Pi. Don't you think so?"

"Thank you for your kind thought," said Wu Yuan. "But my lot is tied with Wu. I owe too much to Fu Chai's father. He asked me to look after Fu Chai, knowing the boy was muddle-headed. I gave him my word, and my word is my bond. I'm obliged to do my best to protect Fu Chai."

"But things have changed, my friend."

"True. But Fu Chai is still my charge. He used to listen to me. In recent years I've offended him with too much remonstration. I can't help it because I want to save him from being wrecked. I don't want his kingdom to be annihilated by Gou Jian. I will have to remonstrate and remonstrate until I die. If he continues to ignore my warnings, the State of Wu will be doomed. Fu Chai will be doomed, and I will be doomed, too. But I don't want my son to share my lot."

Lord Bao Mu felt sorry for his friend, for he knew there was no way to make him change his mind.

"Come here," Wu Yuan beckoned to his son. "Kowtow to your foster-father."

Wu Feng promptly knelt to his guardian and kowtowed three times. Wu Yuan also bowed to Lord Bao Mu. "Thank you for accepting Wu Feng as your son," he said, his eyes wet.

Lord Bao Mu promised to treat Wu Feng as his own flesh and blood. Then he wept, and Wu Feng wept, too.

The next morning, Lord Bao Mu, who held a high position in the court of Chi, ushered General Wu Yuan in for an audience with the Duke of Chi. Wu Yuan tried to counsel the duke to spare the State of Lu and withdraw his troops from the Wen River. The duke promised to consider the issue and invited him to a state dinner the next day.

The Duke of Chi, who had been on the throne for less than a year, was a callow and indecisive ruler. He sought advice from his newly promoted prime minister, Chen Heng. Having just taken the wise counsel given him by the Confucius' disciple, Tzu Gong, Chen Heng naturally advised the duke not to listen to Wu Yuan. He would not allow anybody to foil his plan of consolidating his power by calling back the troops of his opponents.

At the dinner in honor of Wu Yuan, the Duke of Chi expressed his regret for not being able to take Wu Yuan's counsel, because, he claimed, stationing his troops at the Wen River was strategically important to Chi. Wu Yuan tried again to change the duke's mind, but to no avail. Thereupon he reluctantly presented the Declaration-of-War document on behalf of King Fu

Chai, and the dinner ended in bad feelings on both sides.

\* \* \*

Fu Chai convened a meeting with his ministers to discuss the forthcoming campaign against Chi.

"Sire, may I propose that General Wu Yuan take three thousand of his elite troops with him?" Bo Pi made the suggestion deliberately, knowing Wu Yuan would be provoked.

"I'm not going to fight this stupid war," returned Wu Yuan angrily.

The king was appalled. Wu Yuan's refusal amounted to a challenge to his authority. "Do you have reasons to refuse to fight, General?"

"My troops are committed to the defense of the homeland, not for any other purpose. We must be on guard against a sudden attack from Yue."

"The general will please remember that Gou Jian will join our expeditionary forces to fight Chi," Bo Pi said.

"That's a trick to hoodwink us."

"How do you know it's a trick?" Fu Chai demanded, resenting the general's insinuation that he was being fooled by Gou Jian's trick.

"Because I know what kind of a man Gou Jian is."

"What would you say if we defeat Chi and I become the First Lord?"

"Victory over Chi is not impossible. But it will be a worthless victory. You can never become a real First Lord if you don't wipe out your real enemy."

"Out! No more of your nonsense!" The king had enough.

Now that Wu's troops were ready to set out for the north, a ceremonial service was held on the eve of their departure at which Fu Chai offered animal sacrifices to the gods to invoke their blessings for his campaign.

That night he had a strange dream: he saw a rice pot on a burning stove when he was taking a walk outside his palace, but despite the intense heat, the pot did not boil. As he walked on, he saw two black dogs barking at the palace gate and two spades standing against the palace wall. Looking in, he was alarmed that the palace was flooded by water.

Fu Chai woke up in sweat. The next morning he told Bo Pi about his dream.

A fawning smile danced upon Bo Pi's lips. "Congratulations, Your Majesty! Your dream foretells our success. Wu is going to win the war over Chi. The rice pot signifies our vast resources. Dogs barking means rulers of other states vie to pay homage to you. The spades represent the farmers sowing and reaping bumper harvests, keeping our granaries filled to capacity. And the flooding water symbolizes tributes from other nations flowing in like endless streams of water."

"Wonderful interpretation! I nearly thought it was a bad dream."

The king was relieved. But still he was not so sure. He asked General Wangsun Shong to interpret his dream, and the general recommended Gongsun Sheng, a well-known professional astrologer.

"I've heard all his predictions have come true," said the general. "Why not summon him?"

Gongsun Sheng was in the middle of lunch when Wangsun Shong called on him. He was a thin, smallish man in his early sixties, with a pointed nose and thinning hair. He burst into tears the moment Wangsun Shong told him about the king's dream and summoned him to the royal palace to interpret it for His Majesty.

"Your Excellency, the king's summon is my death warrant!"

Wangsun Shong was dumbfounded.

"Please allow me to finish my meal and bid farewell to my wife."

Then he slipped into the inner room, leaving the general standing aghast in the entrance hall.

"My dear," said Gongsun Sheng to his wife, "I knew all along that today is my last day of life because my star tells me so."

His wife could hardly believe her ears. She stared at her husband in consternation. "Last day? What happened?"

"As all was quiet and peaceful this morning," Gongsun Sheng went on, "I began to hope for an escape from death so that I can live with you for another twenty or thirty years to come. But my hope is dashed to pieces."

"Why can't you? I don't understand." His wife was so convulsed with fear that her wrinkled face was drained of color.

"The king had an ominous dream. He wants me to interpret it for him. His envoy is waiting to take me to the palace right away. It is mid-noon now and mid-noon is the worst hour of the day."

"Don't tell the truth," said his wife, barely recovering from her shock. "Tell him he had a good dream, and all will be well."

"I can't do that, my dear," Gongsun Sheng wailed.

"My conscience forbids me to do so. What is ordained by Providence we human beings can't alter. Not only do I grieve over my own fate, but also King Fu Chai's, for his dream revealed that he and his kingdom are doomed to perish."

As he said so, both he and his wife sobbed in despair.

"Your Majesty," Gongsun Sheng said as he knelt down before King Fu Chai, "I entreat you not to go to war with Chi because your dream is a bad omen."

The king's face changed color.

"Your Majesty was walking outside the palace gate in your dream? That means you will have to flee in panic. The rice in the pot could not be cooked? That means Your Majesty, in your flight, will have to eat rice raw. Dogs barking? You will be like a homeless stray dog. The spades leaning against the palace wall? Wu's ancestral temple will be leveled to the ground by Yue's troops. The flood in the palace means that all the treasures in your palace will be pillaged."

"How can I prevent such disasters?"

"Call off the war against Chi immediately."

"Shut up!" The king shouted.

But Gongsun Sheng kept on talking. "Or be prepared to surrender to Yue and let Wu be its vassal state."

"Stop your evil gibberish!"

"If I cherish my life, I would not speak honestly. But I am a loyal subject of yours. I love my country more than my own life. I decided to speak the truth. Please consider my words carefully, Your Majesty."

Fu Chai was furious. He ordered to have the man

beheaded despite General Wangsun Shong's plea for clemency.

Wu Yuan was staying at home on the pretext of being ill. Upon learning that Gongsun Sheng, who was a friend of his, was condemned to death, he rushed to the palace to urge Fu Chai to spare him since Gongsun Sheng was only a professional astrologer.

Before Fu Chai responded, Bo Pi counselled Wu Yuan not to interfere.

"My lord, this Gongsun Sheng is an evil man. How dare he predict disaster on the eve of our expedition? How dare he try to shake the morale of our troops? It's a crime!"

"Of course, it's a crime." Fu Chai snapped, motioning to his guards to take the astrologer to the execution ground.

* * *

It was late in the evening when Fu Chai returned home. Hsi Shih was waiting for him to have dinner together. As the date of the northern expedition approached, she became anxious. Her head told her that the expedition was a good thing for Yue, but her heart did not want Fu Chai to endanger his life. Her head told her that he was the enemy king, but her heart persuaded her that he was a loving husband. She tried to sort out her feelings, but it was in vain.

"How long are you going to be away, my lord?" she asked.

"About two months, my dear. I'm taking Bo Pi and Wangsun Shong with me."

"Is General Wu Yuan not going?"

"No, he'll stay at home. He says he's not going to 'this stupid war' as he calls it. He's too old, anyway."

"But he is most loyal to you."

"That's why I have put up with his impudence. But he is getting on my nerves. He tries to overrule me. He treats me like a child. I don't like that."

"Please be patient with the old general. He means well."

"My precious dear!" Fu Chai gazed at her with a glimmer of new admiration. "You are very kind."

Hsi Shih had mixed feelings about Wu Yuan's not going. On the one hand, she was relieved that domestic affairs would be in good hands; on the other, she was concerned that without Wu Yuan, Fu Chai's victory might not come easily.

As though he read her thoughts, Fu Chai said, "Sweetheart, I'm confident of our victory. You know Gou Jian has dispatched three thousand men to join my forces."

Hsi Shih gazed at him skeptically. "He did? Why?"

"Because he supports our cause."

Gou Jian supporting Fu Chai's cause? That's impossible, Hsi Shih told herself.

"Suppose his troops make trouble on the front line?"

"My dear," Fu Chai laughed, "you sound like Wu Yuan. Our forces are ten times stronger than Yue's. If his troops dare to make trouble, I will kill them off and I will crush Gou Jian once and for all."

Hsi Shih felt reassured. Then she became aware that something was wrong with her own reaction. Good heavens! She was committed to Fu Chai's ruin. But now she worried about his safety. She swore loyalty to Gou Jian. But now she wished Fu Chai could see through him.

"I want to go with you," she blurted out, recovering from her confused thought.

Fu Chai gave her a curious glance. "Sweetheart, this is not like going for a joy ride. This is war—men's business."

His response earned a pouting stare.

"Bo Pi said the Beauty's Palace is half completed," Fu Chai smiled into her eyes. "It will be ready by springtime next year."

"Beauty's Palace?" Hsi Shih beamed. The news sent a thrill of joy to her heart. "I'd love it, my lord."

"After we have defeated Chi, I'll make an effort to win the title of the First Lord. If I succeed, you will be the wife of the First Lord, sweetheart."

"I greatly look forward to it, my lord. I wish you every success."

She forgot for the moment that it was her assigned duty to fan his ambition.

In Fu Chai's absence, she felt lonely. There was no escape from the longing and desolation that filled her heart. There was a void inside her that neither Prince Yiou nor Zheng Dan could fill. Fu Chai's memory, his passionate kisses, his tender, admiring smile, his words of praise, the sweet feeling to be in his arms, his exquisite gentleness, his exciting roughness, ... kept coming back to haunt her days and nights. She could not stop it and did not want to stop.

She liked the man. She had come to care about him despite her efforts to avoid it. She had come to like him more than she had thought possible, more than she was willing to admit to herself. And perhaps, a lot more. *Why, do I not belong to my lord Fan Li?*

Lately there had been days at a time when she did not even think about Fan Li, yet she had genuinely loved him. It was less than two years since they said good-bye to each other, but it seemed ages ago. The memories had become pale since Fu Chai entered her life. More than anything she wanted to be with Fu Chai, to twine herself around him, to crush her mouth against his, to be touched, cuddled, possessed by him. She could not remember if she had felt so passionately about Fan Li. She despised herself for her own weakness, but she could not deny that her feelings had changed.

# CHAPTER NINETEEN

## The Beauty's Palace

THE ARRIVAL OF thirty-three thousand men from Wu boosted the morale of Lu's troops tremendously. Fu Chai let the Lu army engage the enemy first. After all, his men had just completed a journey of one thousand and three hundred *li* and needed to recuperate.

Lu's army of fifteen thousand fought with zeal. But they were up against a much stronger enemy, for Chi had thirty thousand well-trained soldiers. After three days' fighting, both armies were exhausted and casualties heavy. It appeared that Lu's army would not be able to hold their own. At this juncture, Fu Chai threw his men into action.

A fierce battle took place at a point called Ai Ling* between Wu and Chi. Both sides committed their

---

* Present-day Laiwu, Shandong Province.

best troops to the fight. Overcome with thirst for blood, the fighters were bent on killing. Generals confronted generals; soldiers confronted soldiers; battle formations confronted battle formations. Horses neighing, men dying and screaming, swords clashing, salvos of arrows whizzing—a frantic spree of killing possessed all of them. The beating of the drum urged them to advance and the sound of the gong ordered them to retreat.

A valiant commander, Fu Chai brought the fighting prowess of his warriors into full play and struck fear into the hearts of his opponents. Carnage was piled up like mountains and blood formed streams. The moaning of the wounded and the dying was heart-rending. Both sides grouped and regrouped several times. It was not until both Chi's commander-in-chief and the second-in-command were killed in action that Chi admitted defeat. The Duke of Chi was compelled to sign a peace treaty, pledging never to encroach upon Lu's territorial integrity again.

\*   \*   \*

Fu Chai's court was bubbling with activities in celebration of Wu's victory. A national holiday was declared. All government ministers and generals as well as emissaries from other states, who came to pay homage to the king, were invited to a sumptuous banquet. The king read the names on the honor roll, names of those who had rendered meritorious services in the battlefield.

Those who had done a good job at home in support of his expedition were also commended. General Wu Yuan's name was conspicuously absent.

In the midst of the excitement, came King Gou

Jian, resplendent in regal costume. "My Liege Lord," he bowed low before Fu Chai, "I wish to offer my felicitations for your historic victory and pledge once again my unflinching allegiance to you. I am proud to be in your service. Your great name shines over the vast land of China. There is no ruler more deserving to be the First Lord than Your Majesty."

He presented the listings of gifts from Yue which comprised a hundred bolts of silk, nine barrels of honey, five pairs of fox fur, ten boat-loads of bamboo as raw material for making arrows, and a variety of priceless medicinal tonics. On top of these, he offered Fu Chai another eight pretty girls. They were admitted into the song and dance unit of the Wu court like those sent by Yue the year before.

Gou Jian asked to meet with Hsi Shih, saying he had brought gifts from her folks in Zhuluo Village who had asked him to hand their gifts to her in person. Fu Chai readily consented and ordered General Wangsun Luo to take him to see Hsi Shih in the inner palace.

Gou Jian's visit was a surprise to Hsi Shih. She received him in her regal array. Gou Jian was astounded. In all his imaginings, he realized he had not visualized her as beautiful as she truly was. The fetching girl in his memory was now a demi-goddess. Her ebony hair brushed high on her head, topped by a jeweled crown, accentuated the beautiful features of her lovely face. The pale green silk gown wrapped around the waist with a sash of dark green brocade revealed a shapely figure.

One more look, and he regretted having given her away. He had been living an austere life in recent years. But now he realized that the beauty of all his former concubines and his queen put together paled into nothingness compared with this lovely creature who had the ethereal charm of a goddess and the alluring sensuality of a woman in the bloom of youth. How he wished he could strip her naked, grope the soft swell of her breasts and press her warm body against his own!

Hsi Shih knelt down to greet him.

"Please stand up, my fair lady," Gou Jian bent to help her to her feet. Even a slight touch of her arm sparked in him a yearning desire. He stared at her, his small eyes emitting a strange glint that made him seem uglier than he actually was.

"Hsi Shih, you are even more beautiful than before," he said, overwhelmed by a mixed feeling of jealousy and hatred toward Fu Chai. He felt Fu Chai had forcibly snatched this woman from him. He forgot, for a brief moment, that Hsi Shih had been betrothed to his chief general Fan Li, that he had beseeched Fan Li on his knees to give her up to Fu Chai.

Hsi Shih bobbed a curtsy in response to his complimentary remark. Her maid, Ding Hong, came in to serve tea.

"Thank you!" Gou Jian drew from his pocket a small red box containing a pair of gold earrings and gave it to Ding Hong as gift.

When Ding Hong left the room, he grabbed Hsi Shih's hand in a vice-like grip and asked her to sit on the couch by him, hunger for a closer contact gnawing at his heart.

"Lady Hsi Shih," He gave her hand a long squeeze. "It is so nice to see you."

Hsi Shih could not but regard the man with disgust. Beneath her serene appearance, her blood was boiling with loathing.

"I gained permission from Fu Chai to meet you on the pretext of having brought some gifts from your folks in Zhuluo Village." Gou Jian pointed at a carved-wood box he had placed on the table. "I've brought two luminous pearl necklaces, one for you and one for Zheng Dan, a gift from myself and Lady Gou Jian, as a token of our gratitude for your loyal services. I was too busy to get in touch with your folks."

"Thank you, Your Majesty," Hsi Shih freed her hand from his grip. "I'll send for Zheng Dan now." She was anxious to end their meeting.

But Gou Jian stopped her. "There is no need. Please give my regards to Zheng Dan. Lady Hsi Shih, I appreciate your effort in prompting Fu Chai to launch that costly expedition which has consumed his resources to a vast extent. We owe you our thanks. You and Zheng Dan have done good work."

Hsi Shih was silent.

"This is from Fan Li," Gou Jian took out a nice little gift box. "Don't open the box yet. Fan Li says it will take some time before you get the true meaning of his gift."

"How is Lord Fan Li?"

"Oh, he is as fit as ever. He pines for you. But he is too busy to come with me."

What Gou Jian held from her was the fact that Fan Li, urged by himself, had married a woman and was going to be a father soon. In fact, his wife was about to give birth to their first child, and that was why Fan Li decided, with much reluctance, not to come to Wu with Gou Jian.

"Our country is well on its way to recovery," Gou Jian continued. "But we are not ready yet. Wu is still a strong power. If we can remove the one obstacle that stands between us and our victory, we can break our bondage sooner."

"What is the obstacle, pray?" asked Hsi Shih. But as soon as she asked, she knew what obstacle Gou Jian must be referring to.

"Lady Hsi Shih," Gou Jian gazed at her steadily, "the obstacle is old Wu Yuan. He is a very stubborn enemy of ours. And he is in charge of Fu Chai's troops. We must get rid of him by all means. I rely on you to remove this obstacle."

"I'm afraid it'll be very difficult, Sire," Hsi Shih protested feebly. She revolted at such an assignment at the bottom of her heart. "General Wu Yuan's reputation stands high. The king has a great respect for him."

"Fair Lady, Fu Chai dotes on you. Use your charm. Play up to him. The elimination of this old die-hard is very important to us. You must use whatever there is in your power to achieve your end."

Hsi Shih dropped her head, feeling extremely uncomfortable.

"My beauty!" Gou Jian's voice took on an urgent note. "The sooner this old die-hard is removed, the sooner our victory, and the sooner Fan Li will come to take you home. You—and only you—can induce Fu Chai to kill this old die-hard! Do you understand?"

Hsi Shih nodded mechanically.

Gou Jian having left, Hsi Shih opened Fan Li's gift box. What she found was a beautifully carved ivory fan. Upon closer examination, she found tiny characters carved on it. It was a poem Fan Li composed. Read vertically, it was a poem about the four seasons of the year. Read horizontally, it was a poem about landscape. But the true meaning of the poem was to be read diagonally. It was a poem expressing his longing thoughts for Hsi Shih.

Yet the gift failed to arouse any excitement in her heart. It only brought a fleeting nostalgia and an admiration for Fan Li's literary talent, mixed with a faint but lingering resentment, because she believed Fan Li had not done enough to protect her—he had given in to Gou Jian's request too easily. She still loved him, but her love had lost its fervor.

Her thought turned to Fu Chai, a man who loved her with all his heart and soul, a man who would move heaven and earth to please her. She felt guilty having to remain in her role as a secret agent for Gou Jian, a man she loathed. She shuddered at his order to coax Fu Chai to kill Wu Yuan. How could she deliberately poison the king's mind against such an upright man, a man who served him with uttermost devotion? She could never do such a thing in good conscience.

Her thought was cut short by the chirping of a bird from a tree outside the window. She decided not to dwell on her trouble and went to Zheng Dan's chamber to give her Gou Jian's gift.

*   *   *

The opening of the Beauty's Palace was a most exciting event to Hsi Shih. The Beauty's Palace was a misnomer, for it was actually not a palace, but a reproduction of the best sections of her home village Zhuluo.

Spreading over six hundred hectares on the slopes

and in the valley of the Lingyan Hill, the Beauty's Palace was an architectural wonder. Like Zhuluo Village, it had an idyllic setting. But unlike Zhuluo Village, it was built with an extravagance that surpassed the Gusu Tower. Like Zhuluo Village, it had farm cottages hidden among the trees on the slope of a hill. But unlike Zhuluo Village, the cottages were luxury villas in disguise. Like Zhuluo Village, it had a limpid stream flowing through it. But unlike Zhuluo Village, the stream was spanned by a few ingeniously designed arched bridges. Whereas the stream in Zhuluo Village reflected Hsi Shih as a natural-born, beautiful village lass, the stream in the Beauty's Palace reflected Hsi Shih as a gorgeous, noble lady in all her glory. Trees and flowers of various species lined both banks of the stream, diffusing a variety of perfumes all the year round—an additional delight for the king and his consort when they went on boating excursions.

Nature became a living poem. Paths meandered like snakes; pavilion unfolded like lotus leaves; rocks rose like mountain peaks; and the gates opened in the shape of a full moon.

A natural cave was remodelled into a well-furnished chamber to be used by the royal couple as a shelter from the heat of summer. The king named it the "Hsi Shih Cave."

The royal couple loved to drink to the full moon. Hence, the completion of the "Moon Terrace." Around it, a myriad of night blossoms were planted and sweet, refreshing scents drifted in the crisp night air.

The "Lotus Pond" was for Hsi Shih to pluck lotus-seed pods. The water from the "King-of-Wu Well" was used to infuse aromatic, green tea.

To name a few more, there were the "Hunting Island", the "Fishing Village", and the "Winery Town."

The most original invention in the Beauty's Palace was the "Hall of the Musical Floor." Hard wood planks for flooring were set on pilings fifteen feet deep from the surface of the excavated ground. Among the pilings stood thousands of empty earthenware jars of the same depth. The hall would ring with music when human feet touched the floor.

When Hsi Shih walked into the hall, the floor resounded with a melody resembling the chiming of silver bells. This was a most dazzling surprise to her. Fu Chai watched her as she turned in a circle and her expression transformed with wonder.

"Oh my," was all she could say. She knew the place was designed by the most prominent architects of the age, but she had not expected it to be so fabulous. It utterly amazed her.

Seized by an impulse, she started to dance. Thereupon Fu Chai motioned the girls of the palace dance ensemble who had been waiting in the wings to join in, and the sublime music proclaimed that the "Hall of the Musical Floor" measured up to its unique name.

"My love, if you have any idea to make it more interesting," Fu Chai spoke matter-of-factly after she rejoined him, "you have only to tell me."

"No, no," Hsi Shih hastened to assure the king. "It is perfect, my good lord. But I'm afraid it must have cost you a fortune."

"My lady," the king stared at her, his face radiant with inordinate satisfaction. "I want to lay my kingdom at your feet."

Hsi Shih leaned forward to give the king a

thorough kiss, her eyes sparkling with tears.

"What's the matter?"

"I ... just wanted to cry," she said brokenly. "I am so happy."

Never in a thousand years had she expected anything like this. She was deeply touched by the king's extravagant efforts to please her. She felt she should say that she loved him, but the words would not come. Suddenly, she hated her mission. Love was the most sacred emotion of a human being. How could she use an honest man's love as a tool to destroy him? And to destroy him for a mean man like Gou Jian? *It is blasphemy!*

She was ashamed. She despised herself for lacking the courage to put an end to her dishonorable role. She felt she was unworthy of his affection. So even as she was overpowered by his love, she felt uneasy, confused, guilty.

She was tempted to share her thoughts with Zheng Dan, but balked. Lately, she sensed Zheng Dan was privately jealous of her. A distance seemed to have insidiously come between them. It had been a long time since they had a candid conversation. She was not sure how Zheng Dan would react if she was to bare her heart. She was not sure she could trust her friend as she used to.

# CHAPTER TWENTY

## Treason

LATER THAT YEAR, Yue's prime minister Wen Zhong came to Wu for a loan of rice because Yue was hit by a drought. He needed a hundred thousand liters and promised to return the rice once Yue had a better harvest. Fu Chai readily granted his request and told him that Yue could have this much rice as gift.

Wu Yuan was vehement in his protest at the court session the following day after he had learned about Fu Chai's decision.

"What? One hundred thousand liters of rice? No, no! My king!" he said, waving a deprecating hand. "To give that much rice to Yue would reduce our own reserve. I suspect the whole thing is Gou Jian's scheme. I'm sure he's going to use the rice to feed his army."

Increasingly fretting over Wu Yuan's stubbornness, Fu Chai tried to assert his authority by deliberately making decisions in his back, decisions that he knew Wu Yuan would have opposed. He derived perverse pleasure seeing the old general go mad about it.

"What are you talking about, General?" he snorted. "Are you still concerned about Gou Jian attacking us?"

"My king, the war against Chi has used up a lot of resources. It has made our country more vulnerable to attacks from Gou Jian."

"General," said the king scornfully, "you refused to take your troops to fight Chi. Now as we all returned in triumph, you don't even feel ashamed of yourself. Instead, you're harping on your rotten old tune again."

"Have some compassion, Old General!" said Bo Pi. "Yue is our vassal state. Gou Jian sends in tributes every year. We can't just stand by and watch his people starve."

"You," Wu Yuan looked at Bo Pi with contempt, "are a booster for Gou Jian. How much has he paid you?"

"You, you ... " Bo Pi was choked with anger.

"General, that was uncalled for." Fu Chai objected.

"My king, stop acting foolishly," Wu Yuan exhorted. "King Jie of the Hsia Dynasty listened only to his sycophant-ministers and killed his loyal minister Long Fen; King Zhou of the Shang Dynasty also listened to his sycophant-ministers and killed his loyal minister Bi Gan. What happened to King Jie and King Zhou in the end? They both died an ignominious death and their dynasty houses crumbled."

Fu Chai was stung to fury. "You compare me with those ancient tyrants? Get out!" he roared, swinging an arm in a passionate gesture.

"My king, you are nursing a poisonous snake in your bosom," Wu Yuan thundered as he backed out in rage. "If you don't take my advice, you will repent one day."

When Wen Zhong returned with boatloads of fine rice, Gou Jian was elated. As a matter of fact, Yue had abundant grain reserve. Only a small area was affected by poor harvest. But he used it as an excuse to increase Yue's grain reserve as well as test Fu Chai's attitude toward Yue.

"More significant than the rice loan," the king said to his ministers, "is the waning of Wu Yuan's influence in the Wu court. The fact Fu Chai was willing to help us means he has overruled Wu Yuan once again."

"Exactly," said Wen Zhong. "Wu Yuan seems to have alienated himself from his king."

"Hsi Shih must have played a role in it," said Gou Jian, darting a complimentary glance at Fan Li.

Fan Li gave a polite smile. He was proud of Hsi Shih who proved to be more capable and mature than he had expected, which prompted him to wonder whether he did the right thing not to tell her about his marriage. He had asked Yi Yong not to breathe a word to her, for he did not want to add to her emotional stress. He preferred to explain to her himself. He believed she would forgive him if she understood the pressure he had been under. But when would he have the opportunity to tell her?

He loved her as dearly as ever. If they were reunited, Hsi Shih would be his wife and his current wife would have to take the place of a concubine. That was what he had decided before he got married two years ago. It was also the rationale the king used to persuade him. But the fact that Hsi Shih was kept in the dark for so long made him uneasy. If he waited until they were reunited, which could be years away, before telling her, how would Hsi Shih construe his long silence? As yet, his wife knew nothing about his relationship with Hsi Shih. How would she react if she learned the truth? His mind was vexed by these thoughts.

\* \* \*

Since his triumphant return from the north, Fu Chai had been obsessed by the prospect of contending with the Duke of Jin for the honorable title of the First Lord.

The question was: would the Duke of Jin concede his title to him? Much depended on military strength. Now that Wu had become so powerful smaller states were all looking up to it for support and protection. Fu Chai believed he had sufficient reasons to replace the duke as the First Lord. It would be the first time in history for a southern fief ruler to have such an honor. It was true that a higher culture had first developed in northern and central China, in the Yellow River regions. But then the Yangtze River regions, thanks to the vast fertile land and the favorable climate, had also developed a culture comparable with that of northern and central China. Culturally, economically and militarily, there was no reason a northern lord should hold the title for so long. Fu Chai wished to prove that the south was not inferior to the north.

He was in this train of thought when he caught

sight of Prince Yiou passing by his office, a sling in hand, his clothes and shoes all wet and muddy.

"Come here, my boy. You look like a drenched duck. What happened?"

"I fell into a pool in the courtyard," said the prince sheepishly.

"How come?"

The prince gave a facile explanation. "I was in the courtyard when I heard a cicada squeaking on top of a tree. I took my sling to shoot at it. Then I saw a grasshopper climbing up the tree, trying to catch the cicada. But the grasshopper was not aware that a bird was hovering on top, waiting to make a meal of it. So I turned to shoot the bird. I was so absorbed in taking aim I did not notice there was a muddy pool behind me. Before I caught the bird, I lost my balance and fell into the water."

"Foolish boy!" Fu Chai laughed. "You should have been more careful about what's behind you."

"Father," the prince grinned suddenly. "I think the Duke of Chi was also foolish. He ordered his troops to invade Lu, thinking it was easy to take such a weak country. He did not expect that a strong power, Wu, was behind Lu."

"You're quite right, my boy."

"We would make the same mistake, Father," the prince said sardonically, "if we only think of how to subdue Jin but disregard Yue, which is the lurking danger behind our back."

"What? You dare to talk to me like Wu Yuan?" Fu Chai realized that his son was making a point of criticizing his policy by the use of a metaphor. "Get out!"

How dare the old pest instigate his son to lecture him? Fu Chai was furious. He let him teach his son. But he was abusing his trust. The more he thought about it, the more upset he was. His former mentor never seemed satisfied with his performance, never treated him with the respect due a king, and never really endorsed his marriage to Hsi Shih. He had been patient with him, but Wu Yuan seemed not to appreciate that there was a limit to his patience.

Stewing in annoyance, Fu Chai grumbled to Hsi Shih at the dinner table, "The old general is trying to set my son against me."

"The general is a most honest man," Hsi Shih felt compelled to defend Wu Yuan. "He'll never turn your son against you."

"He's poisoning my boy's mind, don't you see?"

"How can you say that, my lord? General Wu Yuan treats him like his own son. Precisely because he's honest, he can't hide his opinion from the prince."

"So, you're on his side?"

"I'm on your side. I want you to be the First Lord. I will feel very proud. But I also want you to be fair to General Wu Yuan."

"Hsi Shih, you have a heart of gold." Fu Chai's anger subsided. "If only the old general knew what a kind person you are. He is prejudiced against you, you know."

"The general may distrust me, but his loyalty to you is beyond question."

"You may be right," Fu Chai murmured.

"I know I am right, my lord," Hsi Shih replied quietly as she poured some wine for him and for herself.

"The general has the right to hold a different opinion. Please respect him."

These days she was tormented by inner conflict. More and more, her double role made her feel ill at ease. She badly wanted to find a way out of her dilemma, to find a compromise. She believed that she had managed to say something in Fu Chai's best interest without betraying her motherland.

* * *

An audience session was in progress in Fu Chai's court. General Wangsun Shong presented the king a map mounted on a mahogany stand. "Your Majesty, I'm pleased to report that the canals are completed. This is how they look like on the map."

"How wonderful!" Fu Chai exclaimed as he examined the map which showed all the states in China with the two newly excavated canals marked in red, one going from Wu to the north to merge with the Yi River in Shandong; the other, going from Wu to the west to merge with the Ji River in Henan.

"The canals will greatly shorten the distance between Wu and northern China," Fu Chai said exuberantly. "They have far-reaching strategic significance for us. General, you have done a superb job."

General Wangsun Shong bowed deferentially. "Thank you, Your Majesty. Please let me know when you want to inspect them." The general had been put in charge of the project after Fu Chai overruled Wu Yuan's objection in a heated argument.

"Your Majesty," said Bo Pi, "I think the canals' completion will usher in a new era in our country's history."

"Precisely." Fu Chai replied. "Let's make the most of them."

"My king," Wu Yuan cut in, unable to suppress his displeasure, "the canals may not be such a blessing as you think. Tens of thousands people have been dislodged from their homes. Many are still waiting to be resettled. The treasury is nearly depleted. And there is a growing public discontent about the increased taxes and corvee duties."

"But the canals will increase our mobility," Bo Pi retorted, "and give us easy access to the north. We stand to gain—militarily, politically and commercially."

"That's your wishful thinking," Wu Yuan snapped back.

Fu Chai was nettled. "Don't be so dismissive, General. The canals will play an important role in extending our influence to the north. Isn't it very obvious?"

"My king, how will you extend your influence to the north if Gou Jian stabs you in the back?"

"You are raising a false alarm again, General." Fu Chai glared at him with disdain.

"I may be repeating myself, but it is for your benefit, my king. Before Gou Jian is eliminated, it is unwise to compete with the northern lords for firstlordship."

"I suppose you don't want me to be the First Lord. You don't want Wu to be the Lord State. But I've always believed in your loyalty, General … "

"Your Majesty," Bo Pi broke in, his face twisted in amused contempt, "how can we expect the general to be loyal to Wu when he has placed his son under the protection of the Duke of Chi?"

"W-H-A-T?" The king was flabbergasted.

"I did send my son to study in Chi," Wu Yuan acknowledged. "But that was several years ago."

"Why didn't you bring him back when you went to Chi to declare war?"

"Why?" Wu Yuan gave the king a wry smile. "Because if Your Majesty keeps confiding in this sycophant and ignoring my warning, sooner or later, Gou Jian will finish off the kingdom you inherited from your father-king, and we will all end up being his prisoners. But I don't want my boy to share my doom."

Fu Chai's face turned purple.

"Your Majesty," came Bo Pi's sardonic voice, "now you see why the general is opposed to your going to the north. He left his son in Chi. Obviously he intends to defect to Chi himself."

"You ... you dare to ... " Wu Yuan was choking with indignation, pointing a trembling finger at Bo Pi.

"Your Majesty, it's not difficult to understand why his friend Gongsun Sheng interpreted your dream as a bad omen. Wu Yuan!" Bo Pi raised his voice. "How did you collude with that evil soothsayer? What were you up to in Chi? Confess!"

This was a calculated insult. Wu Yuan exploded. "You dirty, shameless son of a bitch!" He charged toward Bo Pi, ready to twist his neck. Bo Pi quickly slid behind the king.

"I've always trusted you, General." The king glowered at Wu Yuan. "But you have betrayed me! You have betrayed my father's trust in you!"

With that, he stalked out of the court, visibly shaken.

# CHAPTER TWENTY-ONE

## The Shu Lou Sword

"**PLEASE DO NOT** be so angry with the general, Your Majesty." Bo Pi admonished the king as he followed him into his private chamber. "After all, he has served under two generations."

"That's why I've trusted him and treated him well. But he has no respect for me."

"The general was trusted by your father king like nobody else. He enjoys high prestige among the people—even higher than Your Majesty's."

"But I am the king!"

"Your Majesty had better be patient with him."

Fu Chai regarded Bo Pi skeptically. "Wu Yuan does not like you. Why do you speak for him?"

"I never allow my personal feelings to interfere with my duty," Bo Pi answered with an air of detachment. "It is for Your Majesty's sake that I suggest you tolerate him."

"Tolerate—Tolerate—Why? Why should I? I've had enough." Fu Chai clenched his teeth in anger.

Bo Pi's eyes flashed a peculiar glint. "The general can be difficult at times," he lowered his tone just a notch, "but he commands a strong army. If you push him too hard, he may get out of control ... "

This was a rude awakening for the king. He stared at Bo Pi, then slowly took out his famous sword *Shu Lou* and summoned a courier to his chamber.

"Send this to General Wu Yuan," the king said firmly, a murderous look on his face. "He will know what to do."

\* \* \*

Wu Yuan knew all along that he would die one day for his repeated remonstrations with the king. As the king's courier appeared with the *Shu Lou* in the courtyard of his mansion, he knew his end was at hand.

The *Shu Lou* sword was Fu Chai's family heirloom bequeathed to him by his father. Legend said that the sword was crafted by a master smith who, by quenching its blade in the blood of his twin boys, had bestowed upon it a magical power. The sword was so sharp that it could pierce iron like going into a sack of grain. Its luster as shiny as the stars in the sky, its feel as smooth as the water from a fountain, its texture as translucent as the ice about to melt—it was estimated to be worth a thousand steeds and two towns. And now instead of cutting the enemies, this priceless treasure was given to the king's chief general to cut himself.

Wu Yuan summoned an attendant to send for

his wife. Lady Wu Yuan, a tall, handsome, middle-aged woman, understood immediately when she saw the solemn look on her husband's face. She was calmer than he had expected.

"My dear lady," said Wu Yuan, holding his wife's hands. "I know this would happen sooner or later. My conscience is clear. When I am gone, you will please take charge. I'm glad both our daughters were happily married off. Please give all my books to Wu Feng. I'm comforted that he is out of harm's way. Please give enough money to those among my concubines who prefer to go back to their own homes. They can marry again. Keep well, my good lady."

Lady Wu Yuan nodded, burying her head on her husband's shoulder, her eyes inundated with tears.

"Oh," Wu Yuan wailed in pain, "I worked with King Ho Lu day and night to turn this country into a powerful kingdom. I recommended Fu Chai from among all the princes to become the king. But now he's so confused he can't even distinguish a treacherous official from a loyal official. This country is doomed." Tears ran down his wrinkled face.

"After my death," he said to the courier, "pluck out my eyes and place them over the eastern gate of Gusu. There my angry eyes will condemn the invading Yue troops with burning fire."

The courier knelt before the general. With both hands, he presented the *Shu Lou* sword to Wu Yuan, his eyelids drooping.

Wu Yuan took up the sword. He recalled what his friend Sun Tzu had advised him when he resigned from office after helping King Ho Lu build up a superior army.

"Never tempt your fate. Never press your luck.

And never outstay your welcome. When your mission is accomplished, it is time to leave. When you are at the pinnacle of triumph, it is time to quit. That is the best way to protect yourself."

*Oh, my friend! How wise you are!* Wu Yuan regretted he had not listened to his friend. It was too late now. He had only himself to blame.

The chief general stood upright. Lady Wu Yuan turned her head away. One slash of the *Shu Lou* sword, and Wu Yuan's big body collapsed with a loud thump. Blood spurted out like a fountain from his throat. All the people in the house broke into loud lamentation.

\*   \*   \*

Having learned Wu Yuan's last words from the courier, Fu Chai angrily ordered his guards to go to Wu Yuan's house, place Wu Yuan's body in a leather bag and throw it into the river.

He was still in a foul mood when he returned home that evening.

"What's the matter?" asked Hsi Shih.

"The old pest! He's a traitor!"

"Who?"

"Wu Yuan!"

"That's impossible! There must have been a mistake."

"No, no mistake at all. I've ordered him to commit suicide."

"Oh, no, no!" Hsi Shih's face turned ashen.

"Wu Yuan has betrayed me," Fu Chai said hoarsely.

"No, no!" Hsi Shih stamped her feet. "Wu Yuan's

a good man! Where is he?"

"He is dead."

"You killed a good man!" Hsi Shih screamed, her mind reeling at this most shocking news.

Slowly she sank to her knees. She felt as though the ground underneath her feet was collapsing. *A pillar has fallen! Wu is in danger! Fu Chai is in danger!*

Fu Chai stared at her in consternation. He had never seen her so distraught. He stepped forward to hold her into his arms. Tears forced their way into Hsi Shih's eyes. She was sorry for the old general. She wanted to have nothing to do with his death. Yet she felt she had a part in it. She had contributed to the circumstances leading to his death. A spasm of contrition shot through her. *Oh, forgive me, gods in Heaven!*

"Are you all right, Hsi Shih?" Fu Chai asked anxiously.

He took her cold hands into his. The familiar, gentle touch of his fingers did nothing to take off the chill inside her.

"You are destroying yourself!" she muttered, her face contorted with anguish.

Hsi Shih did not recover from the shock for days. The enormity of Fu Chai's mistake sickened her, frightened her. Yet she cared for him. She wanted to protect him. She struggled with herself and was almost driven to the point of divulging Gou Jian's scheme to Fu Chai, but in the end was unable to bring herself to do so. She hated her ignominious mission more than ever.

A somber atmosphere enveloped the audience session the next day. After the session, Fu Chai asked Wangsun Shong privately, "Why were you so silent, my lord?"

"I was frightened, Your Majesty. Gongsun Sheng was a virtuous man of national renown, but you killed him. General Wu Yuan was a great hero who has given his all to the country, you also killed him. I am not half as good as either of them. How could I not be frightened?"

"I killed them because they were not loyal to me."

"They were being frank with Your Majesty precisely because they were loyal. A good ruler needs people around him who dare to speak their minds, dare to disagree with him, and dare to point out his mistakes."

Fu Chai recalled Hsi Shih's words. He regretted having ordered Wu Yuan's death and felt ashamed that he had been tricked by Bo Pi. And his shame turned into anger.

"I want Bo Pi to die," he roared.

"Please don't," Wangsun Shong made an effort to stop him. "Bo Pi has his faults. But he is still useful. Another killing will terrorize the entire court."

Thus, Bo Pi's life was spared. Wangsun Shong was appointed to be the new chief general. He and his younger brother Wangsun Luo were Fu Chai's cousins. Both were utterly loyal to the king. Wangsun Luo was a born follower with little judgment of his own while Wangsun Shong was a competent army-commander, having served under King Ho Lu and been coached by Wu Yuan.

*   *   *

It was a day set for the rendezvous with Yue's liaison, Lord Yi Yong. Zheng Dan being unwell, Hsi

Shih went alone to the shopping district of Gusu where she first visited an embroidery shop, bought some handcraft, and then slipped into the apothecary's for the meeting. Yi Yong praised her profusely for her effort in having coaxed Fu Chai to order the death of Wu Yuan and presented her a box of gifts from King Gou Jian as a token of His Majesty's appreciation.

On her way back, Hsi Shih sat glumly in the carriage brooding over Yi Yong's words. They brought home to her the cruel irony of the tragedy. Apparently she was given credit for the work of Bo Pi—a man she utterly despised. She did not know whether to laugh or to cry.

Since childhood, she had learned to adore patriots and hate traitors. She had read stories about worthy men who loved their countries more than their own lives. She had also read about greedy men who acted treacherously to the detriment of their own countries. That was why Bo Pi never won her favor despite his ever-readiness to shower compliments on her and please her and why General Wu Yuan's righteousness and loyalty compelled her veneration even though he had treated her harshly. But Wu Yuan was Yue's enemy and Bo Pi, Yue's friend. She was supposed to hate the former and be friendly with the latter. She was supposed to cheer over the death of the former and give encouragement to the latter. Her mind was in a tumult. She felt she was being pulled in two opposite directions. She felt the world she lived in was a world turned upside-down.

# CHAPTER TWENTY-TWO

# First Lord

NEWS OF THE death of General Wu Yuan sent the whole nation of Wu into shock; many people went into mourning. Fu Chai's popularity plummeted. However, his reputation soared abroad in the wake of his victory over Chi. He had secured the leading position among his peers.

At the suggestion of the Duke of Wei who was known for his friendship with Wu, a meeting of the heads of various states was convened in 482 B.C. to elect a new first lord. It was held in Huangchi*, a town on the border between Wei and Zheng, a convenient location to all the states in central China and not too far from Luoyang, the royal seat of Zhou.

As Huangchi was under the jurisdiction of Wei, the Duke of Wei sent out invitations endorsed by King Jing,

---

* Present-day Fengqiu, Henan Province.

the titular ruler of China. The Dukes of Chi, Lu, Zheng and Song as well as the rulers of many smaller states confirmed that they would attend the conference. But the Duke of Jin, the current First Lord, did not respond.

Fu Chai was annoyed at the news. "The invitation is endorsed by King Jing," he said to his newly appointed chief general Wangsun Shong. "How dare he ignore it?"

"He's trying to delay the inevitable."

"I've read about firstlords in history," Fu Chai remarked reminiscently. "The one I admire the most is Duke Huan of Chi. Just think, for nine times, he was acknowledged as the First Lord without resorting to force. No weapons. No war-chariots. It didn't seem too difficult for him to persuade other rulers to recognize his authority."

"But things are not quite what they were like a hundred years ago," Wangsun Shong said. "Now only a show of force can make the Duke of Jin relinquish his title."

"I guess you are right. The Duke of Jin gives us little option."

Fu Chai decided to set out for Huangchi with thirty-six thousand troops via the newly excavated canals, accompanied by Bo Pi and General Wangsun Shong, while leaving fourteen thousand soldiers with General Mi Yong, an able young officer who had been promoted to the rank of commander by Wu Yuan, to be assisted by General Wangsun Luo and the crown prince, to take care of home defense.

\* \* \*

Without waiting for the Duke of Jin, the Duke

of Wei, as the host, announced the opening of the conference.

"I am honored to extend my warm welcome to everyone of you, especially to King Fu Chai of Wu. Since he succeeded his father, King Fu Chai has not only made Wu the strongest and most prosperous country in the land of China, but also demonstrated magnanimity toward his former foe, upheld justice by helping weaker states defend their sovereignty and promoted peace and fraternity among nations. I verily believe we should recognize his merits and choose such a distinguished statesman to be the next First Lord."

One after another, the participants expressed their support for the duke's proposal. But Fu Chai knew very well that the recommendation of the Duke of Wei would be meaningless without recognition from the Duke of Jin.

On the third day of the conference, a messenger from Wu arrived with bad news: Gou Jian had launched a major offensive against Wu. The Yue troops had broken Wu's defense and Wu's forces had retreated into Gusu. General Mi Yong asked the king to return immediately.

Fu Chai was staggered by the report. He felt as if he had suffered a body blow. It took all his strength and will to appear calm.

"Have a good rest for the night," he said to the messenger. "I'll prepare a letter for you to bring back to General Mi Yong tomorrow. But don't breathe a word about Yue's invasion to anyone." He tipped the messenger generously and told a guard to escort him to the guest quarters in the camp.

"If we turn back now," he told Bo Pi and

Wangsun Shong, "all our efforts would come to nothing. We would not only lose the firstlordship, but also run the risk of Jin and Chi joining their forces to attack our troops in the rear."

"Our troops back home should be able to defend themselves for a while." General Wangsun Shong speculated.

"I think so."

"But the Duke of Jin is dragging his feet," Bo Pi said. "He's disruptive."

"There is only one way to solve the dilemma," Fu Chai said decisively, "that is, we bring our troops to his border for a show of force. That's the only language he understands."

"When shall we set off?" Wangsun Shong asked.

"Tonight." Fu Chai replied. Then he whispered to Bo Pi, "Get rid of the messenger quietly before we depart."

*　　*　　*

In Xinjiang*, the capital of Jin, the Duke of Jin, a grey-haired man with finely chiselled features, was conversing with Lord Zhao Yang, his long-time prime minister and chief advisor.

"I have no intention of going to Huangchi," he snorted contemptuously. "Without my concession, Fu Chai can not declare himself the First Lord."

"But the invitation is in the name of King Jing." Zhao Yang, a realist and a supremely cautious man, reminded the duke. "We can't very well ignore it."

Jin was the strongest power among all the states

---

* Present-day Houma, Shanxi Province.

in central China. For the last eleven years, the duke had been recognized as the First Lord. He was not unaware of Fu Chai's challenge to his position. But, to his regret, Wu's rising power could not be checked. Now in his sixties, the duke was not as active and energetic as he used to be, but he was vain, astute and obstinate as ever.

"So I'm left with little choice?"

"If you don't go to Huangchi, Fu Chai will have reason to use force against us. He has a large army stationed on the outskirts of Huangchi. We can't afford to take the risk, Sire. Our troops are not as strong."

Still reluctant to relinquish his title, the duke said, "All right, let's wait and see."

In the small hours of the morning, he was awakened from his sleep by the prime minister who came to report the gathering of Wu's forces on the border.

With the first streak of dawn, Wu's thirty-six thousand men, divided into three huge columns, marching in moving phalanxes, reached the border of Jin. It was a formidable procession. The soldiers of the middle column, headed by King Fu Chai, were all mailed in white colored armor; they had a hundred and twenty standard-bearers holding flags of white color; their arrows were decorated with white plumes; their chariots were painted white and their horses harnessed in white color, too. The left column, headed by Bo Pi, was an expanse of fiery red and the right column, under the command of Wangsun Shong, was the color of the dark night. Suddenly the sky was pierced by the sound of drumbeats and bugles. A messenger was sent to the Duke of Jin with an ultimatum from Fu Chai requesting the duke's immediate presence at Huangchi. The Duke of Jin was compelled to oblige.

Upon arriving at Huangchi, the duke realized he had lost the game. He announced that he was willing to concede his firstlordship to Fu Chai on condition that Fu Chai stop calling himself "king" because there was only one king in China, King Jing of Zhou. Fu Chai readily accepted the condition. He would be a duke outside his own country, but still the king of Wu.

*　*　*

Fu Chai was confirmed as the First Lord at a grand swearing-in ceremony presided over by King Jing of Zhou, China's titular head, Son of Heaven.

The ceremonial hall stood a few *li* away from the conference hall site. It was a huge rectangular structure with a tall gabled roof and beams and pillars of solid oak, festooned with banners of five colors— on the yellow banners were painted the sun and the moon; on the red banners, birds; on the blue banners, dragons; on the white banners, tigers; and on the black banners, snakes and tortoises. Along the walls of the hall were long tables on which various kinds of ceremonial instrument were exhibited—silver and ivory vessels of intricate designs, bronze tripods of varying sizes, drums made of python skin and drum stands made of lacquered wood, oracle bones and tortoise shells for divination—all showing creative imagination and superb craftsmanship.

King Jing, a respectable-looking, well-preserved elderly man with greying hair and beard, was wearing a two-piece silk robe, the upper piece black and the lower piece crimson, embroidered with twelve imperial motifs. The sun, the moon and the stars denoted glory.

The dragon and pheasant symbolized dominion over the natural world. The battle axe and the blue meander design meant temporal power. The flame, water weed, grains of millet, sacrificial vessels and the mountain stood for the five elements of nature: fire, water, wood, metal and earth. His eight-inch-tall imperial crown was topped with a black rectangular board decorated with twenty-four strands of opalescent jade beads, twelve strands suspended from the front brim and twelve from the back, each with twelve beads swaying and clinking with his body movement.

The nobles appeared in full regalia. They all wore crowns, but theirs were decorated with fewer jade beads. King Jing's crown had a total of two hundred and eighty-eight beads. Fu Chai and the Duke of Jin's crowns had two hundred forty beads each. The Duke of Chi had one hundred and twenty-eight beads on his crown and the Duke of Wei had only ninety-eight on his. The lower the rank, the fewer the beads on the crown. The nobles all wore sumptuous robes, but likewise theirs were emblazoned with fewer symbols to correspond to their crown insignia.

The chimes of bronze bells announced the official opening of the ceremony.

"My lords," said King Jing, holding a large silver tray on which was placed a masterly crafted sword with a bejeweled handle cased in a magnificently carved gold scabbard, "as the Son of Heaven, I have the pleasure to confirm the designation of the State of Wu as the Lord State and the appointment of the honorable Duke Fu Chai of Wu as the First Lord. Please join me in offering him our heartfelt congratulations and best wishes."

Fu Chai bowed to the king and accepted the

sword. Amid the solemn, awe-inspiring ritual music, an attendant came up, knelt before him and presented a tray with the left ear of the sacrificial ox and a bronze vessel containing the blood taken from the ear placed on it. Fu Chai dipped his finger in the sacred blood and smeared his own lips with it. Then the tray was passed around to let each of the nobles paint his lips red in the same fashion.

Oath script in hand, Fu Chai knelt down before King Jing of Zhou at the head of all the nobles and began to chant.

"We, loyal vassals to the Son of Heaven, hereby make our pledges:

"We pledge our lasting allegiance to our sovereign lord, the king of the Zhou Dynasty.

"We pledge to protect the royal house of Zhou against barbarian invasion.

"We pledge to uphold justice among the nations.

"We pledge not to substitute our wives with concubines.

"We pledge to honor the worthy and uphold virtue.

"We pledge to provide education to the talented.

"We pledge to appoint officials only on merits and abilities.

"We pledge not to let anyone hold offices by hereditary privilege.

"We pledge to respect the aged, take care of the young and treat travellers with hospitality.

"We pledge to punish those who do not honor their parents.

"We pledge not to obstruct the sale of grains to

needy states.

"We pledge not to alter the embankments of rivers to the detriment of neighboring states.

"We pledge that we, as members of this grand union into which we enter today, will live in peace and friendship."

The nobles chanted after him at the top of their voices. Then Fu Chai placed the oath script in a ceramic jar to be buried with the sacrificial ox. King Jing handed him a long bow and a chunk of sacrificial meat as a token of his appreciation.

"Thank you so very much, my lords!" The king smiled to all the nobles. "I wish you happiness and prosperity."

The bells chimed once again to signify the end of the ceremony.

King Jing of Zhou asked everybody to stay in Huangchi a few more days for sightseeing, little expecting that Fu Chai, together with his entourage and his thirty-six thousand soldiers, was to leave Huangchi the next morning.

# CHAPTER TWENTY-THREE

## Crown Prince

O F HER THREE dwelling places—the Gusu Palace in the city of Gusu, the Gusu Tower on the Gusu Hill and the Beauty's Palace on the Lingyan Hill. Hsi Shih's favorite was the Beauty's Palace. But after Fu Chai had gone, she moved to the royal palace in Gusu to be near to Prince Yiou.

She had become his friend. The death of Wu Yuan had estranged the eighteen-year-old prince from his father. He turned more to Hsi Shih for comfort, taking her into his confidence and trusting her with his private thoughts and emotions.

The prince did not strike her as vainglorious as his father. Though he liked his father to be the First Lord, he expressed doubts about its practical benefit to Wu. He shared Wu Yuan's suspicion against Gou Jian but not his inveterate hatred for Yue. He was curious about

Yue and expressed his wish to visit Yue someday.

Hsi Shih was interested in knowing more about his mother. Fu Chai mentioned his first wife so seldom that she sometimes forgot he had been married.

"My mother was a beautiful woman," the prince reminisced fondly. "She was kind ... intelligent ... very gentle. She never raised her voice when she spoke. She never quarrelled with Father."

"I suppose she always obeyed your father."

"No, not always." The prince's mouth twitched with a mischievous sideways smile. "She had a way of ... handling Father. For example, if Father punished some servant without good reason, she would pretend to be as angry as him and offer to look into the person's offense. After Father had calmed down, she would intercede on the person's behalf."

"Did you father love her?"

"Yes, very much. But she was physically fragile. She fell ill easily. She was only thirty-four when she died."

Fu Chai loved her so completely that Hsi Shih had difficulty imagining him holding another woman in his arms.

The prince gazed at her meaningfully and added. "I think Father loves you more than he loved my mother."

"Why makes you think so?" Hsi Shih's eyes were alight with curiosity.

"Because he had never built a palace for my mother. Of course, even if he had wanted to, my mother would not have agreed. She was frugal and did not like spending money for herself. Before she died, she told Father not to build a mausoleum for her. Just bury her in the Tiger Hill. Father honored her wish. The only burial objects were some clothes and ornaments that she had used."

Hsi Shih felt a mixture of guilt that the Beauty's Palace had cost Fu Chai so much and pleasure that she stood so high in Fu Chai's favor. Perhaps Prince Yiou was right. The king indeed loved her more than his first wife.

"My mother also died young," she murmured. "She left me when I was about your age. I used to have chest pain when I thought of her."

"Do you believe there is life after death?"

"I wish there is, but I don't know."

"I do," the prince mused, "I think my mother knows that you are with Father and me. I think she is glad. She wouldn't like to see Father so lonely after her death. Maybe she helped bring you and Father together. Maybe she is watching over us somewhere."

Tears abruptly sprang to Hsi Shih's eyes. She turned her face away.

"Mother, are you upset?"

Hsi Shih looked back with a wavering smile. "No, I'm happy," she said, dabbing her face with the back of her hand.

\* \* \*

One evening she was reading some poetry after dinner, with Mao Mao snuggling dreamily by her side, when Prince Yiou burst in, his face tense with anxiety.

"Mother, Gou Jian's troops have launched an invasion!"

Hsi Shih was thunderstruck by the news.

"General Wangsun Luo is evacuating all personnel from the Gusu Tower to this palace."

"How ... how can Gou Jian do this to us?" Hsi Shih was at a loss what to do.

"I have to go to the front. I came to say good-bye, Mother."

"My prince, my son, you ... you are too young."

"Mother, it's my duty; it's what I've been trained for."

"Be careful, my son." Hsi Shih placed her hands on the prince's shoulders, her eyes on the verge of tears. "Come back safely."

After bidding goodbye to the prince, she paced up and down her room, deeply agitated.

*Fan Li is coming! That means I can go home with him.* The news came so suddenly. It was too good to be true. She hadn't seen him for three years. Memories of their time together rushed back to her mind and filled her with nostalgia. But her excitement was overshadowed by her concern for Fu Chai and Prince Yiou. Gou Jian was a vindictive man. He would certainly seek their destruction. She must help them. But how? Her mind was thrown into a turmoil.

Yue's invading army, twenty thousand strong, were well-trained and high-spirited. While half way across Lake Tai Hu, they came under the archery attack of Wu's army. Fan Li did not take his opponent seriously, knowing that Wu's best troops were with Fu Chai in Huangchi. He ordered his forces to shoot back, and with a two-to-one advantage in number over their opponents, they made simultaneous landing at three locations.

The fight continued on land. Strong gusts of

northeastern wind blew suddenly to the detriment of the invaders. Under the fearless onslaught of Prince Yiou's men, Yue's vanguard troops ran helter-skelter. Prince Yiou scored an initial victory. But Yue's troops were quickly reinforced. They launched a fresh offensive and a hard battle followed. Brave as Prince Yiou and his men were, they could not thwart Fan Li's overwhelming forces.

Nearly half of Wu's soldiers were killed in action. Prince Yiou, charging at the head of his men, was struck by an arrow in the belly. With a scream of pain, he fell off his horse. Luckily, General Mi Yong hastened to snatch him away from the heat of the battle.

Mi Yong ordered the remaining troops to retreat into Gusu to join the four thousand soldiers under General Wangsun Luo to fortify the defense of the city.

Hsi Shih's anxiety was mounting when she saw smoke rising over the Gusu Tower from the balcony in the royal palace.

"Our troops must be winning the battle," Zheng Dan said, darting a speculative glance at Hsi Shih. "Lord Fan Li must be coming to take you home."

"I ... I don't know."

"Aren't you happy?"

Hsi Shih did not respond. She was caught in a welter of feelings. The idea of going home with Fan Li had always been dear to her heart. However, the sudden realization that she might be leaving Fu Chai pierced her with poignancy. Some significant change had taken place inside her that for the life of her she could not ignore. She had been aware of it for some time, but tried not to think about it because it was just not comfortable to dwell on it.

Her heart ravaged by divided loyalty, she was not sure what she would do if she was forced to choose between Fu Chai and Fan Li. She was not sure whether she should stay with a man who loved her so single-mindedly or leave with a man who had been waiting for her faithfully for the last three years. What she was sure about was that she cared about Fu Chai, deeply. The prospect of Fu Chai being harmed by a victorious Gou Jian sent chills up her spine. She desperately wanted him to come back safe.

She had no news from Prince Yiou for six days since he rushed to the front. She had a foreboding that something terrible was going to happen.

Toward evening, General Wangsun Luo barged in. "Lady Hsi Shih," he announced gloomily, "Prince Yiou's seriously injured. Yue's troops are advancing toward Gusu. They have burnt down the Gusu Tower."

"Does the king know about all this?"

"I've already dispatched a messenger to Huangchi."

The prince was unconscious when he was brought in. His face was white as a sheet and his pulse very weak. Hsi Shih was horrified by the amount of blood that had stained his clothes. His entire lower body was soaked in red. The royal physician, after examining his wound and applying some specially prepared poultice to it, announced that his condition was grave due to the loss of blood.

The prince remained in a coma for two days. On the third day, his body moved a little and his eyes slit open.

"How are you, my son?" Hsi Shih leaned over

him, engulfed by a mixture of guilt, worry and anguish.

"Mother," the prince murmured. His hazy, listless eyes staring into hers, his mouth half-open, he was making an obvious effort to smile.

Hsi Shih fed him the ginseng soup prescribed by the physician. The prince swallowed it down obligingly.

"Son, feeling better?" she asked softly, holding his hand.

Suddenly Prince Yiou's gaze became bright and a pink glow returned to his face. "Please tell Father that I love him," he said in a weak but clear voice. "Ask him to forgive me. I've been cold to him since the death of General Wu Yuan. But I know he regretted the general's death very much."

"Yes, I will," Hsi Shih replied, holding back tears.

"Father is not always clear-headed. He likes flattery and can make unwise decisions. Mother, you have a good heart and a good mind. Please help him."

"I will." Hsi Shih squeezed his hand.

"Mother," the prince's voice suddenly dropped to a whisper. "I love you. You're always so nice to me. I thank you for everything ... "

The prince slowly closed his eyes; his hand became flaccid.

"My prince, my son, wake up! Wake up!" Hsi Shih called frantically, her heart pounding in fear.

Moments later, the royal physician came in. He turned up the prince's upper eye-lid. The light of life was gone. The physician said nothing, but his blank expression told everything.

Hsi Shih collapsed on the floor, nearly passing out. At this juncture, Ding Hong came in to announce that Fu Chai had come back.

\*   \*   \*

On his way home, horrifying news came in succession: The crown prince had been critically wounded; Gusu was under siege; the Gusu Tower was burned down. Fu Chai could no longer hold the news from the rank and file.

All of a sudden, the thirty-six thousand men felt tired. What would have become of their families? What could have happened to their home-towns and villages? They missed their former commander-in-chief, General Wu Yuan. If the king had not killed the lord general, Gou Jian would never have dared to invade Wu. Their morale was sinking, and, to make things worse, they were caught in a driving autumn rain. Their combat spirit was further dampened.

Upon entering Gusu, Fu Chai went straight to the army command center to hear General Mi Yong's briefing.

"What a foul, dishonorable attack!" the king thundered. He ordered General Wangsun Shong to take his troops to join the garrison force in defense of the capital.

Scowling at Bo Pi, he blustered, "It's your fault! You always insisted that Gou Jian would never go against me. Now you see what's happened!"

His words sent Bo Pi shivering.

"My lord," Wangsun Shong pleaded, "the prime minister was deceived like most of us. Right now, the soldiers are all tired and need a rest. I suggested the prime minister use his eloquence to negotiate peace with Gou Jian."

Fu Chai agreed that truce was a sensible option under the circumstances.

"What if Gou Jian turns him down?"

"Our granary holds enough grain to last a few months. What Gou Jian wishes is a hasty warfare. If we refuse to fight and strengthen the security of the capital, Yue's army will be forced to leave before winter sets in."

Fu Chai turned to Bo Pi, his hand on the *Shu Lou* sword that was hanging on his belt.

"Now, go to Gou Jian and negotiate peace with him. If you fail in your mission, I'll cut your throat."

Fan Li had planned to attack Wu as soon as Fu Chai was on his way to Huangchi and storm Gusu by surprise. But the resistance his troops encountered was tougher than he had anticipated. It slowed the progress of the campaign. Now that Fu Chai had come back with Wu's main force and the weather was not in Yue's favor for a protracted war, it would be impossible to take Gusu. His hope to be reunited with Hsi Shih was frustrated.

He was discussing the situation with Gou Jian in the king's camp on the outskirts of Gusu when a guard came in to announce the arrival of Fu Chai's envoy, Bo Pi.

"Bo Pi is coming to sue for peace, my king."

"Shall we agree?"

"Before we withdraw, let's sign a new treaty with Fu Chai. We'll come back to finish him off at a different time."

Gou Jian agreed. He was quite pleased with the result of Yue's surprise attack. In any case, Yue was not in a position to conquer Wu, but the success of this campaign greatly boosted his confidence.

King Gou Jian greeted Bo Pi politely. Bo Pi presented the king the gifts he brought with him—gifts that were as costly as those Gou Jian had yielded to Fu Chai eleven years ago.

"Not that we want to make an enemy of Wu," Gou Jian explained as he thankfully accepted the gifts, "but we want our independence. We can't afford to pay you annual tributes any more. King Fu Chai can still keep the beauties from Yue, though."

Bo Pi was pleased Gou Jian did not try to exact more concessions.

"We won't attack Wu again," said Gou Jian. "Wu must also promise never to attack Yue. It is my hope that Wu and Yue live in peace forever."

A new peace treaty was signed, nullifying the previous one Wu imposed on Yue and granting Yue independence.

Two days later, Gou Jian took his soldiers and sailed for home.

# CHAPTER TWENTY-FOUR

## Confession

A S SOON AS Fu Chai appeared at the doorstep, Hsi Shih ran up to him.

"My lord!" She noticed he was haggard, grizzled, his gaze a little unfocused, his gait a little unsteady. A stifled cry burst from her lips.

"Sweetheart." Fu Chai nuzzled her forehead.

"I was so worried," Hsi Shih gasped. Impulsively she put her hands on him, feeling his face, stroking the bristle of his cheeks and jaw, ascertaining for herself that he was all right. Then, wrapping her arms around his neck, she kissed him hungrily.

"Sweetheart, look, I'm dust and dirt all over. I need a bath."

She helped him undress and removed the boots for him. When Fu Chai came back from his bath, he found her standing by the window, weeping bitterly. He held her in his arms.

"My lord," she said between sobs, "I'm sorry. I'm ashamed for what Gou Jian has done."

"Why, darling? It's not your fault."

"I am a Yue woman. I feel guilty."

"Don't be silly. You can't choose your birthplace. But you and I are one family, aren't we?"

Hsi Shih nestled her head against his broad chest. "Has Gou Jian's army left?"

"Yes. We've signed a new peace treaty with him."

"Gou Jian can't be trusted."

"Don't worry. We shall be on our guard. We'll strengthen our defense. We still have a strong army."

His words set her mind at ease to some degree.

A long moment passed before he asked, "How is everybody in the palace?"

Hsi Shih sensed a falter in his voice. She knew he did not mention Prince Yiou because it was too painful. She clung to him closer without saying a word, tears coursing down her cheeks. Before long she heard him sobbing.

Mentally and physically exhausted, Fu Chai took Hsi Shih to the Beauty's Palace to recuperate, leaving Bo Pi and Wangsun Shong to attend the daily routine of his court for the time being.

Hsi Shih's guilty conscience turned into a deep care for Fu Chai. She decided to pay closer attention to what he ate. Having studied culinary art in the Yue palace, she took it upon herself to prepare a dish or two for him everyday. Dishes that she knew he liked such as Yangtze herring steamed with shredded ham and tips of bamboo shoots, deboned eels stir-fried with ginger and green onion, bean curd simmered in chicken gravy with dried scallop, and swallow's nest.

Fu Chai noticed the change in his food right away. "My darling, every dish is delicious," he said one day as he watched her prepare his favorite delicacy, steamed crabs. He was fascinated by the way she cracked the shells, scraped out the tidbits of crab meat, and had him suck the best and most nutritious part of the crab—the crab roe. "I know why it is so good, sweetheart?"

"Yes?"

"Not only you've got excellent cuisine skills, darling, but you put your heart in the food. You put love in it."

His comment earned him a deep, sweet kiss. But food was just one aspect of life in which Hsi Shih tried to give him more care. When he turned more aggressive in lovemaking, she knew instinctively he was taking out his frustration on her and probably was unaware of it. With a willing heart, she yielded to him completely, answering his passion with utter submissiveness, offering every part of her body for his enjoyment. She told him with her body that whatever he wanted of her, she would give without reserve. Desperately she wished to soothe him, to comfort him, to heal the wound in his heart.

His roughness often left her bruised and sore. When he saw the marks on her body afterwards, he apologized. But he would slide back to his aggressive behavior the next time. Each time she surrendered to him in loving servitude, without resistance, without inhibition. She wallowed in her submission. She found it was a beautiful experience, an experience in which she took pleasure in more ways than one.

It was not until the spring of the following year

that Fu Chai had gone back to normal. He had put on weight; a healthy glow had returned to his face; and his lovemaking had also become fluent.

One afternoon in late spring, Fu Chai found her knitting her brows, her hand on her stomach.

"What's the matter with you, sweetheart?"

"I feel as though my stomach is churning. It happened a few times already."

"You should have told me earlier."

He immediately sent for the royal physician who, after examining her, broke into a broad smile.

"Congratulations, Your Majesty," he said to Fu Chai. "Her Honored Ladyship is expecting."

"My honored lady," he turned to Hsi Shih, "you don't need any medication. Just take a few dried plums if you feel queasy."

Fu Chai was quiet at first, absorbing the news. Quickly his face was transfigured with exultation, his eyes bright with excitement. "Darling," he took Hsi Shih into his embrace, "I'm so happy."

"I want to make you happy," she said, snuggling up to him, hoping the arrival of a baby would, to some extent, assuage his grief over the death of Prince Yiou. "It's going to be a boy, my lord, a chubby, bright boy."

"It could be a girl," Fu Chai replied, kissing her tenderly, "It doesn't matter. Boy or girl ... it's part of you ... of us."

\*     \*     \*

In the autumn of that year, her childhood friend and lady-in-waiting Zheng Dan fell seriously ill.

Since Hsi Shih's pregnancy, Zheng Dan had gone

to meet Yi Yong by herself. Yi Yong told her that King Gou Jian was pleased with the success of his surprise attack, but it fell short of his goal of a full conquest. He would have to wait for another opportunity to vanquish Wu.

He also told her that she and Hsi Shih had exceeded the king's expectations. He did not have any specific assignment for them but asked them to stay alert for any useful information from their vantage point and pass it on at their regular meetings.

Yi Yong noticed Zheng Dan becoming paler and thinner each time they met. Zheng Dan admitted that she did not sleep well, did not have good appetite and sometimes felt dizzy. But she did not know the cause of these symptoms. Before she left, she asked the minister not to let her parents know that she was not well. Yi Yong gave her some medicinal herbs and tonic which were readily available at the apothecary's. He asked her to take good care of herself and suggested that she go in for some moderate outdoor activities.

Zheng Dan had an outing with a few other girls. The following day she had a fever, accompanied with a severe headache and an incessant cough. She was diagnosed as having caught a bad cold. Even though the symptoms of cold were gone after treatment, her condition did not improve.

When she visited her, Hsi Shih was so alarmed by her sickly look she sent for the royal physician for a private talk immediately afterwards.

"What's the matter with Zheng Dan?" she asked.

"Something seems to be bothering her," said the physician. "Her mind is not at peace."

"What do you mean?"

"She appears to be suffering from emotional stress. That's the root cause of her illness. Her cold was just an inducement."

The physician went on to explain how anger would damage the liver which was in charge of metabolism; how worry would affect the lung which controlled the respiratory system; how pensiveness would hurt the spleen which was a crucial part of the digestive system; and how fear would hurt both the heart and the kidney, the former regulated the circulatory system and the latter controlled the reproductive mechanism and aging process.

"Emotional stress is an insidious enemy of good health," he summarized. "It has caused her body to go out of balance, and it is sapping her vital energy. That is why she eats so little, perspires a lot and is short of breath."

"Zheng Dan used to be active and full of energy," Hsi Shih told him. "I never imagined she could have changed so much so fast."

"Worry kills," the physician sighed. "Do you know what is bothering her, Lady Hsi Shih?"

Hsi Shih shook her head. But she should have known, she thought to herself. It had been a long while since she and Zheng Dan had a good chat. They seemed to have drifted away from each other.

The physician told Zheng Dan that she needed a complete rest. But she was resting only physically; her mind remained restless.

In the four years since she came to Wu, she had changed from a vivacious young woman into one who would often sit by the window and stare blankly into the sky, or roam aimlessly in the garden, or give way to fits of weeping.

As Hsi Shih's lady-in-waiting, she was essentially her servant whose duty it was to attend to the needs of her mistress. Both of them understood it was a cover for the sake of their secret mission. But what was make-believe had become reality. Zheng Dan had become a humble maid who was expected to get down on her knees to greet her mistress, obey her will promptly and wait upon her hand and foot. As Hsi Shih had settled in her new role, she seemed to have no qualms about ordering her around. Zheng Dan sometimes wondered if Hsi Shih still regarded her as her equal.

She witnessed first-hand how much Fu Chai loved Hsi Shih while she was being looked upon as a mere underling. She resented that. It was not that she wanted to compete with Hsi Shih for Fu Chai's favor. But Hsi Shih seemed to have it all—the love of Fan Li, the love of Fu Chai, the privileges of a queen—while she had nothing. How could Hsi Shih have such a good time while she was having such a terrible time? She was also pretty, but why was life so unfair for her? Most maddening of all was that Hsi Shih had no real feelings for Fu Chai. But she possessed him, captivated him. *That wily enchantress!*

Zheng Dan understood that Hsi Shih was *supposed* to seduce Fu Chai, yet she could not help feeling jealous. In recent months, when Hsi Shih invited her for dinner or a boating excursion, she often had an excuse for not going. She wondered whether Hsi Shih was sincere or pretending. Didn't she realize that she was the cause of her misery?

Her jealousy turned into spite, and spite turned

into bitterness. Several times she was on the point of pouring out the truth to Fu Chai: their double role, Gou Jian's treachery and so on. But she could not bring herself to do that. She kept everything to herself and continued to pretend as Hsi Shih's friend.

One night she had a dream. She secretly informed General Wu Yuan of Hsi Shih's real mission. The general, in turn, tipped off Fu Chai, who ordered Hsi Shih to be interrogated. Cruelly tortured, Hsi Shih was unable to bear the pain and confessed to being a spy. Seeing Hsi Shih in a cangue, her face bruised and twisted, her body black and blue, she felt a sense of gratification. Then Hsi Shih was taken to the jail's execution ground. Just as the headsman was about to drop his ax, she woke up. She broke into a cold sweat. That she could entertain such baneful thoughts shocked her. How could she be so vicious? Her dream bothered her and she felt disgusted with herself.

As her inner conflicts intensified, they kept haunting her, eroding her soul, eroding her will to live. As a result, her health deteriorated. It was at this juncture that she caught cold.

\* \* \*

The afternoon sunshine stole timidly into Zheng Dan's chamber through the half-drawn window curtains. Hsi Shih was hoping to see Zheng Dan in a better condition. But her heart ached at the sight of her friend lying on the couch asleep, her lusterless long hair loose on her shoulders, and her eyes, with dark circles below them, half closed. Little furrows of unhappiness carved the smooth whiteness of her forehead. Her small rounded chin had become fleshless and pointed. She had noticeably shrunk and was so emaciated that she looked like a young but withering tree, fallen under intense heat. Her breath came in rapid short puffs, her lips parted and her thin nostrils twitching.

Hsi Shih shuddered in sympathetic horror. A sense of bereavement swept over her. She blamed herself for neglecting her friend. She wished she had come to see her more often.

Sitting by her friend's bedside, Hsi Shih tried hard to suppress her tears. A sudden fit of cough stirred Zheng Dan to consciousness. Feeling Hsi Shih's hand stroking hers, she opened her eyes.

"I'm afraid I won't get well, Hsi Shih."

"Don't say that, Zheng Dan. You ... you will get well."

Zheng Dan retrieved a box from her bedside table and gave it to Hsi Shih. "All my valuables are in this box. Please send it to my parents after my death."

Hsi Shih nodded, choking back a whimper.

"Hsi Shih, we haven't talked to each other for a long time." There was a suggestion of cheerfulness in Zheng Dan's feeble voice.

"We can have a good talk now, Zheng Dan. Tell me what's on your mind."

A thin smile flickering in her eyes, Zheng Dan stared at Hsi Shih's beautiful face. Strangely, she felt no pang of jealousy. Hsi Shih was still her friend.

"Hsi Shih, when we were children, we were so happy. We never held a secret from each other," Zheng Dan made an effort to speak. "But now I don't know what you have in your mind. Nor do you know what lies at the bottom of my heart."

"I do miss those days in Zhuluo Village."

"When you and I were sent here, we were committed to Wu's destruction. But now I've come to hate our mission."

Hsi Shih was shocked by the confession.

"Fu Chai has been Yue's enemy," Zheng Dan continued, "but he is not an evil man. You know that better than anybody. True he received annual tributes from Yue. But he has spared Gou Jian's life. Now Prince Yiou has been killed; the annual tributes has stopped; and Yue has regained its independence. Gou Jian already got even with Fu Chai. I don't understand why he is still bent on destroying Wu. Can't Yue and Wu just live in peace?"

Hsi Shih held Zheng Dan's hand tightly.

"In my heart of hearts ... " Zheng Dan paused to take a breath, "I believe you and I should have been envoys of reconciliation between Wu and Yue, not tools of revenge for Gou Jian. Your marriage to Fu Chai should have been used to promote good will between Wu and Yue, not as an instrument for subversion. It should bring peace, not war."

She paused again.

"I've come to regret what I did. I've come to hate Gou Jian's monstrosity. He has instilled the wrong idea of duty in us.... I wish I had done something different.... I wish I had followed my heart.... "

Her voice sank to a faint whisper. "Hsi Shih, Fu Chai loves you. I hope you would influence him.... I hope you would follow your heart and do the right thing.... My dear sister, ... "

Her voice became hardly audible. Her eyes closed. She was releasing her hold on life.

"Zheng Dan! Zheng Dan!" Hsi Shih was seized with panic.

"Hsi Shih, ... you have my blessing.... "

The voice died. The young life of Zheng Dan was extinct. She seemed exhausted, but there was relief on her face.

Hsi Shih sank to her knees and wept aloud, her whole body trembling.

For days she was out of spirits. She brooded over Zheng Dan's words. They were undeniably true, noble. However, it was beyond her power to bring about the reconciliation between Yue and Wu that Zheng Dan had wishfully envisioned. She was not aware that Fu Chai contemplated invading Yue to avenge Prince Yiou's death. If he did, she would do all she could to dissuade him. But would Gou Jian give up his plan of revenge against Wu? She did not hold out much hope of that happening.

# CHAPTER TWENTY-FIVE

## Turning Point

AS ZHENG DAN had died, Hsi Shih had to make the necessary trip for the clandestine rendezvous with Yi Yong at the apothecary's. Disgusted with her mission, she decided not to give away any important information. Nevertheless she was interested to hear news from Yi Yong. She told him that Zheng Dan had died of lung trouble and that she was pregnant. Yi Yong kindly suggested that during her pregnancy she need not come to their periodic meetings if she did not feel well, though he would come as usual.

"How is Fan Li?" asked Hsi Shih. She had not asked after him for a long time.

"Fan Li's got another boy recently. He has a pair of lovely boys now."

The news came as a surprise to Hsi Shih. She had no idea that Fan Li had married.

"When did he marry?"

Yi Yong realized he had made a slip of the tongue. Fan Li had told him early on not to say anything about his marriage.

"F-f-four years ago," he stammered, looking rather awkward.

"I see ... " Hsi Shih murmured, noticing Yi Yong's expression. "Don't worry, Lord Yi Yong. I won't tell anybody."

On her way back, Hsi Shih sat in the carriage, lost in thought. *So, Fan Li has married!* She was not overly disappointed. But why didn't he write her about it? She would have understood. When Gou Jian came last time, he told her Fan Li had been waiting for her. What a liar!

Yes, she did love Fan Li. And Fan Li did love her. But he was not brave enough to defend their love. What would Gou Jian have done if he had refused to give up his betrothed? If he had insisted, he could have made Gou Jian approve their wedding. Gou Jian had to. What could he have possibly accomplished if it were not for the efforts of Fan Li and Wen Zhong?

Her memory of Fan Li, sweet as it was, had paled when she compared Fan Li with Fu Chai. Fu Chai loved her more than he loved his kingdom, but Fan Li loved something else more than he loved her. What could that be? His office as the chief general? His ambition? His country? His king Gou Jian? Oh, what's the point of thinking about him? Right now, she was happy to be carrying Fu Chai's child, and she hoped it's going to be a bright, robust boy.

Suddenly a black bulldog, emerging from nowhere, flew across the road right in front of her carriage. The horse reared in fright, and the next

moment the carriage jerked and overturned. Hsi Shih
was thrown to the ground, her body hitting into a
wooden shaft with a crash.

The driver quickly pacified the alarmed horse and
put the carriage back in place. As he lifted Hsi Shih, he
found, to his horror, that her garment was stained with
blood in the lower part of the back side and she was
groaning with pain.

Back at the Beauty's Palace, Hsi Shih was
immediately placed in bed and the royal physician was
sent for.

It was a case of miscarriage. Another life was
extinct—the life of the darling baby on whom she and
Fu Chai had placed great hopes. What grieved Hsi Shih
even more was that the physician had warned her not
to have any more babies after this. Another pregnancy
would cost her her life.

Disaster seemed to always come in pairs. Since the
death of Prince Yiou, Hsi Shih had been hoping that she
could bear a son for Fu Chai. He needed a successor of
his own blood and she longed for a child of her own to
hold and cuddle and love. The physician's verdict was
like a death sentence to her. She should never have made
that horrid trip to the apothecary's. She had returned
Fu Chai's kindness with betrayal. Remorseful, she cried
bitterly.

"My dear," said Fu Chai, who had been at Hsi
Shih's bedside for days with hardly any rest, "don't cry.
We don't need another baby."

"But I want to have a baby. I want to give you a
baby." Tears were streaming down her face.

"Darling, you are more important to me than the

baby."

"But I am determined to give you a baby, my lord. I don't mind if my labor is to cost me my life."

"No, my darling. You are breaking my heart talking like this. You know, my first wife died in childbirth. I cannot bear another ... " His voice cracked.

Hsi Shih understood. She became quiet. Her hand crept over his.

After gathering himself, Fu Chai said firmly, "I will never allow you to risk your life. You are everything to me. I don't want any baby. All I want is for you to be healthy and safe."

"Oh, Fu Chai, you are a dear!" In all the years they had been together, Hsi Shih had never called him by name.

She snuggled into his arms. Suddenly the dying words of Zheng Dan rang in her ears.

*"Hsi Shih, I hope you would follow your heart and do the right thing."*

Gazing steadily into Fu Chai's eyes, she boldly announced, "Fu Chai, I want to make a clean breast to you of a secret."

"A secret?"

"Yes."

"I don't understand."

"I was sent here by Gou Jian for a purpose."

"Yes, of course."

"I was sent here to spy on you. I am his agent."

She paused, waiting for the impact of her words, waiting for him to absorb the shock—and explode.

Fu Chai was strangely calm. He gave her a baffled stare, seeming unable to comprehend her statement. Then a soft laugh escaped him.

"My darling," he put a hand on her forehead. "You are running a fever. Your face is flushed. You are imagining things."

Hsi Shih averted her gaze. "No, I'm not," she said dully. "I am telling you the truth."

"I'm also telling you the truth, my sweet," he returned. "You know, I used to have a bodyguard who had a similar condition. Once in a battle, his horse was struck by an arrow. The horse fell dead, and he fell unconscious. When he came to, he began to imagine things. He warned me to be careful because he saw a shadow behind me. It was all his hallucination. But of course I appreciated his loyalty to me."

Thus Fu Chai dismissed her confession as delirious ravings. Clearly, he did not understand her. But his disbelief was strangely comforting. She lifted her gaze. A wobbly smile curved her lips. "I'm sorry, my lord. Please forgive me...."

She sounded as though she was apologizing for talking feverish nonsense, but in fact she was apologizing for being Gou Jian's agent to spy on him.

He pulled her closer, hugging her to his muscular body. "You need a good rest, my sweet dear."

Why did Fu Chai refuse to believe her confession? Was it because the truth was too terrible and he did not want to know? No, he did not believe her words because she could never be a spy in his eyes. Because he loved her too much. She reasoned to herself.

Relief flooded her. Hsi Shih trembled. At this time, her maid, Ding Hong, brought in a bowl of stewed herbal medicine.

"Come on, my sweet, drink it up and have a good sleep." Fu Chai took over the bowl from Ding Hong.

Hsi Shih took the medicine like an obedient child. She smiled at him with a sweetness never seen in her eyes before.

"I love you, Fu Chai!" She said fervently, pressing a deep, warm kiss on his lips when he bade her good night.

*I love Fu Chai. I adore him. He is an extraordinary man. He is my lord, my king, my husband. I don't want to deny it any more. I must follow my heart. I must take care of Fu Chai. I must protect him from harm, from Gou Jian! I'm going to throw in my lot with Fu Chai. That's my destiny, my mission in life. From today on, from this very moment, I'm no longer Gou Jian's agent. I'm free! Free to love!*

Her thoughts thus cleared, she felt as though she were liberated from bondage. She sank into a peaceful sleep. When she woke up the next morning, she removed the necklace, the hairpin and the anklets that Fan Li had given her and put them away. This was a turning point in her life. She was no longer torn between Fu Chai and Fan Li. She knew how much Fu Chai loved her. She owed him too much. She was to return his love, double-fold.

\* \* \*

Hsi Shih made a quick recovery. It was also a cathartic process for her. Now her single preoccupation was the succession of Fu Chai's family line. She wanted to have another pregnancy. But Fu Chai was adamant that she should not risk her life, saying he could adopt one of his nephews to be his heir. However, that was not a satisfactory solution to her. It afforded her no relief. She wanted to make amends. Nothing short of procuring a girl to be Fu Chai's concubine to bear him a son would make things right.

One day, at the sight of Ding Hong playing with some children in the courtyard, her eyes flashed an indescribable ray of joy. She had an inspiration— Ding Hong was to be the candidate! She could hardly wait to talk to Fu Chai. That evening she prepared one of Fu Chai's favorite dishes, crucian carp soup with dried mushroom and slices of ham, and she donned an exquisite pink silk gown embroidered with floral designs. She greeted Fu Chai with a bright smile when he returned home.

"My precious dear," the king noticed her euphoric mood. "You look exuberant."

"I have good news for you."

Fu Chai saw a mischievous gleam in her eyes as he contemplated, but his mind was a blank.

"Would you like to guess?" Hsi Shih asked.

"I'm afraid I can't, my dear. You may as well tell me."

"I want to offer Ding Hong to be your concubine."

Fu Chai's face froze for an instant, but it quickly relaxed into a smile. "What made you think so, sweetheart?"

"Your family line must continue. Ding Hong is not only pretty but also very healthy. She will be able to bear a baby boy for you."

"Let's talk about that later," he replied nonchalantly.

"Let's talk about it now."

"I don't need a concubine, my sweet."

"You do. It is my responsibility to find one for

you."

"But I didn't ask you to."

"No, you didn't. But it's my duty to make sure that your line will continue."

"Hmm." Fu Chai was struck by the earnest resolution in her tone.

"I will kill myself if you reject my offer."

Fu Chai stared into her eyes: Hsi Shih had never bluffed.

"All right. I accept your offer."

"Wonderful!" Hsi Shih hugged him, grinning with delight. "I'm so happy. I'm sure Ding Hong will be very happy too."

Holding her in his arms, Fu Chai brushed her lips in a husbandly kiss. "But, sweetheart, I love you alone in the whole world."

At the dinner table they discussed the details of the arrangement. Hsi Shih was satisfied with Fu Chai's cooperation.

* * *

Ding Hong's promotion brought about a joyous anticipation in the Beauty's Palace. Hsi Shih gave her a gorgeous pair of ruby bracelets as wedding gift and helped her choose costumes and jewelry suitable for her new status of Royal Concubine.

On her first nuptial night, Ding Hong was chaperoned by Hsi Shih to an elegantly decorated bed-chamber where Fu Chai was waiting. Fu Chai's pleasant manner put Ding Hong at ease right away. A willing slave to His Majesty, Ding Hong served the king with all her heart.

Twice a month Hsi Shih took a trip to the Ancestral Temple of Wu to pray. The temple was located on the Tiger Hill on the northwestern edge of Gusu. Fu Chai's first wife and his father, King Ho Lu, were both buried here. Legend had it that three days after Ho Lu's burial, a white tiger appeared on the hill to protect his tomb.

Hsi Shih had to walk some twenty *li* from the Lingyan Hill to get to the Tiger Hill. She would go alone in the disguise of a peasant woman, carrying a basket of cookies, fruit and incense.

As a rule, most Wu people went to the temple once a year during the Ching Ming Festival in early April to offer sacrifices to their ancestors and sweep their ancestral tombs on the hill. For the rest of the year, the path to the temple was largely deserted.

The rough hilly road was punishing to her bare feet, but Hsi Shih was happy, genuinely happy. Even though she could ride, she chose not to. For one thing, it would be too conspicuous to go on horseback; for another, walking there in bare feet was a way to express the sincerity of her prayer as well as her contrition. At the foot of the Tiger Hill, there was a small river to be crossed. A ferry could be hired at a nearby village, but the water was not deep. Hsi Shih decided to wade through it to avoid the attention of the locals.

Behind the altar in the temple stood a tall table on which were exhibited the soul tablets of the Royal House of Wu. After placing the fruit and cookies in the vessels on the altar, Hsi Shih lighted three sticks of incense. Holding them in her hand, she knelt down and began to pray in a soft voice:

O our royal ancestors in Heaven,

With this first stick of incense, I beseech you to bless Fu Chai with a good son.

With this second stick, I beseech you to bless Ding Hong with good health.

With this third one, I beseech you to bless Wu with good luck and peace.

She put the incense sticks in a large bronze tripod in front of the altar and kowtowed three times to the tablets.

She went to the Ancestral Temple regularly, rain or shine, and her prayers were answered. The following year, an angelic, chubby baby boy was born, to the great delight of Fu Chai. He named the boy Wei, which meant greatness.

# CHAPTER TWENTY-SIX

## Tea Peddler

"HSI SHIH DIDN'T show up, did she?" Gou Jian asked Yi Yong who had just returned from a secret trip to Wu.

"No, she didn't."

"It's nearly a year since you told me she had a miscarriage. What's going on?"

"She may still be recuperating."

"I doubt it," Gou Jian snapped, his face turning grim. "Since Ding Hong became Fu Chai's concubine, Hsi Shih should have time to come out to meet you if she still cares about her mission."

"She must have reasons."

"What reasons?" the king snarled. "Pooh! The bitch must have gone over to the enemy. That's why she has not given us any intelligence for so long."

Yi Yong was astonished by the king's foul language.

"Sire, we should give Hsi Shih the benefit of the doubt," Fan Li said, upset by Gou Jian's suspicion.

The news of Hsi Shih's miscarriage deeply disturbed him. He felt he was at least partially responsible, and prayed everyday for her full recovery. But the king apparently did not appreciate her sacrifice. The king was a suspicious man by nature. An ingrate. That he knew and could put up with. But he would not allow him to slander Hsi Shih. Since her accident, Fan Li had been haunted by guilt. He was ashamed he had not protected her. Now her honor was being attacked, he must defend her.

"We should give her credit for what she has done. Maybe there is nothing urgent for her to report."

"Nothing urgent?" Gou Jian darted him a sharp glance. "Hsi Shih is no longer working for us. She's turned a traitor. A traitor!" he bit out between his teeth.

Scowling at Gou Jian, Fan Li returned bluntly, "No, she is not." His voice strained with the effort to suppress his anger. Suddenly King Gou Jian became abominable to him. He would have required little provocation to slap the king in the face. His hands clenched against the urge.

Just as he and his chief general appeared to be on a collision course Gou Jian looked away. "Ugh, you still love her?" Abruptly his tone turned gentle.

"Yes, I do," replied Fan Li, stone-faced.

"I admire your faithfulness, my lord."

"Please be patient with her, Your Majesty," Fan Li said tersely.

"You are right." Gou Jia seemed to calm down. "I should be more patient. I'm sorry I was in a bad mood today. Thank you for your good counsels, my lords."

The tension was diffused. The ministers bowed and backed out, shocked by the king's outburst.

Gou Jian dropped into his chair. The exchange with his advisors had done little to mollify his wrath. Hsi Shih's blatant disobedience must not go unpunished. But it should not become an issue with his ministers. His fingers kept tapping on the wooden arm of the chair until, almost imperceptibly, a vicious smile played on his lips. His slanting eyes flashed a strange light. Then he nodded as if he had made a momentous decision.

\* \* \*

Azalea and Rose, court-maids in the Beauty's Palace, were walking trippingly down the gentle slope of the Lingyan Hill. The air was chilly, but the birds were twittering, the trees were in leaf and spring was very much in the air.

Dressed in colorful palatial livery, they were heading for the marketplace at the foot of the hill where fish, meat, poultry, fruit and fresh vegetables were being sold from early morning to noon every day. They enjoyed visiting the marketplace from time to time. It was a world far removed from the neat, perfect existence of the Beauty's Palace, and yet it was only a short distance away and provided a welcome change. The smell there was not sweet, but it was alluring. The noise there was not pleasing, but it was exciting.

Azalea was a young woman of spirit. She was pet-named Azalea because of the glowing color of her cheeks. Her friend Rose was so called for having the same healthy complexion. They were eager to see what the peddlers were offering, hoping to find something interesting to fritter away a few coins on. They toured around, but, to their disappointment, did not find anything that struck their fancy. Then they heard a female voice.

"Fair ladies, do you want some tea? Dragon Well tea?"

They turned around and saw a country woman beckoning to them. The two walked up to her stall. The woman, clad in a blue top over blue trousers, had a weather-beaten face, but the features of her face were perfect. Her skin was dark, yet somehow she did not look like a peasant.

"Fair ladies," she gave them a toothy smile. "I have excellent tea leaves to sell. They are the new crops of Dragon Well."

"You must be from Yue," Azalea said to the woman, remembering Hsi Shih mentioning that her favorite tea, Dragon Well, only grew in Yue.

"Yes, fair lady. How do you know?"

"Because you speak the same dialect as our mistress." Rose answered for Azalea.

"Who's your mistress, pray?" The woman's eyes widened.

"Lady Hsi Shih."

"Oh, I've heard of Lady Hsi Shih. Does she live here?"

"Yes," Rose said, pointing to Hsi Shih's villa, which was bathed in the golden rays of the morning sun on the slope of the Lingyan Hill. "Look, that is the palace where she lives."

"Palace?" The woman cast a quizzical gaze in the direction of the villa.

"Yes. It looks like a farm house from outside, but

inside it's a palace," Rose explained.

"How do you like Lady Hsi Shih?"

"Well, she is very beautiful, very kind and generous."

"Lady Hsi Shih is beautiful inside and out," Azalea added.

"Miss, you travelled all the way from Yue to sell your tea?" Rose asked sympathetically, noticing the woman's grimy, leathery feet that resembled horse hoofs rather than a part of human anatomy.

"Yes, I have to support my family. Would you like to buy some tea?"

Rose took out some silver coins from her purse. "Give us some real good Dragon Well. We're going to present it to Lady Hsi Shih."

"Of course." The woman took a pinch for the girls to have a sniff. "I guarantee you can't get better tea from any other place."

The girls smiled their approval and a deal was easily struck. As they walked away with a bouncing step, the woman turned her appraising gaze to Hsi Shih's villa.

The fourth watch, about three hours before dawn, was the darkest moment of the night. The moon was faint; the stars, hardly discernible. The Beauty's Palace was wrapped in shadow.

A dark figure in tight-fitting black outfit had stolen into it.

With inaudible steps, the dark figure climbed up the walls of Hsi Shih's two-story mansion, landed on the balcony of her bed chamber, easily pried open the latched door and slipped in. The dark figure was none other than the woman tea peddler who had met with Azalea and Rose a few days ago.

Holding a candle she had lit on the oil-lamp outside Hsi Shih's bed chamber, she tiptoed to the four-poster bed which was curtained around by silk gauze, drew the curtains apart and peered down.

Hsi Shih was sleeping. Her beautiful face seemed to have made an effect on the intruder who leaned over for a closer look. Suddenly Hsi Shih raised her leg and kicked the intruder in the shoulder. The woman nearly lost her balance. The candle dropped from her hand. Another kick on her chest, and she was knocked down.

Hsi Shih slept badly that night. A premonition kept her on the alert these days when she was not with Fu Chai. She felt someone moving in the room. When her seemingly closed eyes sensed the light of the candle, she knew the intruder was close by and seized the moment to lash out.

Barely had she jumped down from her bed when the woman propelled herself forward with a rolling action. She wrapped her left arm around Hsi Shih's ankle and pulled her leg forward. Hsi Shih fell backward. The woman followed through with an elbow strike. The next moment she was on top of Hsi Shih, pinning her arms to the floor. With great effort, Hsi Shih forced her hips upward and twisted her body to the side to throw off her opponent.

Now both were on their feet. Hsi Shih attacked first with a left jab, but her opponent blocked it. Next Hsi Shih drove her right hip forward and delivered a right punch, and then twisted her left hip forward and struck out with her left arm. Both blows hit her opponent on the head. Unfazed, the woman counterattacked with a series of whirlwind punches before Hsi Shih could evade. The impact made her dizzy, but she managed to shoot a hard low kick at the woman's groin. The woman, however, was a far better martial artist. When Hsi Shih attempted to clinch her, she used her momentum to grab her right arm, and, with a swift leg movement, swept Hsi Shih's right leg out, throwing her to the floor.

"Make no noise!" she ordered in a threatening whisper. She was on top of Hsi Shih again, bearing down heavily on her with both knees against her chest. "If you shout, I'll kill you right now." Hsi Shih felt something hard pressed against her neck—fingers as hard as iron that threatened to stamp life from her.

"Who are you?" she gasped, astonished to hear the assassin speaking in a female voice with Yue accent. "What do you want?"

"Never mind who I am," the woman stared down into her face. "My job is to punish bad people. But I don't punish without giving the reason. I am ordered by King Gou Jian to kill you because you are a traitor to Yue."

Hsi Shih's heart dropped in sickening plunge. "No, I am not. I'm not a traitor."

"You are lying." The woman gave her a stinging slap in the face and Hsi Shih grimaced.

"No, I'm not," she protested. "I'm innocent of your accusation."

"Innocent?" Another hard slap landed on her face.

"Yes," Hsi Shih asserted stubbornly. "I am a traitor to Wu, to King Fu Chai." Irony washed through her voice. "I should be punished by King Fu Chai, but not by King Gou Jian."

The woman seemed baffled by her response.

"All right." She took out a rope and hogtied Hsi Shih into a grotesque form. "My knife is never tainted by the blood of an innocent person." After picking up the candle which was still burning, she placed it in front of Hsi Shih. "Now tell me your side of the story."

She seated herself on a chair in the corner of the room, her own face hidden in the dark.

In a low, trembling voice Hsi Shih told her how she was chosen to be sent to Wu, how she collected intelligence and passed it on to Yi Yong, how she had a dreadful accident during one of such meetings, and so on and so forth. When she had finished, she broke down and started sobbing.

"Stop crying!" came the woman's stern voice.

Hsi Shih checked her tears.

"Why did you stop spying for King Gou Jian?" Her interrogator's tone became milder.

"Because my mission is completed. The king has had his revenge."

"But ... but that is not something for you to decide."

"Well, I've decided not to be a spy any more," Hsi Shih said flatly. "I don't believe in endless feuding."

A brief silence passed. "You ... like Fu Chai?" The woman asked impassively.

"Yes, I do," came Hsi Shih's firm reply.

"What kind of a man is he?"

"King Fu Chai is a good husband," Hsi Shih said after a pause, a little offended by the intrusive question. "He's a great husband. I love him, and he loves me," she added defiantly. There was even a note of triumph in her tone. "But I've never betrayed my motherland. And never will. Whatever you decide to do, I want you to know the truth."

A long silence ensued. The woman sat motionless, seeming oblivious of the form squirming helplessly before her under the flickering candle light. Hsi Shih sensed her inner struggle, a conflict between obeying the king's order and making up her own mind about her captive.

The agony in her cramped limbs becoming unbearable, her whole body soaked in sweat, Hsi Shih let out a muffled groan. Her groan roused the woman from her study and she stood up. Hsi Shih shivered with terror when she beheld the glint of a dagger in her hand. She meant to scream but her voice came out in a croak: a breath clogged in her throat. The pattering of unshod feet coming toward her, she closed her eyes. Her mind went blank....

Now the footstep stopped. She felt her face scraping against some rough fabric.

"I believe you are a good person, Hsi Shih," the woman's husky voice cascaded. "I will not carry out the king's order...."

Suddenly Hsi Shih collapsed. She fell sideways, her head knocking against the woman's feet. The woman bent down to cut her free from the ropes. But Hsi Shih did not move. The woman knelt by her and began massaging her temples. Moments later, Hsi Shih regained consciousness.

"Are you all right, Hsi Shih?" the woman asked softly. "I'm sorry."

Hsi Shih panted, her body tingling. "May I know your name, miss?"

"I'm the Virgin of the Southern Forest," she said,

extending her hand to stroke her.

"Ah, I've heard about you, Virgin," Hsi Shih said weakly. "I've always admired you."

"Thank you, Lady Hsi Shih. Please accept my apology."

"Thank you for sparing me my life, Virgin. But King Gou Jian never forgives anyone who goes against his will."

"I understand. I can't stay in Yue any more."

"Do you have a family?"

"No, I don't. But Master Chen Yin and I are engaged to be married."

"Master Chen Yin? I've heard about him, too. Does he know about your assignment?"

"No, the king ordered me not to tell anybody. It's top secret. I intend to go back and tell Master Chen Yin what happened. We both have to leave Yue before the king finds out."

The Virgin's massage was miraculously effective. In the space of half an hour, the pain in Hsi Shih's body had largely disappeared. She stood up, walked to the bedside cabinet and took out a bag of gold coins. "Virgin, you will need money on your travels."

"Thank you, Lady Hsi Shih," the Virgin made a deep bow. "Your life is still in danger. King Gou Jian may send another assassin."

"I will be on my guard."

"I won't forget your kindness, Lady Hsi Shih. I hope we will meet again some day."

The Virgin turned to the balcony, ready to leave.

"Just a minute, Virgin. How do you know I am sleeping alone tonight?"

"I don't," the Virgin smiled sheepishly. "But it is

the night of a new moon. So I guess the king is probably sleeping with his concubine."

Thus saying, she went out through the balcony, disappearing into the dark night. The Virgin had guessed correctly. Fu Chai was with Ding Hong that night in another villa.

According to the imperial tradition, the king's sex regime was regulated by the wax and wane of the moon. He should sleep with the women in his harem on the correct days of the lunar calendar. The king usually slept with a lesser-ranking woman when there was a new moon. As the moon gradually grew in size from the beginning of the lunar month, he would shift his favor from lower-ranking ladies to higher-ranking ladies. When the moon was full, he would sleep with the queen. This way his potency would be enhanced by previous unions with women of lower ranks before he had his intercourse with the queen. Because the king symbolized the sun and the queen the moon, the best time to join each other was when there was a full moon. At such time, it was believed, there was a perfect harmony between the two cosmic symbols of the male and the female.

# CHAPTER TWENTY-SEVEN

# Dream

HSI SHIH CHANGED into a full-length gown the following morning to cover the rope marks on her limbs. But the pallor on her face did not escape Fu Chai's notice.

"Sweetheart, are you all right?" he asked at the breakfast table.

Hsi Shih shook her head. "I didn't sleep well. I had a nightmare."

"Tell me about it."

"I dreamed Gou Jian broke into my room. He was trying to kill me."

Fu Chai puckered his brows.

"I tried to fight him away. I screamed for help. But he overpowered me. His hands were on my throat. I almost choked.... "

"Then ... "

"In the nick of time, you dashed in and jumped upon him."

"Did I kill him?"

Hsi Shih shook her head. "He escaped."

Fu Chai chuckled gently. Obviously she had not completely recovered from the after effect of the wreck of the horse-and-carriage.

"I'll send for the physician," he murmured, his fingers gently touching her forehead.

"Physician? What for?"

"He'll give you some medication to help you sleep."

"But he can't protect me from Gou Jian," Hsi Shih was all seriousness. "My dream warns me of danger. We must take proper precautions."

Fu Chai's eyes flashed an understanding twinkle. Right away he summoned the chief guard of the Beauty's Palace and ordered him to place more guards on night shift and heighten the overall security.

Then he turned to Hsi Shih. "I'll also have the physician give you some medication, darling, so that you can sleep better. Would that be all right?"

"Yes." Hsi Shih was pleased that her improvised story would result in more protection for her without unduly worrying Fu Chai.

\* \* \*

A year after the arrival of the boy prince, Ding Hong was expecting again. Hsi Shih wanted to wait upon her. Ding Hong declined. During her first pregnancy Hsi Shih had been her's most willing servant. She and Gao Lan had attended on her with great solicitude. They made sure that she had plenty of rest, fed her with good, nutritious meals so that she could produce nourishing milk for the baby, and did everything possible to keep her in high spirits, because, Hsi Shih said, a happy mood would have a beneficial influence on the baby.

But Hsi Shih was the royal consort. Ding Hong was uncomfortable to have her as her maternity nurse again.

"Lady Hsi Shih, I would be happy if you just let Gao Lan look after me."

Hsi Shih gladly obliged and assigned a number of maids to help Gao Lan in her nursing role. In due course, Ding Hong gave birth to a baby girl. Fu Chai named her Min, meaning smart.

Hsi Shih took on the responsibility of taking care of Prince Wei. She became the boy's favorite playmate. She would held him in her arms and sing to him, and as she sang, she would lean back and forth, tickling the boy immensely. She would get down on her hands and knees and crawl after the little boy, or crawl ahead and let the little boy chase after her.

When the weather got warm, she would take him to Lake Tai Hu, often spending a day there, romping on the shore, splashing in the water, shuffling their feet in the sand that glistened in the sun like silver. In the morning she would take him on a treasure hunt to find clams and oysters in the sandy muck, or give him a pink pebble or a heart-shaped shell that she had found and tell him to find something like them. In the afternoon they would sit on the top of a dune to watch rabbits hopping at random, field mice scurrying around, fishing boats gliding past the gleaming surface of the water under the setting sun.

Another of her favorite activities was to draw in the sand with a stick. It was a wonderful way to teach the boy how to write. As many Chinese characters resembled the objects they stood for, it was easy to draw a picture. For example, the word "sun" was a square with a dot in its middle; "moon" was a crescent with a smile, "man" looked like somebody walking; "woman" looked like a mother holding a baby; and the word "good" was formed by putting a woman and her child together. Some words were easy to identify with the pictures they symbolized. Others required imagination.

To encourage the boy to become creative, Hsi Shih would draw his attention to the many pebbles on the beach and ask him what they look like. Most pebbles were ordinary, but some looked like fish, some like birds. Some resembled human beings. Some reminded the boy of the numbers and Chinese characters he had learned. He also drew funny pictures of his own invention in the sand.

He quickly learned to play with Mao Mao who instinctively knew how to be his friend, but he needed encouragement to make friends with birds on the beach who would wait gingerly when he was snacking on cookies or fruits and then move in to snatch leftover crumbs.

Sometimes Fu Chai would join Hsi Shih on the lakeshore playing with the boy prince or take them for a pleasure ride on horseback.

Fu Chai had resumed his work routine. For more than once, Hsi Shih warned him that the peace treaty with Yue was a fake, and asked him to guard against Gou Jian's treachery. Fu Chai said he would, but Hsi

Shih was not sure whether he had really understood her message. In any case, Wu's treasury was being replenished; its army was conducting regular maneuvers; its status as the Lord State remained unchallenged. For the next few years, all was peaceful between Wu and Yue.

\* \* \*

Hsi Shih spent most of her time in the Beauty's Palace. She doffed her courtly costumes in favor of the native clothes of Yue which seemed more in tune with the idyllic surroundings. Rather than sumptuous garments encrusted with gems, pearls and embroidery in gold and silver thread, she preferred lighter gowns made of vibrantly hued silks and brocades. The climate being mild, she was clad frequently in a tight-fitted, short blouse and wide trousers, with colorful belts around her waist, a gold ring on her exposed navel, colorful anklets and matching toe-rings on her feet—she had long stopped wearing shoes except on ceremonial occasions.

These were the happiest days in her life. The trauma caused by her miscarriage was completely healed. Emancipated from a troubled mind, she enjoyed every moment with her adored king to the fullest extent. She loved him for his big-heartedness, his devotion, and his faith in her.

With nature remodelled into enchanting landscape, the Beauty's Palace was a paradise on earth. In summer, the enamored couple would spend many a sweet night in the "Hsi Shih Cave." In autumn, they would drink to the full moon in the "Moon Terrace." On days when Fu Chai did not hold court sessions, they would go horseback riding or hunting in the woods on the "Hunting Island." They would dangle their feet in the limpid water of the "Lotus Pond," go fishing in the "Fishing Village," or swim, undressed like fish, leaving all the worries of the world behind them.

There were days of communion that bound their spirit in blissful accord and nights of lovemaking that blended into a sweet dream. It was a miracle to wake up the next morning and realize all this was not a dream. Yet Hsi Shih still felt it was like a dream. A dream that was too good, too idyllic to be true. She wished it would last a lifetime. No—a lifetime would not be enough. It must be an eternity.

"You would never leave me, Fu Chai?" she asked one morning after a hugely enjoyable night.

"Never," he assured her.

"Fu Chai, you are the best man I've ever known."

"But you haven't known that many, darling." A chuckle stirred in his throat. He cupped her lovely face in his hands and looked into her lustrous dark eyes. "I love you more than my life, more than my kingdom."

Fu Chai cherished the time alone with Hsi Shih. Her beauty would never lose the power to fascinate him. He wondered what he had done to merit her presence in his life. He must be a very lucky man, and he was full of gratitude.

# CHAPTER TWENTY-EIGHT

## Rice Relief

"MY LORDS, I think we have done enough to ensure a victorious invasion," said King Gou Jian at a meeting with his advisors. "This time we will finish off Fu Chai once and for all."

Six years had passed since he launched the surprise attack on Wu and won a partial victory. He grew more and more impatient about launching another invasion.

"We are stronger than ever before." The king went on to cite his reasons. "Our population has doubled; our treasury is full; our granaries have three years' grain reserve. Externally we have befriended Chu in the south, Jin and Chi in the north. I have even given my daughter to the king of Chu to be his concubine. Every year we present these states with generous gifts to forge good relationship. Above all, we have a strong army, well-trained and well-equipped."

Wen Zhong expressed his reservation. "Sire, there is no doubt our army is stronger than ever, and our diplomacy has done much to isolate Wu. But we should wait a little longer."

"Why?"

"Because Fu Chai still has a large army. He can put up a stiff resistance. Even if we win the war, the cost will be enormous."

"When is the right time, my lord?" The king puckered his brows.

"The right time has to be provided by the enemy through their own mistakes like what they did last time."

Not satisfied with Wen Zhong's vague answer, the king turned to Fan Li. "What is your opinion, my lord?"

Fan Li was just as anxious as Gou Jian, as a matter of fact. Since Hsi Shih stopped meeting Yi Yong, he had tried repeatedly to contact her through her father, but received no response at all. Her father said she was fine, but Fan Li suspected she had changed. He could hardly fail to notice that the king had stopping mentioning her. He might have suspected the same thing and did not want to embarrass him by asking him about her. Even though he had his own family, Fan Li had never stopped yearning for her, never stopped loving her, never stopped thinking of her, not for a single day. But reason told him the time was not ripe. Fu Chai had a sizable army. There was no guarantee that Yue would win, and he had no appetite for another partial victory. He did not want to go into Wu and come back again without Hsi Shih. Victory must be assured before the next war was started.

"The days won't be too long," he told the king. "Your Majesty has done a splendid job in preparing Yue for victory. But we have to examine how things stand with the enemy. In that regard, victory depends on three factors: the earthly factor, the human factor and the heavenly factor. The decrease in Wu's treasury is the earthly factor; the death of Wu Yuan and the folly of Fu Chai is the human factor. If we just wait till the heavenly factor arrives in good time, we can annihilate the State of Wu with little effort."

Gou Jian felt Fan Li's argument carried more creditability. After all, Fan Li should be as eager as he was to attack Wu because of Hsi Shih. If, in Fan Li's judgment, the time was not yet ripe, then he should suppress his impatience and wait until an opportunity presented itself.

He had not realized until much later that Hsi Shih's presence in Wu provided a powerful incentive to his chief general to work towards *his* goal. He regretted having sent the Virgin of the Southern Forest to kill her a few years ago. Luckily Hsi Shih had survived. Otherwise the consequences would have been awful. He shuddered to think what Fan Li might do if he had found out about the assassination attempt. So when the Virgin had left abruptly, he was in fact relieved.

\*   \*   \*

Gou Jian did not have to wait long. In the year 474 B.C., a severe crab pest caused famine in Wu. The paddy fields were swarmed with crabs feeding themselves on rice crops. By the time the farmers exterminated them, they had already missed much of the planting season. The harvest was poor.

Fortunately, there was a considerable amount of

grain reserve. Fu Chai ordered the national granaries to be opened and rice doled out to the starving populace.

When news of rice shortage in Wu reached Gou Jian's court, Fan Li suggested that Yue send rice relief to Wu.

"This is a good opportunity, my king. Give Fu Chai some rice, reaffirm our friendship, and he will slacken his vigilance against us."

"I'm not going to feed my enemy, my lord."

"I've got an idea, Your Majesty." A devious smile appeared on Wen Zhong's face. "I'll have the rice half-steamed beforehand."

"Half-steamed? What for?" asked the king.

"Because," Wen Zhong lowered his voice to emphasize, "Wu is bound to save a portion of the rice as seeds for the next sowing season."

"Bravo!" Gou Jian clapped his hands. "My lord, only you can come up with such a wonderful idea."

Fan Li frowned but kept quiet.

"My king, isn't it too ... " Yi Yong stuttered, thinking the scheme too vicious.

"No, not at all," Gou Jian interrupted him. "My lord, that is the heavenly factor for us to fight a winning war. Don't you recognize it?"

\*　\*　\*

In the spring of the following year, Fu Chai was fretting about the dwindling rice reserve when Bo Pi came in with a letter from Gou Jian in which he stated that Yue was willing to donate a hundred thousand liters of rice. Fu Chai had not at all expected this goodwill gesture from Yue. A warmly-worded reply was dispatched and soon Yue's foreign minister Yi Yong arrived with a shipload of rice.

"My master is grateful to Your Majesty," said Yi Yong when he was cordially received by the king, "for the help you extended us last time. Now he heard about what has happened in your land, he says it is his duty to return kindness for kindness done to him."

"It's very kind of Gou Jian to offer us such a timely aid." Fu Chai's bitterness over the loss of Prince Yiou had long since faded. "I really appreciate."

Yi Yong requested to meet Hsi Shih to convey greetings on behalf of the villagers of Zhuluo. He was taken to her residence promptly.

The Beauty's Palace was at its best in spring. The air was permeated with the sweet scents of flowers, and the scenery was a riot of color. Yi Yong gazed at every corner with wonder. It was his first time to visit this famed place.

After crossing a winding, tree-shadowed path and climbing a flight of stone steps, he was led into a building whose exterior resembled a farm cottage. Inside, it was an ornate palace with carved wood balustrade, padauk furniture, silk rugs, satin draperies, walls decorated with landscape paintings, and ceilings painted with flower-and-bird designs. What a fantastic place to live in, Yi Yong marveled.

With her pet cat Mao Mao by her side, Hsi Shih received Yi Yong in her magnificent queenly costume.

"Your Excellency, it's nice to see you again." She greeted him with civility.

Yi Yong was exultant. "How wonderful to see you, Hsi Shih! How have you been? I've missed you."

Hsi Shih did not answer; she just smiled. Yi Yong

had not seen her for seven years. Nicely tanned, she was beautiful as ever, and carried herself with a poise and elegance that she had not possessed before. With her ripe mouth and blooming cheeks, she wore the look of a content, well-pleasured woman. Yi Yong was curious to learn about her life in Wu and to find out the reason why she had stopped coming to their secret meeting. He liked the girl and was genuinely concerned about her well-being. He had many questions. But the reserve of her manner discouraged him from asking her any more. Still he had to fulfill the task assigned by Fan Li.

"Fan Li misses you badly; he is anxious to know how you are doing." He presented a letter from Fan Li, together with a box of gifts for Hsi Shih.

"I'm all right," Hsi Shih replied, ignoring the letter. "I am grateful that Fan Li remembers me. But I'm afraid I cannot accept his gift. I've made up my mind—he has his family, and I have mine. He has to understand. Please wait. I'll be right back."

She went inside and returned with a big parcel. "Your Excellency, please take this parcel back to Fan Li. It contains all the gifts he has given me over the years except the necklace. I'll keep it as a memento. Tell him I will always cherish his memory. But I've decided that I am another man's woman, and I will live and die as wife to my lord, King Fu Chai of Wu."

Yi Yong was at a loss what to say.

"Please take care, Your Excellency. I bid you farewell."

With that, Hsi Shih ended the meeting. She felt as though she had relieved herself of a heavy burden. She did not hate Fan Li, but she had long ceased caring for him. She would never forget him. He did love her. His love for her was true love until that fatal moment when he decided to give her up.

She decided to keep the necklace Fan Li had given her when they were betrothed. A symbol of pure love. But the fond memory associated with it had become so remote and abstract that it could hardly cause a stir in her heart anymore except for a wisp of nostalgia.

\* \* \*

The rice from Yue seemed to be of good stock. Just as Wen Zhong had anticipated, a significant portion was saved as seed-grain for the following year.

It was too late when Fu Chai realized that Gou Jian had played a malicious trick on him. For two years in a row, there was a crop failure in Wu. Though there was still grain left in the national granaries, the quantity was far from enough. Fu Chai dispatched envoys to other countries to seek assistance. But only the Duke of Lu and the Duke of Wei offered some limited aid.

Hsi Shih was deeply distressed to see the influx of refugees into Gusu. Small babies were carried by their parents in baskets hung on either end of a bamboo shoulder-pole; old and sick people were placed in wheelbarrows pushed by able-bodied men. She heard that in some areas, people had to eat tree barks, sea-weeds, grass and even rats to survive. She had not believed Gou Jian would be so caring as to send rice relief to Wu. She had suspicions. But she had never expected that such a sinister scheme as sending rice seeds that would not grow would have been played on the people of Wu.

They were innocent people—just like the people

of Yue. How could Gou Jian do this to them? Why didn't Fan Li stop him? Did Yi Yong know what he was delivering? Was this the way to wreak revenge on Wu? It was simply too vicious, too inhuman. She was furious and felt ashamed as a Yue native.

# CHAPTER TWENTY-NINE

## Invasion

FAN LI WAS robbed of speech when he received Hsi Shih's parcel of returned gifts. Her act cut him to the heart.

Since Hsi Shih stopped communicating with him, he suspected that she was no longer faithful to him. The news brought back by Yi Yong confirmed his worst fear. Fu Chai had turned the tables and seduced her. Even though it was not totally unexpected, it shattered him nevertheless. But he could not blame Hsi Shih, could he? Hadn't he betrayed her first by his own marriage? She had been Fu Chai's captive for so long. She was flesh and blood after all. It was his fault—and his fault alone. He should never have let her go to Wu in the first place. What a fool he had been!

He had lost. He had lost his beloved to the enemy king. Fan Li moaned in pain. No word could express his agony. And he had no one to share his sorrows with. His wife had died recently. Even if she were alive, he could not expect her to be sympathetic. But he refused to give up hope. Hsi Shih's pledge of love was still fresh in his memory. Perhaps there was still a chance to win her back. The fact that she was still keeping the necklace he had given her—*as memento*, she had said—meant there was still a soft spot for him in her heart. Her feelings for him might not have vanished entirely. He was determined to reclaim his beloved. Once they were reunited, he would make her so happy that the memory of Fu Chai would be dispelled like a fog under the sun. He made a silent vow to himself.

\* \* \*

Gou Jian was gloating over the news that the famine in Wu was to last another year after Yue's rice donation and that people were fleeing their famine-stricken homeland. He ordered to have refugee centers set up along the Wu/Yue border. Signposts were put up to inform the refugees that Yue was offering them free rice. As the word spread, many people of Wu rushed over to the border, grateful to their former enemy.

Gou Jian held a meeting with all his ministers. He was convinced that time had come at last for him to have his revenge on Fu Chai.

"My good lord," he said to Fan Li, "you mentioned the human factor, the earthly factor and the heavenly factor. Isn't the famine in Wu an act of the gods in Heaven? Don't you think the heavenly factor is highly in our favor now?"

"The time has come," Fan Li said most assuredly.

"Your Majesty's patience will be richly rewarded. I've already made up a detailed plan of action for your examination. Brave though he is, Fu Chai can do nothing to save himself from doom."

After discussing with his ministers, Gou Jian decided that the invasion was to begin in autumn. Two months before the expedition, the king issued an order to the nation.

"Those who had enlisted for military service must report to their assigned unit within a month. Death penalties will be imposed on late-comers as well as those who fail to show up.

"If both the father and the son of a family are in the service, the father may go home; if the sons of a family are all in the service, the eldest one may go home; if a family has only one son, he may be exempt; those servicemen not physically fit enough for fighting will be placed in the support unit; those who are too weak will be sent home."

Yue's forces fifty thousand strong consisted of a land force of forty thousand, a naval force of four thousand, and an elite troop of six thousand personally commanded by Gou Jian.

As they were ready to set out, Gou Jian held a review on horseback. With his characteristic eloquence, he delivered a rousing speech to his soldiers, accompanied by vehement gesticulation.

"Soldiers, you are about to fight for our country. You are the most valiant fighters I have ever set eyes on. You have spent long years of training. Now you are going to reap the rich fruits of your toils. Fortune is smiling on you. She will bestow a reward worthy of your valor.

"We shall vanquish our enemy. Remember the humiliation and injury we suffered at their hands. It is time to finish what we left unfinished nine years ago. It is time to destroy our enemy once and for all. I, as your leader, command you to punish them with your mighty sword and burn them with your indignant flame. Remember when you triumph, you will receive rewards greater than you were wont to desire. But you must not loot or harm innocent civilians, for this time we shall stay in Wu as victors and whatever our enemy possess will become ours.

"Soldiers, you must conquer or die. If death is to be your lot, better meet it in battle than in flight. Remember this is a great war, but a great war need not be a difficult war, for we, the attackers, have the advantage. We are much more confident and courageous than our foes who are on the defensive. Soldiers, if you are determined in your mind to win victory, then victory will surely belong to us."

The assemblage broke out in thunderous cheers of "Long Live the King!"

\*     \*     \*

Vessels moored to the northern bank of Lake Tai Hu carried Wu's naval force of six thousand under the command of General Wangsun Luo. A land force of three thousand was garrisoned on shore under the command of General Mi Yong. Seeing endless columns of Yue soldiers continually gathering on the southern bank, Wangsun Luo hastily sent a messenger to Fu Chai who was in the Beauty's Palace with Hsi Shih. Yue's troop movement was ominous. It called for immediate attention. The royal couple left for Gusu that same night.

An emergency meeting was held the following day. Apart from those under Wangsun Luo and Mi Yong, Wu had another forty thousand men. Fu Chai gave Bo Pi ten thousand and put him in charge of the defense of the capital. He himself and Chief General Wangsun Shong would go to the front with the remaining thirty thousand. The king decided to leave with his troops in three days after drawing up a plan of campaign.

On the eve of his departure, King Fu Chai attended a prayer service to ask gods' favor for his army, and hosted a farewell banquet in the magnificent dining hall of the Gusu Palace attended by all his ministers and generals. Jars of fine liquor were served as well as meat and delicacies. Everybody ate and drank to his heart's content. Everybody toasted to the health of the king and the victory of his army. But the atmosphere was subdued. Send-off parties were also held in the army barracks. Each soldier could eat and drink as much as he wanted.

Fu Chai came home late, half-intoxicated. Hsi Shih had prepared his favorite dessert, swallow's nest stewed with crystal sugar and osmanthus flowers. He took it with keen relish.

"My king," Hsi Shih said with a concerned expression, "Gou Jian's coming with a big force this time."

"Don't worry, darling. We're ready for him."

"Gou Jian is a crafty man. Be careful."

"No matter how crafty he is, we are going to defeat him."

Hsi Shih found it hard to share Fu Chai's confidence. "Gou Jian must have been preparing this for a long time. Don't underestimate him."

"Darling, we are going to wipe him out once and for all. I swear."

Apparently that was all he intended to say on the subject. Hsi Shih was about to ask another question when his mouth came down fervently on hers.

Fu Chai had scarcely had time for her for the last few days. He was aching for her. He kissed her with eager impatience, savoring her mouth with deep forays of his tongue while his hands searched her body with urgency.

They made love three times that night. Both were insatiable, urged on by the knowledge that this was the night before the king departed for a battle that would determine the fate of his kingdom. Every sensation, every pleasure took on an extra dimension.

He kissed her greedily, groped her insistently, and smelled and tasted every inch of her body as though he could never have his fill. His thrusts corresponded to the caress of his fingers, sending intense pleasure rippling through her whole being like a warm, breaking wave, filling her, overwhelming her. For more than once Hsi Shih was driven to such ecstasy she felt she was melting away. She draped herself over his chest, relishing the powerful length of his body. They remained locked together for a long time. A life time of love compressed into this night. An eternity of happiness crowded into these precious moments.

Tired, Fu Chai quickly fell asleep. But Hsi Shih could not. She had a premonition that this might be their last night together. The forthcoming battle were fraught with danger and grim consequences; the future of Wu hung in the balance.

The night was as silent as the grave. In the soft candlelight of the bed chamber, she watched Fu Chai's expression as he slept. His face was handsome even in sleep. His mouth twitched intermittently. There was a frown between his dark brows. A surge of love gushing from the depth of her heart, she wanted to spread herself over his warm, muscular torso and make love to him for one more time. Unable to help herself, she stroked his forehead, and his frown smoothed away. Her fingers slid to his ear, his neck, his shoulder. He murmured slumberously as though he was responding to her even in sleep. Not wanting to wake him up, she withdrew her hand.

Weighed down by her premonition, she burst into sobs. She had to grab a corner of her quilt and pulled it over her face to muffle her sobbing. A long time passed before she calmed down and became drowsy.

When she woke up, her half-open eyes met a ray of brilliant sunshine beaming into the room through a crack between the satin curtains. She rolled over. There was no Fu Chai beside her. He is gone.

Hsi Shih reared upwards in panic. There were matters of import she had wanted to talk to him about last night but she had been distracted. After a few sleepy blinks, she jumped down from her bed and dressed herself with alacrity. She ordered her guards to get her horse ready, hurried through her breakfast and then leapt on the horse and raced off, leaving her guards and servants standing agape at the gate.

In the army barrack, Fu Chai had finished his

conference with Bo Pi and other officials who bade good-bye to their king and left. Just when he was ready to depart with the soldiers, Hsi Shih burst in on him. Looking stirringly smart in her riding gear, she was gasping, her chest heaving, her face gleaming with a mist of perspiration.

"Take me with you, my lord!" she said breathlessly.

"Why did you come here, sweet? You should stay at home."

"I want to go with you," she persisted.

"It's war, sweetheart. I don't want you to suffer with me"

"My lord!" Hsi Shih went down on her knees, holding his legs in her arms. "I want to be with you no matter what," she begged frantically.

"Darling, I must go without you."

But Hsi Shih would not move. She stared up into his face in supplication, her eyes brimming with tears until his face was a fluid blur.

"Now, now, don't cry, sweetheart!"

"I'm scared."

"Don't be scared! We have a good army. We will defeat Gou Jian."

She buried her face in his knees and sobbed.

"Darling ... " He stroked her tenderly.

"I love you, Fu Chai," she said. She felt a quiver run through him at the words. "I love you," she repeated.

"Hsi Shih, stop crying! I am the happiest man in the world because of you. I am forever grateful to you."

Hsi Shih would not stop. She felt she owed him too much. And she was not sure whether she would be able to requite his love.

"Darling, you can't come with me. I will send you messages."

"I'll go mad if I have to wait in the palace."

"You have things to do in the palace."

"I'll do anything for you." Hsi Shih stopped crying, raising a tear-stained face to her lord.

"Take care of my children. That is your responsibility."

Hsi Shih gave Fu Chai an emphatic nod, her shoulders trembling, but the look in her eyes was firm. Reaching up to him, she kissed him with desperate ardor, her lips pressing to his in a kiss that her subconsciousness told her was farewell.

*　　*　　*

After the departure of Fu Chai, the palace was enveloped in an atmosphere of gloom. There was widespread fear among the populace of Gusu.

Hsi Shih was plagued with a sense of foreboding. As a matter of precaution, she decided to find a safe haven for the six-year-old prince and the four-year-old princess as well as for her their mother Ding Hong and her faithful maid Gao Lan in the event that the worst should happen.

Fortunately, she had a loyal guard, Wang Zhong, who she felt could be trusted to help her with this all-important responsibility. A few years ago, Wang Zhong's father, while serving as a housekeeper at Bo Pi's residence, had offended his master, for he was found to have been secretly carrying on an affair with one of Bo Pi's concubines. Bo Pi threw him in jail to be executed. Wang Zhong begged Hsi Shih to intercede with Bo

Pi, and she did. As a result, his father's life was spared. The elder Wang had since returned to his home in the country to take care of his farm.

Hsi Shih discussed her plan with Wang Zhong who, after consulting his father, offered to let his father be the guardian of the child prince and princess as well as Ding Hong and Gao Lan.

In complete secrecy Hsi Shih escorted the children and the two ladies to Wang Zhong's home. The Wang family lived in a remote and sparsely populated village. Their house, located on a hillock amidst heavy clusters of bamboo, was spacious enough to accommodate the newcomers. Wang Zhong's father promised to take good care of the ladies and the children. They were to be given the new name Wang and identified as relatives of the Wang family in the future. Hsi Shih left with the Wang family an amount of gold worth a fortune.

Parting with the two ladies and the children was a painful ordeal. She nearly fainted.

# CHAPTER THIRTY

## Revenge

ONE AUTUMN NIGHT in the year 473 B.C., under cover of darkness, the right and left wings of Yue's navy, commanded by General Zhu Jicheng, sailed across Lake Tai Hu simultaneously for a two-pronged attack on Wu.

It was not until the fleet of both wings was more than halfway across the lake that torches were lit on each vessel.

Under bright torch light members of the crew were standing on the decks, weapons in hand, each wearing a shiny suit of armor and a shiny helmet.

Each vessel was well-decked-out, wooden dragon heads, painted black, white, crimson and golden, stretched high on the stem with big, fierce eyes and drooping whiskers. Fluttering from the masthead were flags bearing the big character "YUE."

The oarsmen intensified their efforts, their oars cutting the waves, speeding the boats toward the northern bank of the lake amidst rumbling drumbeats and a great clamor from the crew.

The battle formation of Yue's fleet looked formidable. Assuming Yue had opened a flanking assault to envelop him, Fu Chai divided his troops to intercept the invaders, leaving only a small force in the center.

This was exactly what Fan Li had hoped for. He immediately ordered Yue's main force, the central wing, to drive into the gap and made the crossing by stealth. They were so silent and so efficient that not until they had reached the forward position of Wu's camp were they noticed by the sentries, and by then it was far too late. Wu's troops were thrown into disarray.

Panic-stricken, Fu Chai hastily turned back. His forces were attacked not only by Yue's central wing that was awaiting them, but by Yue's flanking troops which had now made their landing. After a bruising battle, Fu Chai was forced to retreat to the town of Zuili.

The next twenty days saw three major battles between the armies of Wu and Yue. The first one was fought near Zuili. It was here twenty-three years ago that Gou Jian had defeated Fu Chai's father, King Ho Lu.

Well-trained, well-fed and superbly disciplined, the soldiers of Yue were ferocious. Wu's troops were by no means in their best form. Famine had demoralized them. Although there was adequate food reserve for the troops, their thoughts were with their own folks, many of whom having joined the general exodus from the famished land. It was no wonder that the battle ended in their defeat, and they were forced to retreat again.

The second battle was fought in a key strategic location called Li Ze*, about thirty *li* south of Gusu on the eastern tip of Lake Tai Hu. Again, the Wu army lost.

The third and most decisive battle was fought on the outskirts of Gusu. The Wu army sustained a crushing blow. Both General Mi Yong and General Wangsun Luo were killed in the last-ditch struggle and Chief General Wangsun Shong suffered a head injury. Fu Chai decided to pull back into Gusu, only to find that Yue's army had already cut off his retreat. He was compelled to flee southwest to the Gusu Hill. By the time he and Wangsun Shong reached there, the number of their troops was reduced to only four thousand.

\* \* \*

The Gusu Hill was practically a desolate, forsaken area. The remains of the Gusu Tower burnt down by Gou Jian's troops nine years ago were still visible. Fu Chai and his followers were fatigued and hungry. General Wangsun Shong searched around the place and picked up some raw rice with husks on to serve as meal. As there was no stove for cooking, Fu Chai had to chew the rice raw and swallow it with cold water.

He sighed a deep sigh as he recalled the words of the astrologer Gongsun Sheng—the man he had killed on account of predicting that one day he would have to eat rice uncooked.

No sooner had Fu Chai and his company finished their meal than drums and horns and shouts of Yue's soldiers were heard. Surrounded like an animal at bay, Fu Chai remembered what General Wu Yuan once said,

---

* Present-day Wujiang, Jiangsu Province.

"Fan Li is a man of great talent. Use him or kill him."
If he had listened to Wu Yuan, Gou Jian wouldn't have
been able to destroy him. How foolish of him to have
killed the loyal general!

"Your Majesty, I'm compelled to report that we
can no longer hold out," Wangsun Shong declared in a
cracked voice, a doleful look on his face. "The soldiers
are starving."

At the end of his wits, Fu Chai wrote a few lines
on a piece of cloth, tied it to an arrow, and shot it toward
Fan Li's camp.

> *"Esteemed Lord,*
> *"Do you remember the old saying, 'When flying
> birds are exterminated, even the best bow will be
> cast away. When wild rabbits are killed off, even
> the best hunting dog will be cooked.' I beg you to
> spare me, for I will always be grateful. I beg you
> to help preserve Wu, for it will also serve your best
> interest. Please pull back your troops and let me
> return to my capital with my men."*

Fan Li read the letter several times, struck by
certain perceptiveness that he had not expected from a
man like Fu Chai. But the game was over for Fu Chai.
No matter what he did, his fate was sealed. Fan Li wrote
a reply and had it sent to him in the same manner.

> *"Your Majesty,*
> *"At the time of the Battle of Guiji, Heaven
> gave Yue into the hands of Wu. But you did not
> appreciate the heavenly favor. Now as Heaven
> has given Wu into the hands of Yue, it would be*

*against Heaven's wish if we should decline the offer. Think for yourself. Do you deserve your throne?"*

Fu Chai was dismayed. "Fan Li is right," he said to Wangsun Shong. "What a fool I was to have let slip the opportunity of wiping out Yue!"

Wangsun Shong just stood by with his head hung, knowing they were at the end of their rope.

"Go to Gou Jian," Fu Chai said despondently, "and tell him I am ready to offer my kingdom to be his vassal state. Ask him to spare us."

A blood-stained bandage round his head, Wangsun Shong approached Gou Jian's camp, crawled on his knees and asked for an audience.

"Your Majesty," he threw himself at Gou Jian's feet, "my master Fu Chai sent me to beseech you for mercy. If you spare his life, he is willing to offer his kingdom to you as your vassal state."

Gou Jian smirked as he looked at Wangsun Shong, revelling in the perfect vengeance that he was to exact from Fu Chai soon.

"Doesn't Fu Chai have any sense of shame?" Fan Li addressed the Wu envoy. "He killed a loyal general, trusted a sycophant minister, forgot his promise to his father and acted against the will of Heaven. Does such a man deserve to be a ruler?"

Gou Jian kept quiet.

"Tell Fu Chai," Fan Li continued, "we do not accept his surrender. The only thing left for him to do is to accept Heaven's punishment."

Gou Jian listened, expressionless, marvelling at

what a terrible mind-reader Fan Li was. He did want Fu Chai to die an ignominious death, but did not want to say the word. Thank heavens, Fan Li had said it for him.

Bending his head low, Wangsun Shong fell on his knees when he briefed Fu Chai on what had happened.

Fu Chai sighed. "So this is the will of Heaven."

The following day Wangsun Shong offered to appeal to Gou Jian again.

Gou Jian listened to his supplication with a funereal smile on his face. "General, please tell your master that as he spared me my life twenty years ago, so will I spare his."

Wangsun Shong's heart leapt with hope. "Thank you so very much, Your Majesty." He hastily kowtowed to Gou Jian. *After all, Gou Jian has shown some mercy.*

But mercy was not in Gou Jian's vein. His pleasant tone promptly changed into a harsh one. "Tell Fu Chai I will allow him to live till the end of his natural life, alone, that is, on the Island of Yongdong*. But he is not allowed to take his consort or any servant with him. There are five hundred inhabitants on the island. They will feed him. My offer is final."

For an instant, Wangsun Shong was dazed. Gou Jian's offer amounted to a death warrant. Yongdong was an island in the East China Sea under Yue's control. To live there would mean life-long captivity.

"What are you waiting for?" It was Fan Li speaking again. "Tell Fu Chai to accept His Majesty's generous offer, and Fu Chai will live the rest of his life in peace."

Gou Jian frowned. Did Fan Li mean to be sarcastic

---

* Present-day Zhoushan Island, Zhejiang Province.

by calling his offer a generous one?

Wangsun Shong came back, despair written on his face. Fu Chai understood that all hope was lost. As Wangsun Shong related to him Gou Jian's words, he wearily dropped his head. It was worse than death to accept Gou Jian's offer. How could he leave his land forever? How could he desert his ancestral temple forever? How could he live without Hsi Shih?

*Oh, my father-king, forgive me! Forgive your foolish son!*

Tears of regret streamed down his cheeks. Sitting on a stump, he remained in a pensive mood, sadness imprinted on his tired face. He tore a square of silk from his garment and wrote a letter to Hsi Shih. It was his dying message to his most beloved. After finishing the letter, he stared vacantly at the muddy ground for a long time, reliving every moment of rapturous intimacy he had with Hsi Shih. Then he looked around and carefully hung the letter on a tree beside him.

Accompanying him were only General Wangsun Shong and two faithful attendants. The others had already deserted. Turning to Wangsun Shong, he said, "I am ashamed to live on. And I can not face my father-king and General Wu Yuan in the other world. After my death, please cover up my face."

He drew his sword *Shu Lou* from its scabbard. One sweep of his arm from the left to the right across his throat, and his robe instantly ran red with blood. The king of Wu fell dead.

Wangsun Shong turned around and told the two attendants to follow a narrow path amid the bushes and return to their homes. After their departure, he cut off a corner of his own yellow-colored garment and covered

Fu Chai's face with it. Then he fell on his knees.

"My king," he wailed, "You've always treated me like your own brother. But I have been a poor aide to you. I'm ashamed of myself. Wait for me. I'm coming to join you and continue to serve you in the other world."

He stood up, bowed three times in the direction of Gusu, and fell on his own sword.

*   *   *

Earlier, while Fu Chai was being pursued by troops under the command of Fan Li, another army of Yue was dispatched to encircle Gusu. Inside Gusu, Bo Pi was directing the defense of the besieged city. He had not heard from Fu Chai for ten days. Five days ago, he knew that all three battles were lost, and with them, the might of the Wu army.

Gusu was a strong fortress. The moat was deep and wide; the battlements, solid and secure. However, the food supply was running short, and the morale of the soldiers was eroding. Gou Jian's army had set up camps around the city to cut it off from the outside world.

Word came that Fu Chai had fled to the Gusu Hill and the situation was hopeless. It was only a matter of time before Gou Jian won a complete victory. Bo Pi decided to negotiate a peaceful surrender.

He wrote Gou Jian a letter in which he falsely claimed that Gusu could withstand Yue's attack for months on end. But if Gou Jian promised not to kill or loot, he would cease all resistance and surrender in order to avoid unnecessary bloodshed. Bo Pi was concerned that Gou Jian's humiliating experience in Wu as a slave might cause him to retaliate against the people of Gusu.

Gou Jian's reply came quickly. He welcomed Bo Pi's cooperation, saying that it was not his intention to maltreat the people of Wu. Since Wu was going to be part of Yue, they would be treated the same as his own people. He pointed out that his troops had been feeding the starving population of Wu as a matter of fact. As long as his troops were not attacked, he would guarantee the safety of the residents of Gusu. He demanded that Bo Pi should make sure the Gusu Palace and all official buildings were kept intact.

Bo Pi promised that he would honor the king's request and asked Gou Jian to issue a proclamation publicly stating his peaceful intention. He would have it posted in all public places in Gusu to ensure a bloodless surrender. Gou Jian agreed. The proclamation was duly drafted and sent to Bo Pi.

At the end of four days' intense negotiation, Bo Pi believed he had secured the best possible terms for his surrender. Thereupon he issued a statement to the people of Gusu appealing to them not to offer resistance to the occupation force.

At daybreak the following morning, the city gates of Gusu were thrown wide open.

# CHAPTER THIRTY-ONE

# Lady Gou Jian

IN THE ROYAL palace in Gusu, every day was an anxious day and every night a sleepless night for Hsi Shih. With Fu Chai absent from the palace, Hsi Shih felt extraordinarily weary. Her only companion was Mao Mao, the white cat Prince Yiou gave her. She was wearing no make-up, her hair disheveled, her clothes stained, her beautiful face care-worn. She had been like this for days.

Leaning by the window, she stared blankly at the desolated palace garden. A gust of wind sent falling leaves spattering on the ground. She could see smoke and fire rise to the sky in the distance; she could hear drums and horns beyond the walls, mixed with the reverberation of hideous noises inside the city. Then came an eerie quiet. *Why? Has the battle ended?*

Her sixth sense told her that Wu had lost and

the city was about to be overrun. Apprehension for Fu Chai's safety gripped her.

She hoped that some messenger would come to bring her news of Fu Chai. As no news came, she let her mind drift back to her childhood days: the cheerful bustle in the marketplace of Zhuji; the street fair in the square of the Temple of King Yu; the brook where she washed silk floss with Zheng Dan....

She thought of her parents. She knew her father was well-provided for. She often wrote to him and sent him money. But they had never had any deep communication.

She thought of Fan Li. Their first encounter, their betrothal, and their final embrace. The recollections always ended in bitterness. Had it not been for Fan Li, she would not have acted against her will; had it not been for Fan Li, Prince Yiou would not have been killed; had it not been for Fan Li, Fu Chai would not be in trouble now. What was Fan Li's love compared to Fu Chai's? Fu Chai's love was boundless. Fan Li's love had limits.

She recalled how General Wu Yuan put her on a level with two evil women in history, Mo Shi of the Hsia Dynasty and Da Ji of the Shang Dynasty.

She was certainly not like them. But why didn't she stop playing the shameful double role earlier? If she had told Fu Chai the whole truth before General Wu Yuan's death, things would have been different. She was the culprit! The culprit who caused the ruin of the man who loved her more than his kingdom.

She recalled the dying words of Zheng Dan—and Prince Yiou. But it was too late, much too late now. And it was she who was to blame for all this. Hadn't she helped divert Fu Chai's attention from his duties?

Hadn't she helped deplete Fu Chai's treasury by building the Beauty's Palace? Hadn't she encouraged Fu Chai to go on the expedition to the north? Hadn't she passed on vital information to Lord Yi Yong at their clandestine meetings? That was how she returned Fu Chai's love! The man who had placed every confidence in her!

Of all her contradictions, none was more striking, more ironic than the fact that she despised Gou Jian, yet she had worked for him faithfully until it was too late to remedy the harm she had done.

Remorse seized her. With a heart heavy as lead, she sobbed bitterly. She became drowsy and fell asleep. She woke up a few hours later feeling somebody stroking her face. When she opened her eyes, Mao Mao was crouching by her pillow, rubbing tears on her cheeks with his furry body. He stared affectionately into her eyes, and then touched her nose and her chin with his paws, and purred.

Hsi Shih smiled. Mao Mao was trying to comfort her. She gained a lot of satisfaction from raising him—he had grown from a tiny kitten to a magnificent animal, and there was a strong bond of love and affection between them.

Her thought wandered to Prince Yiou, to Prince Wei and Princess Min. The knowledge that the child prince and princess were out of harm's way with Ding Hong and Gan Lan brought her some consolation. *I am not Mo Shi. I am not Da Ji. I never will be! I am a good woman!*

\* \* \*

Hsi Shih was praying. She was praying for the safety of Fu Chai, for Wu, her adopted country. She did not remember praying so poignantly ever in her life before.

There was a sudden knock at the door. Startled out of her tranquility, Hsi Shih answered the door with trepidation. Two soldiers in Yue uniform dashed in.

"Are you Hsi Shih?"

"Why, yes."

"Come with us."

"Who are you?" Instinctively Hsi Shih backed off, sensing evil.

"Don't move," came a sharp command. The next moment the blood-dripping tip of a sword was pointing at her breast.

One of the soldiers took out a rope, twisted her arms behind her back and fastened her hands tightly.

"What do you want?" Hsi Shih struggled in futility.

A sharp slap across her face, and she was nearly knocked down. A straw rope was instantly wound around her mouth. Its coarse edges cut the corners of her mouth, bit into her tongue and effectively gagged her. Then she was forcibly dragged out.

Out of nowhere Mao Mao burst out and confronted them in the pathway. He was hissing angrily, his glinting green eyes staring at her kidnappers, his back arched, his tail lashing. The two men tried to brush him away. Suddenly Mao Mao lunged forward and slashed one of them on the arm that was trying to keep Hsi Shih from struggling. Startled, the man screamed in pain and let go of his hold on her. Mao Mao's action took Hsi Shih by surprise. She never imagined her sweet, meek pet could be so fierce, so gallant.

Mao Mao leaped for the second man. But before he

could sink his fangs into his arm, the man grabbed him and threw him to the ground. Mao Mao was momentarily stunned. The first man pulled out a sword and struck at him. Mao Mao deftly evaded. The man cursed and struck again. Again Mao Mao dodged his blow.

Mao Mao did not make any more attempt to rescue his mistress—it was obvious the odds were against him. As she descended the doorsteps outside her residence, Hsi Shih heard a forlorn snarl at her back. Mao Mao was saying good-bye to her, she thought sadly. He must feel frustrated. Silently she thanked him for trying to help her.

At the gate of the inner palace, she saw, to her horror, the bodies of two of her guards—one being that of Wang Zhong—lying in a pool of blood. She was dragged into a waiting carriage, thrown onto the floor, and the carriage sped off at once.

Face down, Hsi Shih rolled side to side with the motion of the carriage. To steady her, a guard placed his booted foot on her back.

*I am being kidnapped! But by whose order?* A sense of doom descended upon her as one of the soldiers put a chain around her neck—a cold, heavy, black iron chain, the kind that only a felon was made to wear.

They treated her like a criminal. They would not dare to do so without permission. Whose permission? Obviously, they were going to kill her. But she must not die yet; she's waiting for news from Fu Chai. He might still be alive; he might come back at any time.

An hour later the carriage stopped by a river. One soldier tugged at the chain to pull her up and she was made to walk stumblingly after him while the other stayed by her side, pulling the rope that bound her hands to twist her arms upwards. Each time he jerked the tether, it brought a grimace of pain to her features. But the man showed no pity. As she staggered along, Hsi Shih knew all too well that she was probably on her way to be executed like a convicted felon. But why? On what charge? She closed her eyes, and resigned herself to the worst that was to happen to her.

She was dragged across a reedy marsh along the river and then hauled onto a big boat. The soldiers threw her on the deck with a thump. Her whole body was burning in pain. Presently the boat started moving.

"Lady Hsi Shih, I haven't seen you for ages. How are you?" It was a woman's voice. It sounded familiar. She opened her eyes and there stood Lady Gou Jian!

With a jerk, the soldier behind her lifted the rope that tied her hands, and forced her to kneel before Lady Gou Jian. Hsi Shih felt as though her arms were dislocated. Her face contorted in agony, she groaned, but her groaning was muffled.

"You are beautiful—even in this outfit," Lady Gou Jian said with a ring of triumphant sarcasm in her voice. Her gaze slashed over Hsi Shih.

She stepped forward, grabbed the chain on Hsi Shih's neck, and pulled it up. Hsi Shih was forced to confront her face-to-face. Lady Gou Jian had visibly aged. Her face was wrinkled, her eyes emotionless, and the corner of her mouth twitched with insolent amusement.

Hatred smoldering in her heart, Hsi Shih wanted to spit at this woman, but the rope gag was bruising her tongue, nearly choking her. Still, she managed to cast a defiant look at her.

"No wonder Fu Chai likes you so much." Lady Gou Jian sneered and shook the chain on her neck. "You must have enjoyed your time with him; you must hate parting with him, eh?"

She gave the chain a hard tug; Hsi Shih almost fell down backwards.

"I cannot help feeling sorry for Fu Chai. He has been fatuous enough to love such a treacherous woman."

Hsi Shih felt insulted. But she admitted there was some truth in Lady Gou Jian's words. Yes, she was guilty. Fu Chai loved her, and he lost his country because of her. She deserved to be punished. But certainly not by this woman.

"Thanks to your good service, finally we had our revenge on the enemy. Your seductiveness has ruined Fu Chai. Now you will be coming back, I'm worried that King Gou Jian might also be seduced, for seductiveness is in your nature."

Lady Gou Jian had been planning Hsi Shih's kidnapping for a long time. Her husband used to have a number of concubines in the royal harem, but he loved her more than any of them, for none of his concubines was half as intelligent and as pretty as her. But Hsi Shih was different, very different. Now that Gou Jian had defeated Fu Chai, Hsi Shih was to be his captive. Lady Gou Jian could well imagine what was going to happen.

"If that should happen," she told Hsi Shih, "it would be disastrous for Yue. Don't you agree? Lady Hsi Shih, you're a patriotic woman. I'm sure you wouldn't want our king to follow Fu Chai's footsteps or it would defeat the purpose of your sacrifice in the last twelve years, wouldn't it?"

These words were delivered slowly and deliberately, obviously premeditated. Sarcastic as them were, Hsi Shih sensed the fear beneath them.

"Twelve years ago," Lady Gou Jian reminisced,

twisting her face into a hideous grin, "I asked a great favor of you. I'm grateful to you for your sacrifice. Now I'm going to ask you for another great favor. That is: To protect the king of Yue from your seduction, you will please throw yourself into the water. When you are gone, gone too will be your seductive power. It is best for you and best for your country. Good-bye."

Thus saying, she let go of the chain and walked away, but not before she spat in her captive's face. The soldiers stepped forward and lifted Hsi Shih's arms from behind, ready to drag her to the port side of the boat.

"Just a minute," Lady Gou Jian turned back. "Hsi Shih can swim. She grew up by the river. I'm sure she wouldn't mind getting some help from us."

She gestured to a third soldier who at once brought out a huge millstone weighing at least a hundred catties*. There was a chain attached to it through a hole in the middle. The soldiers lifted the rope that bound Hsi Shih's hands against her back, causing her to lurch forward with her face down on the deck. They fastened her feet to the millstone with the long chain and began dragging the millstone to the port side of the boat.

*So this is the end of my life. Forgive me, Fu Chai. I am leaving you against my will. Only in my next incarnation can I requite your love.* Hsi Shih wailed silently, her beautiful face wet with tears.

Just as the soldiers lifted up the millstone and were about to hurl it into the water, twang! an arrow shot through the throat of one of them. Then came a second shaft and a second guard was shot in the chest. Both died an instant death. The crew was thrown into a panic.

---

* A hundred catties is equivalent to a hundred and ten pounds.

# CHAPTER THIRTY-TWO

# Reunion

AMID A FANFARE of trumpets and salvos of applause, King Gou Jian led his troops into Gusu through the eastern gate of the city. He smiled benignantly at the lines of humbly bowing Wu officials who were led by Bo Pi to welcome their victor. Twenty years ago he had come here as slaves of Fu Chai. Now he was the conqueror! His patience, his hard work, and his long years of plain living had finally borne fruit. *Revenge is sweet.*

In triumph, the king did not notice that his chief general Fan Li had sneaked away. Fan Li could not wait to meet Hsi Shih. He raced to the Gusu Palace to look for his beloved. The Wu guardsmen standing sentinel outside the palace, recognizing him to be a ranking Yue officer, did not try to stop him. They were under orders to protect the palace but not to offer any resistance to

Yue's army.

Fan Li went straight to the king's family quarters, but Hsi Shih was nowhere to be found. When he came out of the inner palace, he saw two men in palatial livery lying dead at the entrance that he had failed to notice earlier. A jolt of alarm went through him. He returned to the main gate of the palace.

"Where is Lady Hsi Shih?" he asked the head guard.

"Lady Hsi Shih has just been taken away by two soldiers in Yue uniform."

How could any Yue soldier come here before him? His face turned white.

"Where did they take her?"

"I don't know. They drove away in a carriage. Lady Hsi Shih's tied up and gagged."

A wave of horror rolled over him.

"Sir, I saw them heading in the direction of the Wusong River," another guard said helpfully. Wusong River was a creek in the southeast of Gusu that linked Lake Tai Hu with the Yangtze.

*Hsi Shih's life was in danger!* The realization made Fan Li insane. Shortly before the invasion started, he had managed to get in touch with Master Chen Ying and the Virgin of the South Forest. Both of them were now in his hire. He was so disgusted when he learned of Gou Jian's earlier attempt to assassinate Hsi Shih that he decided to leave Gou Jian's court as soon as he was reunited with Hsi Shih. But he had not anticipated Hsi Shih would have been taken away with such diabolical swiftness.

He rushed the water front to board a boat that he had prepared in advance. He had meant to take Hsi Shih away with him in that boat.

Though of the same size as Lady Gou Jian's boat, Fan Li's was lighter and faster. Luckily he arrived in the nick of time. After shooting the two soldiers, Fan Li jumped onto Lady Gou Jian's boat. Sword in hand, he was ready to kill anyone. The crew members were frightened out of their wits when they recognized the chief general and scampered into the inner cabin as fast as their feet could take them.

"General Fan Li!" Lady Gou Jian tried to appear calm.

"You, you ... " There was a strange expression on his face, at once brutal and contemptuous.

"I am doing this for ... for the sake of the king, for the sake of the kingdom," Lady Gou Jian stuttered. She was shaking in her shoes. She had never seen Fan Li in a rage.

Staring at her with a lethal dispassion, Fan Li cursed between his teeth, "You wicked woman!"

Lady Gou Jian stood aghast, almost frozen in terror.

Fan Li quickly turned to Hsi Shih, unfastened and ungagged her and then carried her onto his boat. As his boat was sailing away, he turned back, notched an arrow and shot down the sail on Lady Gou Jian's boat.

\* \* \*

Hsi Shih was dazed by what had happened, but dimly, she was aware that Fan Li had saved her life. Her eyes closed, she let Fan Li place her on a bunk in the cabin.

"Hsi Shih, it's me! It's your Fan Li!" Fan Li spoke in a soft but anxious voice.

*A stunning beauty she still is!* Fan Li told himself as he rubbed her bruised face with a towel and warm water. Suddenly Hsi Shih opened her eyes. She rolled off the bunk and backed off a few steps, giving Fan Li quite a start.

"Hsi Shih, it's me! It's your Fan Li!"

Hsi Shih did not respond. She shot a distant stare at him. Her eyes were alert but cold.

Fan Li stretched out his arms to reach for her. But she held up a hand to keep him at bay.

"Hsi Shih, speak to me, please!" he implored.

"Where is Fu Chai?" she demanded with a stony expression on her face.

A pang of jealousy shot through Fan Li's heart. He was loath to talk about Fu Chai.

"Hsi Shih, I've been waiting for this day for twelve years. My thoughts have always been with you.... "

"Where is Fu Chai?" Hsi Shih repeated, staring hard at him.

Fan Li realized he could not possibly expect her to be indifferent to Fu Chai's fate. But if she knew Fu Chai had died, she might feel easier to come back to him. It would be a shock. He had to prepare her mentally before breaking the news to her.

"I'll take you to him if you so wish," he said, striving to appear serene.

The boatman was applying the oar with full force and the boat sailed out at top speed. Hsi Shih seemed to calm down and sat at a small table in the middle of the cabin.

"Hsi Shih," Fan Li began to tell his story. "I must tell you I have married and my wife has died. I married because King Gou Jian ordered me to do so. I respected my wife. She was a nice woman. But my heart is always with you. I can't love anyone else in the world. I love you. I love you alone."

*He is taking me to see Fu Chai. So Fu Chai is still alive.*

"Hsi Shih, remember what we promised each other twelve years ago?" Fan Li continued. "Remember the vow we made to each other—*till the mountains rot, till the seas dries up?*"

*They must have taken him captive. They must have locked him up in a dungeon cell.*

"Hsi Shih, I want to be with you. I want to spend the rest of my life with you. We will enjoy life together. We will never separate."

*Never separate? Where is Fu Chai? Where are we?* At last Hsi Shih picked up the thread of Fan Li's monologue. She stepped onto the front deck.

The night was deepening. The boat had sailed out of the city. In the distance, she saw the gaunt outlines of the Gusu Palace. The trees on both sides of the river, enveloped in darkness, were black shadows against the evening twilight. Occasionally there was a faint glow coming from a farmhouse near the bank of the river. Suddenly she became nervous and turned back into the cabin.

"Where are we going?" she asked. "Are you taking me to see Fu Chai?"

Fan Li's lips twitched but did not utter a word.

"Where is Fu Chai?" Her voice became urgent.

"Fu Chai ... Fu Chai is dead."

Hsi Shih had more or less expected bad news, but she had hoped against hope that some miracle might happen in the last minute. Now the confirmation of Fu

Chai's death had shattered all her hopes.

"When did he die?" she asked after a long pause.

"Three days ago."

"Where?"

"In the Gusu Hill."

"How did he die?"

"He killed himself. He refused to surrender." Fan Li decided not to tell her the whole story.

"He had a letter for you." He took out from inside his gown the square of silk which he had unfastened from the tree branch where Fu Chai had left it.

Hsi Shih unfolded the letter, her fingers shaking terribly. The message read:

> *"My Darling,*
> *"I thank you for the long years of your sweet company. You have made my life supremely happy. A king may have many conquests. But not every king is so lucky as to have a beautiful, loving wife like you. I am going to die. Please forget me and find love again. I want you to be happy. Good-bye, my dearest love! Keep well!"*

Hsi Shih clutched the letter to her bosom, her eyes bearing an absent look. Then she closed her eyes and sat still. There was no trace of tears on her pretty face: extreme grief had rendered her incapable of crying.

A dreadful silence shrouded the cabin. Fan Li brought a cup of tea to her. But she did not move.

A long moment passed. Slowly Hsi Shih opened her eyes and gazed at Fan Li. She noticed his greying hair. He was getting old but the look in his eyes and the tone of his voice remained the same. She felt a pang of pity for him, and her eyes grew tender.

"Hsi Shih," Fan Li said hopefully, "I have quit my post for good. I've bought a comfortable mansion in a quiet town in the north, far away from Wu and Yue, for us to enjoy our life together. Does that sound agreeable?"

"My lord," came Hsi Shih's calm voice, "before I go away with you, I would like to burn some incense for the soul of Fu Chai."

Fan Li opened a small cabinet on the table, took out a bunch of incense sticks from the top drawer and handed them to Hsi Shih. They had been placed there by the boatman who often prayed to the gods. Having picked out twelve, Hsi Shih lit them up on the oil lamp.

"I won't be long," she said to Fan Li.

Slowly she stepped onto the rear deck, incense sticks in hand, her pretty face in absolute repose. There was even the suggestion of a smile on her lips. Facing the shadowy city of Gusu, she fell on her knees and kowtowed three times....

Fan Li waited in the cabin, eased by Hsi Shih's peaceful looks. Of course she was distressed. It was only natural. He must be patient. Time was the best healer. In a few months, she would have forgotten her pain. And he would have the reward of being patient. He would win her heart eventually by being kind and loving and understanding. He felt a surge of hope and confidence.

Suddenly there came a loud splash. What could that be? Fan Li felt a chill. He hastily rushed to the rear deck. But Hsi Shih was not there.

"Hsi Shih! Hsi Shih!" he shouted in alarm.

There was no answer.

*Hsi Shih has thrown herself into the river!* Without a second thought, Fan Li plunged into the water. The boatman, an excellent swimmer, plunged in his wake. It was a black night. There was no moon, no starlight. The current of the river was swift. Groping in the dark for a long while, the boatman heard the sound of someone struggling in the water. He hastened to grab at the drowning body and pulled it up onto the boat. It was Fan Li.

"Leave ... me ... alone," Fan Li mumbled in a feeble voice. "Go try ... again."

The boatman dived again.

Lying on the deck, all drenched and gasping, Fan Li waited and waited. Finally the boatman returned, exhausted. His search ended in failure. The rapid flow of the water was merciless. It seemed that the dark night and the swift current had swallowed up Hsi Shih.

Hsi Shih was thirty years old. Her body was never recovered.

Grief-stricken, Fan Li returned to the cabin. In the dim candle light he saw something glittering on the table. It was the gold necklace Hsi Shih had left behind. He stared at it, motionless as a clay sculpture.

"Sir, shall we continue our journey?" asked the boatman.

"By all means," Fan Li murmured.

He took out a cloth pouch from inside his gown and produced an embroidered silk handkerchief. It was the souvenir Hsi Shih had given him on the day of their betrothal. He wrapped the necklace in the handkerchief, put them in the pouch and then placed the pouch back into the inner pocket of his garment.

# CHAPTER THIRTY-THREE

# Celebration

K ING GOU JIAN granted a respite for three days and invited officials of both his court and the former government of Wu to a grand banquet on the third day in the Gusu Palace. He spent the night in Fu Chai's luxurious bed chamber which Bo Pi had specially prepared for him. When he woke up the next morning, the first thing that came to his mind was to find Hsi Shih. His revenge could not be complete without possessing this ravishing beauty. He would make her his concubine, his slave. He would make her do things that Lady Gou Jian would never have tried.

Taking two guards with him, he went looking for her in Fu Chai's inner palace. He saw many pretty women, but Hsi Shih could not be located. He was bewildered. Asked where the great beauty was, Bo Pi said he had not the faintest idea, and nobody else had, either. It was at that moment that Gou Jian noticed the absence of Fan Li.

*Fan Li has disappeared! He must have taken Hsi Shih away, just one step ahead of me!* Fan Li had a trenchant mind. He must have divined his intentions. He must have slipped away while he was parading his victorious troops through the streets of Gusu. Gou Jian suddenly remembered his promise to Fan Li that he would personally bring Hsi Shih back to his arms as soon as Yue defeated Wu. But that promise was made under duress, and he would not honor any promise made under duress.

*How dare Fan Li forestall me?* Gou Jian gnashed his teeth in rage and immediately ordered a general search for Fan Li and Hsi Shih, and another search for Fu Chai's little son and daughter and their mother Ding Hong, but all to no avail.

At the banquet on the evening of the third day, he received a message from Fan Li, a petition for resignation from all offices.

> *"It is said that if a king is in disgrace, his loyal subjects ought to forfeit their lives. When Your Majesty was in captivity, I, your servant, preserved my worthless life only because I wanted to do my bit in restoring the kingdom and avenging the nation's shame. Now as the enemy state has fallen, and Your Majesty has spared my life, I am too ashamed of myself to stay on in office. I petition Your Majesty to allow me to spend the remaining days of my life amidst mountains and valleys and trees and flowers to enjoy the beauty of Nature."*

Anger was smoldering in his heart. Gone. Fan Li was gone, having taken away his booty—the beauty of all beauties.

He wanted to seize the runaways—at once. But he knew better than to try to overtake Fan Li in his flight. Whatever Fan Li plotted to achieve, nobody would be able to foil.

He forced himself to appear calm and feigned grief over the loss of his chief general. Wiping his imaginary tears with his sleeve, he ordered, in the presence of all the banqueters, to have a gold statue made in commemoration of his loyal Chief General Lord Fan Li.

\* \* \*

King Gou Jian decreed that the capital of Yue be moved from Guiji to Gusu, a city he had fallen in love with at first sight twenty years ago. He ordered to have the bodies of Fu Chai and Wangsun Shong buried on the Tiger Hill by the side of the tomb of Fu Chai's father, King Ho Lu, and organized a funeral ceremony at which he loudly chanted prayers to the gods for the repose of their souls. He praised Fu Chai's valor as a soldier—a manifestation of his magnanimity toward a fallen foe.

He also officiated at a splendid memorial service in honor of General Wu Yuan, which was attended by the members of the general's family, many Yue officials and officials of the former Wu regime as well as members of the public.

"Lord General Wu Yuan's name should go down to posterity," the king proclaimed, "and his patriotism and loyalty should be a shining example for everyone."

All those present were impressed by the king's graciousness toward his former enemy. But Wen Zhong remembered how the king had taken General Wu Yuan as Yue's worst foe. If captured, Gou Jian had once said, he would tear the general limb from limb by tying him to the legs of five horses and then making each horse run in a different direction. *My king is a different man now,* Wen Zhong marvelled.

When Bo Pi was summoned to Gou Jian's court, he expected to be appointed to a high position given that he had been friendly to Gou Jian all these years. He was grossly mistaken.

"My lord, why didn't you follow your king?" Gou Jian asked coldly.

Bo Pi could not believe his ears. He prostrated himself before Gou Jian.

"Be ... because I want to serve Your Majesty." Suddenly he lost his usual eloquence.

"You've been treacherous to your master," Gou Jian sneered. "How can I trust you?"

"Your Majesty," Bo Pi felt a deadly chill running down his spine. "I've saved your life. I've helped you."

A sardonic laugh escaped Gou Jian. "You saved me but you betrayed your master. You helped me because you were greedy. I have to kill you to show how a traitor's life should end." He motioned to his guards to come forward.

"P—please, please let me live for old time's sake," Bo Pi begged.

He cast an imploring glance at Wen Zhong, but Wen Zhong turned his head away. Bo Pi kept kowtowing until his forehead cracked. Blood was trickling down his face, mixed with sweat and tears. Gou Jian cast a disdainful look at him and ordered his summary execution.

"Please have mercy on me! I don't deserve this! Please have mercy!" Bo Pi wailed as he was being dragged out to the execution ground.

"Did I do the right thing, my lords?" Gou Jian asked his ministers in the court.

"Yes, Your Majesty," they answered in unison. "Long Live the King!"

\* \* \*

Wen Zhong received a secret letter from Fan Li.

*"My Dear Friend,*

*"You are a smart man. Having worked with King Gou Jian all these years, you must have seen through him. He is a mean, suspicious man. An ingrate. A hypocrite. In adversity, he needs able counsellors like you. In triumph, he will not tolerate any one whose intelligence exceeds his own. He will allow them to share sorrows with him, but will grudge them the joys of victory.*

*"I was grateful to the king for promoting me to one of the most powerful positions in Yue at a young age and entrusting me with great responsibilities which I took great satisfaction in fulfilling. My reservations about his character had not diminished my loyalty, because my sense of duty obliged me to work with him in the interests of Yue. I have allowed my duty to take precedence over my marriage and my sacrifice has been no small.*

*"Now that victory is won, I don't feel duty-*

*bound any more. I have decided to leave Gou Jian's court and go elsewhere. I have waited long enough. My children have already been escorted out of the country by Master Chen Yin and the Virgin of the Southern Forest.*

*"I believe it is high time that you quit office lest you will find yourself in the role of the hunting dog after the wild rabbits are killed off as predicted by Fu Chai before his death. Please consider my advice carefully. Thank you for what you have done for me all these years. I cherish our friendship. I hope we would meet again."*

Wen Zhong read the letter over and over again, yet he could not make up his mind to quit office. Fan Li had a point, but the king was a different man now, he thought to himself.

# CHAPTER THIRTY-FOUR

# Lord Tao Zhu

TWO YEARS AFTER Yue's victory Yi Yong resigned from office. The former rotund, thickset minister had grown fatter. He spent a lot of his time touring various places in the vast land of China. One day he travelled to Linzi, the capital of the State of Chi, nearly two thousand *li* from his hometown Guiji.

Linzi was the most prosperous city Yi Yong had visited so far. It was considerably larger and more populous than Guiji. People here appeared generally taller than southerners, and they were definitely dressed better, mostly in fine linen and woollen garments. The wealthier wore furs and eider down. The marketplace in the center of the city was a bustling scene. The noise was deafening. Vendors shouting from the rows of souvenir stalls, cooked-meat stalls, vegetable stalls, grocery stalls, and travelling soup kitchens were competing for his attention. There were entertainments too. A team of five musicians were playing zither, pan-pipe, flute, drum and bells at one end of the marketplace. At the other end, a sword juggler was tossing and catching four knives while his monkey was walking around the ring of spectators begging for money with a bowl. Whoever contributed a silver coin would be thanked by the monkey with a bow. Whoever put in a copper coin in the bowl would get the coin thrown back at his foot right away. Fascinated, Yi Yong lingered around in the marketplace for a good part of the day. He bought an exquisite tea set with tiny silvery spots on its dark brown glaze. This was a local specialty, for Linzi was well-known for its ceramic art and pottery.

Leaving the marketplace, Yi Yong sauntered into a quiet and more affluent area of the city. There were few pedestrians; only horse-drawn carriages were going up and down the wide, clean, tree-lined boulevards. Most of the horses were caparisoned with breastplates and bridles gilded with gold and silver. As he was strolling past the residence of Prime Minister Chen Heng, he espied a respectable-looking couple, the man in his mid-forties and the woman in her early thirties, walking out of the splendid residence, escorted by a grey-haired man who was small of stature but imposing nonetheless, probably the prime minister. They bade good-bye to their host and were heading for a luxurious carriage in front of the gate. They were elegantly dressed in the fashion of the aristocrats of Chi, but their voices seemed oddly familiar.

Seeing the man help the woman onto the carriage, it suddenly dawned upon Yi Yong that the man was none other than Fan Li and the woman Hsi Shih. Yi Yong darted toward them, but was stopped by the guards near the gate before he could get close. Yi Yong craned his neck to have a clearer look. *Why, there is no mistake about it!*

Fan Li was grizzled, but his features had undergone little change, handsome as ever. The woman was Hsi Shih; nobody else had her unique beauty. A feeling of camaraderie sprang up in him. He was elated. Nothing could make him happier than a chat over a cup of wine with his good old friend Fan Li—together with Hsi Shih!

"Fan Li!" Yi Yong waved to his friend, so excited that his heart almost jumped out.

The man turned around. His eyes flashed a gleam of recognition, but immediately his face assumed a blank expression.

"You're mistaken, sir," he said curtly. "I'm not Fan Li."

"I'm sorry," Yi Yong apologized.

As the carriage drove away, Yi Yong asked one of the guards who the honorable guests were.

"They are Lord and Lady Tao Zhu."

Turning away disheartened, Yi Yong shuffled along the boulevard. *Lord and Lady Tao Zhu? No, they are Fan Li and Hsi Shih! There is no mistake!*

He decided to run after them.

"Fan Li!" he called out, wheezing and puffing due to his corpulence.

But the carriage sped up and soon disappeared into the distance in the twilight of the evening.

For a long time, Yi Yong could not calm down. As he felt hungry, he found a restaurant and dropped in. To his astonishment, he ran face to face into a man and a woman with a baby in her arms. They were walking out of the door. Their faces were also familiar. He tried to remember who they were. Yes, they were Master Chen Yin and the Virgin of the Southern Forest! He saw them earlier in the day with Fan Li and Hsi Shih, seemingly either as their companions or bodyguards or both. Yi Yong decided not to accost them. Something told him that they might not welcome the opportunity of being identified by him.

Lying on his bed that night, Yi Yong kept thinking of his experience that day—it was somewhat surreal. *Life is like a dream,* he said to himself.

The next day when he came back in the evening after some more sightseeing, the innkeeper gave him a letter, saying that it was delivered by a courier. Yi Yong had a hunch that it had something to do with his encounter the day before. He opened the letter as soon as he entered his room. It came from Hsi Shih.

*Your Excellency,*

*I hope everything is fine with you. Perhaps you would like to know what has happened to me since we last met.*

*The moment Yue's army entered Gusu, I was abducted by Lady Gou Jian who wanted to put me to death. But Fan Li managed to thwart her scheme and saved me from the jaws of death. By then he had seen through Gou Jian. He had prepared a sailing boat to take me with him to a distant land. But I wanted to be with Fu Chai. After I had learned of Fu Chai's death, I threw myself into the river.*

*I believed only by joining him in the realms below could I repay his vast bounty; only by reuniting with*

*him in the other world could I requite his limitless
devotion; only in death could I find peace of mind.
To die for love meant true happiness to me.*

*Miraculously, I survived. I was spotted by an
elderly fisherman who pulled me out of the water.
He lives in a fishing village by the river. He was
very kind and let me stay in his house. He and his
wife treated me like their own daughter. But I was
depressed. I felt I had gotten a reprieve I did not
deserve.*

*It was the fisherman who ultimately lifted up
my spirits. After hearing my story, he told me that I
had requited Fu Chai's love and redeemed my sin by
the act of drowning myself. Although Fu Chai was
in the other world, he certainly should have known
what I was trying to do and appreciated my gesture.
But the fact I had survived meant my days on earth
were not yet over and that a happy life was ahead of
me.*

*The fisherman's words were powerful and I knew
he was right. A few months later, I was reunited
with Fan Li when he came to the fishing village,
making inquiries about me, the fishing village being
in the vicinity of where I had jumped into the water,*

*Fan Li has repented his fault and I have forgiven
him completely. I am living a happy life. My mind is
at peace. I've also managed to get in touch with my
father. Naturally he was relieved to hear that I was
all right.*

*I am writing to you because you are a good man.
But please do not tell anybody else about this and do
not look for me, or Fan Li, for you will never find
us. Take care!*

Yi Yong breathed a deep sigh, overcome by a sense of nostalgia. He was grateful to Hsi Shih for letting him share her secret. *My God! Life is a dream.*

As he was touring around China, Yi Yong soon left Chi for Lu. There he intended to visit some of Confucius' disciples, for the great master Confucius had passed away in the year 479 B.C.

Convinced that Lord Tao Zhu was Fan Li, Yi Yong wrote him a letter care of Chen Heng before he departed for Chi. The envelop was prudently addressed to Lord Tao Zhu and there was no mention of Hsi Shih in the letter.

> *Dear Lord General,*
>
> *It was a pleasant surprise to run into you in this part of the world. You must have good reason to assume a new identity. I will respect that.*
>
> *Let me tell you what happened in the two years after you had left. King Gou Jian gradually became estranged from those of us who had faithfully worked with him. The prime minister, like most of us, had sensed something wrong with the king's demeanor and began to absent himself from court sessions on the pretext of illness.*
>
> *One day about half a year ago, the king went to visit him. He praised him for his distinguished services, and then made a curious statement, "We have wiped out Wu. But Ho Lu, Fu Chai, and Wu Yuan were all tough guys. What should we do if their ghosts contrive to take revenge on us? You have to check up on them."*
>
> *Wen Zhong was confounded. He was about to ask the king what he really meant when the king stood*

*up and bade him good-bye. Then he found that the king had left the famous sword Shu Lou on the table, the sword with which Fu Chai had ordered Wu Yuan to take his own life. Wen Zhong understood. The following day he killed himself.*

*Lady Wen Zhong disappeared a few days after she had told me about the king's visit and her husband's sudden suicide. But the king claimed that the prime minister had died of illness. Subsequently I and many other meritorious ministers resigned from office on the pretext of either old age or poor health. We came to realized what kind of a man the king is, just as you had done much earlier.*

*Wherever you are and whatever your pursuit is, I wish you and your family best of luck.*

\* \* \*

Lord Tao Zhu was the richest man of the land. Two years ago, he and his wife arrived at the small, picturesque town of Tao* in southwestern Chi with two children and a snow-white cat. Earlier he had bought, through a middleman, a beautiful piece of land and a stately mansion on the outskirts of the town. There he and his family came and settled down in comfort.

The sudden appearance of this strange, wealthy couple had caused quite a stir in the neighborhood and people were eager to befriend them. But Lord Tao Zhu and his wife kept to themselves most of the time. The neighbors all agreed that Lady Tao Zhu was the most beautiful woman they had ever seen.

Lord Tao Zhu was engaged in trading business.

---

* Present-day Dingtao, Shandong Province.

In a few years, he made a fabulous fortune. Those associated with him also prospered. And the town of Tao grew into a boom town for inter-state trade and commerce.

Despite his reclusiveness, Lord Tao Zhu had left such a profound impression that even now when the Chinese refer to a very rich man, they would say, "Oh, he is as rich as Lord Tao Zhu," just as when they refer to a very beautiful woman, they would call her "Hsi Shih."

There is no record that Lord Tao Zhu and Fan Li were one and the same person, that Lady Tao Zhu and Hsi Shih were one and the same person. No record whatsoever.

# EPILOGUE

**G**OU JIAN REPLACED Fu Chai as the First Lord. But his firstlordship was short-lived. As our story happened in a period of bloody wars in Chinese history, all the self-styled kingdoms, in their scramble for power and supremacy, rose and fell by turn.

As smaller and weaker countries had been swallowed up by larger and stronger powers, the number of warring states eventually dwindled to only seven by the mid-fourth century B.C. from some one hundred and twenty in the eighth century B.C.

Yue had been annexed by Chu. Among the seven, the State of Qin, seated on the western frontier, became the strongest. In 256 B.C., Qin's force seized the royal capital of Luoyang, putting an end to the Zhou Dynasty. Within thirty-five years, the king of Qin brought the entire China under his control and assumed the imposing title of "The First Emperor."

The First Emperor was one of the cruelest tyrants in history. For fear that people with knowledge might be dangerous to his despotic rule, he had hundreds of scholars buried alive. For protection against invasion by barbarians, he ordered the construction of the Great

Wall at the cost of innumerable lives of common people who died from forced labor.

Dynasties rose and fell, but the legend of Hsi Shih lives on. Her name is synonymous with "beauty" in the Chinese language.

# ACKNOWLEDGMENTS

I would like to thank the entire Better Link Press staff for their enthusiasm and hard work.

I am grateful to Wu Ying, chief editor of the award-winning *English-Chinese Dictionary*, for the critical role she played in the publication of this book.

A good story is a joy forever. It transcends time, space and race and touches the heart of many. I have many friends, colleagues and readers in America and China to thank for their encouragement and for the pleasant hours I spent with them telling them the story of the *Siren of China*.

I would like to give special thanks to Constance Yang and Bea Nguyen who read my earlier drafts and gave me invaluable suggestions.

I must also pay tribute to Liu Danzhai, a renowned Chinese artist, whose work inspired and graced the jacket design.

I appreciate the remarkable job that Yuan Yinchang Studio did for this book.

I dedicate this book to my parents who fostered a habit of reading in me in my early childhood.

# ABOUT THE AUTHOR

Born in Shanghai, Michael Tang majored in English Language and Literature at East China Teacher's University. In 1980, after winning first prize in a worldwide English Competition sponsored by the BBC, he went to Britain to study and graduated with honors from the London School of Economics. In 1983, he entered Harvard Business School and graduated in 1985 as the first Harvard MBA from mainland China since the founding of the People's Republic in 1949.

He is the author of three best sellers published in China and the acclaimed *A Victor's Reflections and Other Tales of China's Timeless Wisdom* published by Prentice Hall Press in 2000.

Michael Tang can be reached through his website www.michaeltang.com.